30 Days Hath September

Larry Morris

Table of Contents

Part One – **Inception**

Chapter One

Chapter Two

Chapter Three

Chapter Four

Chapter Five

Chapter Six

Chapter Seven

Chapter Eight

Chapter Nine

Chapter Ten

Chapter Eleven

Chapter Twelve

Chapter Thirteen

Part Two – **Perpetuation**

Chapter One

Chapter Two

Chapter Three

Chapter Four

Chapter Five

Chapter Six

Chapter Seven

Chapter Eight

Chapter Nine

Chapter Ten

Chapter Eleven

Chapter Twelve

Chapter Thirteen

Chapter Fourteen

Part Three – **Parlay**

Chapter One – The Bet

Chapter Two – Progress

Chapter Three – School

Chapter Four – Jimmy's Back

Chapter Five – The Talk

Chapter Six – Attempt

Chapter Seven – The Snake

Chapter Eight – Moving Along

Chapter Nine – Daq's Friend

Chapter Ten – The Neighbor

Chapter Eleven – The Tantrum

Chapter Twelve – Daquiri

Chapter Thirteen – Goodbye Neighbor

Chapter Fourteen – Laila's Fifteen Minutes of Fame

Chapter Fifteen – Intel

Chapter Sixteen – Lessons/Date Night

Part Four – **Abduction**

Chapter One

Chapter Two

Chapter Three

Chapter Four

Chapter Five
Chapter Six
Chapter Seven
Chapter Eight
Chapter Nine
Chapter Ten
Chapter Eleven
Chapter Twelve
Chapter Thirteen
Chapter Fourteen
Chapter Fifteen
Chapter Sixteen

Part Five – **Finale**
Chapter One
Chapter Two
Chapter Three
Chapter Four
Chapter Five
Chapter Six
Chapter Seven
Chapter Eight
Chapter nine

Authors Note

In Loving Memory of

Lindsay Jacobsen

*Never Forgotten
Always in our Hearts*

30 Days Hath September

This is a work of fiction. Any similarities to persons living or deceased, places, or events, is purely coincidental. Many of the places depicted in this book, which is set in Palm Springs, are completely fictitious and designed for the purpose of this story only.

Copyright, 2023

By Larry Morris

All rights reserved.

Part One

Inception

Chapter One

The Santa Anna winds were particularly gusty this warm summer morning in Palm Springs. The palm trees in the back swayed and rustled as their palm fronds gave off a distinct susurrus. The small windmill feature planted in the ground near the palms added a rhythmic tune as an almost inaudible squeak spoke with every spin of the blades.

Alex lay on his back listening to the outdoor sounds and the quiet of the bedroom. He glances at the clock radio on the nightstand next to his bed. 5:15AM, the alarm will go off in another 45 minutes and his Monday can start. Oh Yes, another Monday morning sales meeting to enlighten us all on how we are to do our jobs...the job that Alex has been doing for the last 32 years. Oh, and a special bonus...today is August 14th and that means the added benefit of the second Monday of the month which brings the delightful sale numbers for the previous month. And of course, the inevitable discussion of whether you made your last month's quota. All of this being presented by a young hot shot half our age and who has never spent one day in the field selling.

Alex, a sales representative, works for a heating and air conditioning company called 'Desert Air" with the tag line 'But, it's a dry heat!' It had been a family-owned business for over 50 years and Alex had become an intricate part of the business and family over the years. The owner and his wife ran the business entirely the way they wanted, and that way was to treat everyone that worked there like family. Alex learned everything there was to know about the heating and air conditioning business, especially the cooling end as the desert heat of the Coachella Valley can be quite intense. When he first started, he worked as an apprentice and absorbed copious knowledge of all aspects of the business. He evolved into sales and soon became a top salesperson and consultant, earning a very good income. He loved his job and the family he worked for, especially their son who was roughly the same age as he was. He was the main repairman, and they worked together very compatibly. About five years ago he was killed in an auto accident while driving in an unexpected dust storm just outside of Palm Springs. It was a devastating time for the family and for Alex.

A few years after that tragedy the owner and his wife retired and sold the business to a large national chain, it was the right move for them, but was devastating for Alex. The family aspect of the business was gone, and the new company looked only at the bottom line and cut all the services and commissions they could, just to earn more profits. After 30 years of doing business the right way, Alex struggled mightily with the new corporate way.

He had just turned 63 a few months ago and was now struggling with the possibility of retirement. He was in the process of penciling out the financial end of the process but had not made any firm decisions yet. He had been smart with his earnings over the years and had a sizeable 401K in place, but with the possibility of 20-30 more years of life, he had to be sure.

He shook away his bad thoughts about the day ahead of him and rolled slightly to his left and looked at Ellie sleeping next to him. He smiled and carefully brushed away a tuft of hair from her eyes. She stirred slightly and turned her head away but did not wake up. Old Maurice was curled up at the end of the bed and when he saw that Alex was awake, he moved to his 'good morning' position which was about 6 inches from Alex's face, then did a soft meow and a gentle tap to the face with a furry paw. Old Maurice was an orange tabby cat weighing in at a robust 17lbs and still pretty darn spry for his 13 years. "It's the same thing every morning Maury. Do you really think I would forget how the system works?" He whispered as he stroked the big kitty and smiled as he listened to his loud purr. This went on for another few minutes and the clock now said 5:30.

"OK, I guess it's time to get up." With this announcement Maurice moved down to the foot of the bed and waited in a sitting position. Alex leaned over and switched off the alarm, which was there only for an emergency back-up, as sleeping till 6 in the morning was an unheard-of event in this household. Now he rolled fully over to his left side. "Ellie, time to get up." No movement. "Come on baby girl, time to rise and shine." Still, no movement. He stretched across and brushed her hair away from her eyes again and she scowled and pulled away. "Come on baby, open your eyes. Want something to eat?!" That seemed to do it, Ellie stood and stretched, thrusting her nose downward and pushing forward till her head was in the air and her back and butt got sufficiently stretched. She wagged her tail as she looked at Alex and then scampered down to the end of the bed and jumped on old Maurice and playfully chewed on his ear which earned her a whack across the face with that big furry paw (no claws). She jumped off the bed and with a loud bark ran down the hallway, then a slight right into the dining room, and to the back door. The morning had officially started at the Barton household. Ellie is a two-year-old West Highland white terrier with an overabundance of energy and personality.

When the back door opened, she ran out and quickly went potty, then just as quickly back into the house and into the hallway where she jumped on Maurice again and the two of them proceeded to have their morning wrestling match (just for fun) while Alex fixed her breakfast.

"OK Ellie, heeeeere's breakfast!" And in a flash her nose was buried in her bowl happily munching away on her fresh food breakfast. Alex went to the back door and locked it and turned to watch her eat. The back door led out to a sizeable patio and graveled backyard with the palm trees and various bushes and cactus; and of course, a patch of artificial grass that had affectionately been named 'Ellie's drop zone.' He stood in the dining room and to the right was a large kitchen with an island and four tall chairs and the stove top. Behind the island were the cabinets, microwave, dishwasher, and kitchen sink. Where Ellie was eating her breakfast was a doorway into the great room or living room (your choice) and a wall that angled across the kitchen and dining room with the opening to the dining room at the far end. If you didn't go into the dining room from the hallway, it led to another archway to the great room and foyer to the front door. The great room housed the sofa and two overstuffed chairs at the front of the house with a large picture window looking out into the front yard, it also was where the television and the fireplace were located.

Alex went to the hallway and walked back toward the master bedroom which was at the end of the hallway on the left, which housed the master bath and a dressing area that had a door leading to the back yard. On his right was a large bedroom which he had turned into an office and straight ahead was the main bathroom. A sharp right at the bathroom and there was another bedroom to the left and straight ahead was the utility room with a sink, a washer and dryer, and a door to the garage. Also in the utility room were cabinets above the dryer that held the cat's food, which was where old Maurice sat looking up at.

"Yea, you're next buddy." Alex lifted Maurice up onto the top of the dryer. Now, he used to jump up there, but recently age had taken its toll and now he was fine with being lifted. Of course, it would be much easier to feed him on the floor, but Ellie tended to help Maurice finish his meal, even without permission. Alex put a little canned food in a dish and a scoop of dry in another and water in a third and he had a happy kitty.

He walked out of the utility room and stood in the hallway looking toward the dining room. Ellie sat there with her head tipped and ears standing straight up, and a wave of emotion filled Alex. He glanced a look into the master bedroom and saw the picture on the nightstand of him and Faith on their 30th anniversary in Hawaii at a luau. He had his arm around her, and they both were smiling and holding a Mai Tai. That was 2 years ago. Shortly after that celebration, Faith was diagnosed with pancreatic cancer. Ellie was purchased as a companion and source of enjoyment for Faith during her survival fight. Ellie proved to be all of that, and much more. His 2 girls, as Alex referred to them, were rarely apart and the bond they had was truly beautiful. That bond lasted only 18 months when Faith lost her valiant battle against a very aggressive form of cancer. And now Ellie, especially in the morning, often will give him the look she was right now, a look that said, 'where's Mom?'

Alex swallowed away the lump in his throat, blew a kiss toward the picture and went to the master bath and readied himself for the day ahead…only he had no idea what the day ahead had in store for him.

Chapter Two

The hot August wind blew into her face as she walked toward what they were calling home now. On this Sunday night each step she took hurt after her friend Jimmy had given her a 'fun poke'. Daquiri had just turned 13 and Jimmy, who was 22, was her friend that took her under his wing since she was now homeless and living on the streets.

Daq and her two sisters lived in their car with their dad in a homeless camp near the airport. As she walked toward their car, she thought about what she was going to tell him about where she had been. She knew if he found out about Jimmy and what he had done to her, he'd kill him. Her Dad could have a bad temper sometimes and she knew this would set it off. So, she was thinking of a story to tell him that would save Jimmy and still let her hang with him. She rubbed the red mark on her face, this wasn't going to make convincing him any easier.

Daq thought about the life they had had before Shalia died in a car accident. *'Shalia was Dad's wife and mother to Daq's 5-year-old sister. She had been a very good Mom to all of us and she worked at a lawyer's office, so we had more money and lived in an apartment. Dad worked sometimes and he was sick sometimes. When he was sick, Shalia always took care of him. I know that Dad took drugs that he wasn't supposed to, and that's what Shalia was trying to help him with. But when she died, Dad fell completely apart and started taking more drugs. We had to leave the apartment and now we live in the car at the homeless camp near the airport in Palm Springs. Dad goes out and works sometimes and gets some money, so we have a little food, but it sure isn't fun like it was in the apartment with Shalia. Dad is always depressed and sad and he worries a lot about us. That's why I hang with Jimmy because I make some money doing things for him like deliveries, going and giving people messages and now he's telling me I can make a lot more with a new idea he has, which I don't want to do, but I can make more money.*

Last week he made me let him have a 'fun poke' as he called it, but it wasn't fun for me. I know it's called having sex and it's supposed to be fun cuz guys pay money to do it, but for me it just hurt. But afterwards I got to go and have a hamburger at Jack in the Box where it's air-conditioned, and I got to have the big burger with fries and coke. That was good. But today the fun poke hurt even more and when I told him I didn't like it, he slapped me across the face real hard and left this red mark.

"Now look what you made me do goddammit!"

"Ow Jimmy! What did I do?! You didn't need to slap me!" I started to cry.

"I'm trying to help you and your sisters and all you can do is whine about it hurts! I told you that it was your first times, and it would hurt a little, but it'll get better the more you do it. That's what I was doing today, trying to make it hurt less."

"But it really did hurt more this time, worse than the first time."

"Look, it will get better and not hurt so much. Maybe we can do it again tomorrow, wait...I can't tomorrow, but Friday I'm free for sure. You know, before you do it with this other guy on Saturday night."

"What! What are you talking about? What other guy?"

"Look Daq! You said you need to make money for your sisters and your dad. And *this is how you can do it. I'm going to give you ten dollars every time you do a fun poke with another guy. Ten dollars! You do 2 guys in one day and that's twenty dollars. And I'll buy you dinner after each day that you do it with somebody. Now that will help your family a lot!"*

"Jimmy...I don't want to...I don't like it and if my dad finds out he'll kill both of us."

"He better not find out! We talked about this; you have to keep this a secret. And...you are going to do this, you said you would work for me to earn money...and this is it! And if you think you're just gunna say no I don't want to now...think again! I have a lot of guys that are interested in this and even one guy that wants to fun poke your little sister...and that one would be worth twenty, maybe thirty dollars to ya...and don't worry I'll protect her. So, you see, I have plans and you're going to do what you said you would!"

"I never said..."

Then Jimmy grabbed my throat. "I said you are going to do this...and you will or you're going to get hurt." He rubbed along the red mark on my face..." This is nothing compared to what I could and will do to you...you understand? Now, I'll see you Friday, same place and same time." His breath stunk and his body odor was so strong it made me gag. But I nodded my head. Now I had to find a way to get to Jimmy's house by 3:00 PM Friday.

As Daq walked toward their car which was sitting in some bushes at the camp next to a row of tents and makeshift shelters, she was scared, she was hurting and now she had to come up with a lie that would satisfy her dad. And on top of all that, what was she going to do about her little sister? She couldn't just let some creep do a poke on her!

As she rounded the corner for the final jaunt to her car, she noticed police lights flashing around where their car was parked. She intently watched as she got closer, then she saw her two sisters standing next to a police officer who was talking to the girls. Daq then saw that the eight-year-old was crying and the five-year-old was sucking her thumb. She broke into an all-out run and when she got to the police officer she screamed, "What happened!" Right then the eight-year-old started crying uncontrollably and ran into Daq's arms. Then the five-year-old began crying. The police officer quickly comforted the child and moved to where Daq was standing.

"Are you related to these two?" She said in a compassionate and concerned voice.

"Yes...these are my sisters!" Right then she waved at the five-year-old to come to her and when she did then she had both sisters wrapped up in a hug. "What's going on?!" Just as she was about to ask her next question, she saw a gurney with a sheet covering a body, rolling toward an ambulance. "Oh No...is that my dad?!" She then started to cry herself. The police officer guided them a few feet away from the scene where not as much activity could be seen.

"What is your name?"

"Daq."

"Dack?"

"Yes…short for Daquiri."

"OK. How do you spell that, and what is your last name?"

"D-a-q, and Smith is our last name."

"And these two are your sisters, correct?"

"Yes."

"Can you tell me their names?"

"What happened?" Daq started to cry again. "Is my dad dead?"

Right then the eight-year-old spoke up. "Yes, Daddy's dead Daq."

"You saw him?"

"Yea."

"I'm sorry Angie…I'm so sorry you had to see it. I should have been here." She responded through her tears.

The police officer spoke up again. "I'm really sorry about this for all of you. And after I get your names, we can take you somewhere safe and cool where you can rest and get some food till what we know to do next. OK?"

Both Daq and Angie nodded.

"What's your little sister's name?"

"Laila."

"All of you have the same last name?"

Daq squeamishly nodded an affirmative.

"OK, let's get you into a squad car where it's cooler and then we will get you out of here." She led them to a car, made sure they were comfortable and gave Laila a teddy bear, the other two girls chose not to hold a bear. The three girls were treated wonderfully and overseen with great care by the PSPD.

Chapter Three

Alex finished his morning 'get ready' routine at around 6:30, right on schedule. The temperature, even at this time of the morning, was 89 degrees and supposed to get to a high of 117. So surprisingly, even the executives at this tight-ass corporation had relaxed the dress requirements. So, Alex was dressed in Khaki pants and a white shirt with a palm tree logo.

Now he would take Ellie out for a quick walk and give her and Maury fresh water for the day. Ellie was good at being left alone for the day, she had plenty of toys and chew bones, and a retired neighbor would come over around noon every day that Alex worked and let her out for a midday potty walk. Now old Maurice had special privileges while alone during the day. He had been the only pet in the house for ten years before the introduction of Ellie. Now, that past decade of peace and quiet was severely compromised. So, Alex had a pet door installed in the wall just above the washer in the utility room that led out to the garage, which is air conditioned, and 'lo and behold' there was what Alex called, Kitty City. There were carpeted stations, boxes, ramps, and ledges that he could play, walk, and relax in, all in the peace and quiet of the garage, not to mention his litter box was there. Alex would always place a step on the floor in front of the washer before leaving each morning so Old Maurice could easily get to the top of the washer and the exit to kitty city. Life wasn't too bad for the pets at the Barton house.

Now it was time to start the journey to go see the wizard, the wonderful Monday morning wizard of sales meetings! Just as he got Ellie's leash from a cabinet in the kitchen, the doorbell rang.

"This is a bit early." He said aloud to Ellie as she bounded to the front door. Alex told Ellie to sit and stay while he opened the door, which she did. Alex came face to face with a police officer standing at the door with a solemn look. His gut rolled and his breath came to a stop. He suddenly was back at the hospital with the doctor that had this same solemn look, telling him that Faith had passed away while he had gone home for a few hours of sleep and pet care. He forced himself to take a ragged breath and said, with a slight waver in his voice, "How can I help you officer?"

"Are you Mr. Barton? Alex Barton?"

"Yes."

"Mr. Barton, last night a man died at a homeless camp near the Palm Springs airport and was tentatively identified as a Robert Smith. And you were also identified as his father. Is that correct?"

"No, I don't know any Robert Smith. Must be some mistake. How did you even get my name attached to this?"

"A young girl identified you as his father. A girl that was apparently living with him and identified as his daughter. Her name was..." he pulled out a notebook and said, "Dak? Short for Daquiri?"

"Oh my god! Oh, my dear god!"

"Sir? Are you alright?"

Alex looked at the cop and gasped as he tried to intake air into his lungs. His face turned white, and he felt his equilibrium start to falter. The officer grabbed his arm and led him to a bench that sat under a small tree next to the walkway to the front porch.

"Sir...do I need to call an ambulance? Are you having a medical emergency?

"No..." Alex shook his head. "No, I just need a minute...If this is..." Alex put his hands to the side of his face and dropped his head down toward his lap. "If this is what I think it is...this is a major shock to my system." Right then Ellie had sensed enough conflict in the situation and started barking. Alex lifted his head and looked at her and raised a hand and made a patting motion at her. "It's OK baby girl. It's OK, come here." He now patted his hand next to him and she jumped to the bench and leaned against him, skeptically staring at the cop. Alex looked up and said, "Let me try to explain. Yes, I have...had...a son named Robert, but I know nothing about a homeless camp, or the name Smith. The last time I saw him was about thirteen years ago, when he left our home and never came back." Alex looked at the officer and realized how that sounded, even though it was true. "Why don't we step into the house officer?" The officer nodded and they stepped into the entry. Alex closed the door and said, "I know that sounds a bit weird, but my son was diagnosed with schizophrenia about twenty years ago and…" He realized that the officer was not here for the story of his mentally ill son. "Well, let's just say it has been a very difficult situation. So, when you asked if this could be my son, I was certain that was incorrect…until you used the name Daquiri. He had a daughter with that name and I'm guessing that's not a real common name."

"No, it's not. Uh, she has two other sisters that were at the scene also."

"What! Two Sisters! Are you sure?"

"That's what I have been told. Mr. Barton. Why don't you come to the police station and make a conclusive identification and talk with the officers that were at the scene and an investigator. And I'm sure that child services will be involved. Can you come now?"

"Of Course. I have a few loose ends I must take care of with work, and here, before I can go but it shouldn't take long."

"Actually, you're not under arrest or under any suspicion, so come when you can. I can let everyone know when you'll be there."

"No more than an hour. Thank You."

"Certainly, I will let them know. Go to the main station and ask for Detective Halloran."

Alex saw the officer out and then went into the great room and sat in one of the chairs. For about 5 minutes he processed what he had heard. Then the realization of the situation hit him, in his heart, he knew he had lost his only child last night...the child he had assumed was dead for the last thirteen years. Ellie sat with him.

Chapter Four

Jimmy Braxton was a miserable little son-of-a-bitch. He was a meth addict with little or no redeeming qualities. He would sell his own mother for a fix. He hadn't done that, yet, but he had stolen money, clothing, food, and jewelry, anything he could get his hands on from her. He had a RAP sheet as long as his skinny, pock marked arm. His personal hygiene was virtually non-existent. His clothes, the few he had, were dirty and ragged. The house he lived in was outside of Palm Springs in a condemned area that many people didn't even know existed. He had lived there with another addict until one day when the roommate went missing for a few days. Jimmy found him in another house in the same area, dead. He apparently had OD'd and died alone in this abandoned desolate house. Jimmy knew this was a nobody, a homeless transient, so Jimmy buried him in the desert sand a few hundred feet from the house he found him in. He figured nobody would know or miss him and at least he got buried. Perhaps a redeeming quality?

He was mean, violent, conniving, un-educated, and had virtually no conscience...and now he had his grimy hands on Daq, an easy meal ticket if he had ever seen one. Young, pretty, homeless, and needed help...perfect! She wanted to protect and provide for her little sisters, even better. He had never been involved in sex trafficking before, especially in children, but 'what the hell'! There was money to be made. He was surprised how much interest there was in young children, even in the eight-year-old. He knew he could book Daq at $100 damn easily at least three or four times a week and that was good money for him even if he had to give up $10 to her and a burger. Now the eight-year-old...that was going to be more, but he had some work to do to get that arranged, but he was confident he could pull it off. Meeting Daq was one of the greatest things to ever happen to him. He had to make sure that this Saturday, being this was her first time with someone else, it had to go good, real good. He would have to be sure the new guy was nice and gentle, and he also knew he would have to be special nice to Daq after it was over. A sacrifice for sure, but hey, ya gotta do what ya gotta do...at least till you get her trained...and good and scared.

***

Alex looked at the clock and saw that it was 6:55. He picked up his cell phone and called his sales Manager Tom. He wasn't looking forward to this conversation, actually any conversation with that egotistical jerk, but he knew it had to be done. He punched in the numbers on his cell phone and listened as the phone rang.

"Tom Wilkerson!"

"Morning Tom this is Alex Barton."

"Yes?!" (A curt response.)

"Tom I'm going to have to miss the meeting this morning, there has been a death in my family."

"Really?" (An even more curt response.)

"Yes, and I have to go this morning and take care of a few things."

"Who died?" (Another curt remark with an accusatory tone.)

Alex paused while he thought to himself *'that really shouldn't matter to this conversation...as a matter of fact it really is none of your business.'* "Actually, it's my son..."

"I didn't know you had a son!"

Again, he paused. Now Alex was getting angry. *'Who the hell does this jerk think he is? What the hell does that have to do with anything? It's none of your fucking business.'* "Well, that's hardly the point Tom..."

"Alex, you know how important these meetings are!"

That churlish remark hit Alex abruptly and all the frustration and animosity he had for the company he worked for took him to a different level of anger. "I tell you my son died and all you can say is how important your little Monday morning meetings are?! That has to be the most callous, and un-feeling remark I have heard!"

"Now listen Alex..."

"No, you listen Tom. These Monday sales meetings are ridiculous at best, you have no idea what you're doing, and what should be an enjoyable and inspiring session for the employees, so they would want to go out and sell and make our customers happy; are instead tedious, boring and ponderous. Perhaps if you had even a smidgen of experience that wasn't written in a textbook you might understand how to handle salespeople and customer service staff. So, here's what you can do with your stupid little Monday morning...'really important'...sales meeting! You can stick it in your ass! What was once a very prominent part of Palm Springs where thousands of customers sang our praises and promoted our service to others; is now just another conglomerate that doesn't give a shit about anything except making money. Which you just proved in spades with your cold-hearted comment about my son! So, I won't be at your sales meeting this morning...you little shit!" Then, he punched the 'end' button on his phone. He thought to himself that now was one of those times that he wished he had an old land-line telephone that sat on your desk, so he could have slammed the receiver down.

He sat for a few minutes cooling down after his tirade. Then he smiled and silently said to himself, *'Well, I'm sure that this will make my decision about retiring a lot easier.'*

Chapter Five

He pulled it together and realized he had an actual important meeting ahead of him. He went into the kitchen and splashed water on his face and looked at Ellie sitting on the floor next to him. He reached down and petted her and said, "It's OK baby girl." She had become distressed about the energy he was giving off. "Everything's alright." He lifted her up and kissed her on top of the head and gave her a hearty skritch on the neck. She responded by wagging her little tail furiously and licking him in the face. He took her out back and let her go potty again. Then headed down the hallway and out the utility room door into the garage. He glanced at kitty city and the elaborate set-up for his cat. As he stood looking for a few seconds he re-focused on what the next few hours would bring. He opened the car door and…

THUNK!

"Goddammit Maurice!" Old Maurice loved to lounge on one of the higher platforms in kitty city and when Alex would start to get in the car, he would jump off the platform and land on the car roof right in front of Alex. The object of this game was that he would then get a head and neck scratch and a couple of good pets before he had to get down. He didn't do it consistently, so it would come as a surprise, and Alex was always amazed that it always seemed to scare the hell out of him every time it happened.

***

Alex got to the police station almost exactly at the time he had said. He stated who he was and why he was there to an officer behind the reception desk. A few minutes later a distinguished looking gentleman dressed in a suit with no tie, and a young lady casually dressed in shorts and brightly flowered short sleeve blouse, came out to the lobby.

The man spoke first, "Mr. Barton?"

"Yes."

"I'm detective Jim Halloran, and this is Officer Lucy Chen who was on duty at the scene last night."

Officer Chen then spoke, "I'm very sorry for your loss. The girls were upset, and I tried my best to be as convivial as possible."

"I appreciate that. Where are the girls?"

Detective Halloran spoke up, "They're at child services right now. They spent the night there last night. We'll get you over to them right away, but we have some questions first and of course we need you to identify the body as your son."

"OK, let's get started. Do we need to go to the morgue?" As the three headed down a corridor with a series of doors on both sides.

Officer Chen gave a humorous chuff and said, "No, this isn't an episode of 'The

Naked City." Then turned quickly toward Alex somewhat chagrined and said, "I'm sorry, I wasn't making light of the situation, it's just that people have a certain image of this procedure."

"I took no offense." Alex smiled at her. "I am curious though, how does someone your age know about episodes of 'The Naked City.'"

"It is some of the best loved old shows that we all watch here at the precinct. But I shouldn't have said what I did."

"No worries."

Right then detective Halloran opened a door and said, "Here we go. Just sit anywhere."

Alex sat down and Officer Chen sat across from him. Detective Halloran had a file folder and opened it and laid a picture in front of Alex. "Can you identify this person?"

He stared at the photo intently and finally said, "Yes, that is my son. Robert...Bobby."

Alex choked, then swallowed hard, took a deep breath. "Robert Barton."

"Are you positive? It has been a long time since you saw him last."

"Yes, I'm positive. He looks the same, and there on the left side of his neck is a clover shaped birth mark.

"We're very sorry for your loss."

"Thank You."

"We have some questions…"

"I do too. How about I tell you my story concerning my son, then you can ask your questions. My story may shed light on the situation."

"OK, please go ahead." Detective Halloran took out a note pad and pen ready to take notes.

"Bobby was born in June of 1993. My wife and I were ecstatic at having a child and so looking forward to raising a son. For the first five years everything was bliss, we doted on that boy, and he was our everything. It wasn't until later in his sixth year that we noticed discernible problems that were aggressive and disturbing. Behavioral issues arose and what was most disconcerting was his lack of emotion through it all. He really seemed like he was void of emotions. An example of that, which to me was one of the most telltale signs of sociopath tendencies, was this story. In the second grade, when he was eight, a classmate of Bobby brought to show and tell a model scale replica of Palm Springs. She and her father had worked on this for years, painstakingly carving out buildings, streets, landmarks, and painting everything so that it matched the actual colors of the city. It was quite impressive, and one could tell a great deal of time and effort, and love went into the project. The class and teacher made a big deal out of the project and praised the little girl for her work and diligence to the project. At some point Bobby poured a small can of red paint over the project. A couple of his classmates saw him do it and we were called into school that evening. He sat in the principal's office with his teacher, the principal, Faith and I, the little girl and her father...with absolutely no emotion at all. He sat blankly looking at everyone in the room and even when the little girl began to cry, I could see in his eyes...he didn't care. When asked why he did this, his answer...*'because everyone had talked about her show and tell enough, it was my turn next.'* When Faith and I talked to him at home, there was nothing there, just like an empty seashell."

"Quick question...who is Faith?"

"Faith was my wife; she died around six months ago."

"Oh, I'm sorry to hear that. Please continue." He was taking copious notes.

"The following few years didn't bring any major traumas, but there was always a hint of that un-emotional kid always present. Faith chose not to acknowledge it, but I watched it closely. When he hit his teenage years, things got worst. Bobby became fascinated with working out and being strong and tough. So now, with his lack of emotion and a strong physical body to go along with it caused more problems to pop up. There were a lot of fights and altercations with other kids and regardless of the reason, he was always an empty shell, no emotion just a blank stare that said he had no feelings about any of it.

He dropped out of school when he was fourteen and ran away from home. He lived on the streets with some very unsavory people and that's where he got into the drugs. He refused to come home and if we did find him and bring him home, he'd be gone in a couple of days.

We tried everything we could to bring him back home and get him help. After a couple of years, we managed to find and get him some help. The doctor worked with him for a few months and diagnosed him as a schizophrenic sociopath. Not a good combination. We tried everything we could, but he didn't get better. He'd leave and be gone for extended periods of time, and we never knew what or who he would be when he came home. He attacked Faith one day and damn near killed her. Was choking her on the kitchen counter and she was convinced that he meant to kill her.

Luckily, she was able to grab a knife from the knife block and stab him in the side just under his right shoulder. Stunned, he ran out of the house. I'm sure if he would have stayed, he would have killed her.

We tried everything to get him into an institution after that, which isn't easy with the current laws on institutionalizing people. When he found out that we were trying to get him to a facility like that, he was gone, and we hadn't seen him for months. Until, one day he showed up with a wife and child. Apparently, he had been seeing this woman for a few months before the stabbing incident and she had gotten pregnant during that time.

Barbie was her name, and she was a real special girl. For example, she announced to Faith and me that the baby's name was Daquiri (mis-spelled on the birth certificate of course), and I quote...'*because that's what Bobby and I were drinking the night I let him fuck me without a rubber.*' A real charmer...with an obvious proficiency in the English language. She was an evident drug addict and fraud artist, who didn't care about anything except what she could get for herself. They approached us for a 'loan' so they could get started on their new life together. They stayed with us for a few nights and one evening I asked her if I could have sex with her for $1000. She was hiking up her dress before I finished the sentence. So, as I watched her get into a dog style position, I asked her another question. *'How about no sex, but I give you $2000, and you just leave and never come back.'* Her response? *'Damn straight! I'll even throw in a blow job. For that much you deserve at least a BJ.'* When I asked her about Bobby and her daughter...her answer? *'Hey, I'm ten years older than him, he's only 16 for Christ's sake I can't babysit my whole life away.'*

And your daughter?

'Never liked kids much, so naaww, not interested, she'd have a shit life with me anyway. You should keep her.' I paid her the two thousand and she left. Oh, she did ask about the blow job again, stating that she was pretty damn good at it and wanted to show me just how good. I said I would

decline that experience even though the offer, as pristinely presented as it was, was indeed difficult to resist. We never saw her again.

Bobby and Daq stayed with us for about four months, and then one day they were gone. Stole all the money he could find, took my debit card and used it twice for a total of $600. Daq was less than a year old and we haven't seen them since that day. That was the beginning of 2010. We tried mind you, God...we tried. But every search, every lead, every hope just vanished after a few years. We went to a counselor for therapy for over a year and finally we started living our lives, always mindful of Bobby, but no longer as a part of our lives. The councilor convinced us that we had to treat this as a death. In fact, our belief was that he had died at some point and Daq was somewhere...but that we would never know exactly where she was, or if she was even alive. A sad and tragic part of our life, but one that we could do nothing about and that we had to find a way to move on.

Now, I find out he's been alive all these years and he has two other children?"

"Apparently, that is correct. The child services counselor will talk with you about that. She has spent all night with them and is talking to them now. She should be able to give you more information." Detective Halloran replied.

"When can I do that?"

"Soon…she wanted the rest of the morning to evaluate the children more extensively. When we're finished, I will call and find out a time. However, we want to talk to you a bit more about last night. You see, there was a note left, addressed to you."

"Was it a suicide note?"

"We don't know. He died of an overdose of heroin, which we know. But whether it was intentional or accidental we may never know.

"Can I see the note?"

"Absolutely, just a few more quick questions and we will leave you alone to read it. By the way, it was marked confidential, and we have not opened it."

They were true to their word, a few simple questions later and Alex was left alone in the room with the letter from his son. His hands shook as he opened it, and he could feel the emotion building inside. It was addressed to:

Alex Barton...My father
Confidential
Please Dad...Read this!
Dad,
I am in a lucid state right now, and they come fewer and fewer now, so I wanted to write this to you now and want you to feel like it comes from your son...I mean your real son, in a state of mind that is thinking straight, knows what he is saying and saying what he knows to be the right and proper thing.
I hope if you're reading this, you still will allow me to call you Dad. I know I have been gone and not in touch for

the last thirteen years and for that I am so very sorry and regretful...Especially since I just learned about Mom dying. I've been back in Palm Springs for about the last month. My intentions were to contact you but when I heard about mom, I knew I couldn't ever come back. Even if you would have permitted me back into the family, I don't think I could have lived with all this hanging over my head. Frankly I don't deserve it.

After I left, I ended up in Denver living in a commune type lifestyle. We'd stay with different people we met; we never had a home of our own, we were like nomads just getting by however we could. I would find jobs to bring in some money and even occasionally we could afford to get an apartment and actually have a home of sorts. But that was generally short lived, and we would be back on the streets and living our homeless lives.

After about 4 years I met Sandy, who was another junkie, but she at least had a house. She had gotten it from her family somehow in a will, or at least her parents got the house and gave it to her. She became a house for junkies and made money however she could...and I think you know how she made most of it. But I was considered her main guy, so when she got pregnant after about a year...I became a father again.

Dad...my life was pure shit...I was drugged up all the time, I would have schizoid episodes and be gone for days and weeks. I was always in a state of depression...and always knew what a shit father I was. God only knows what my girls went through. But I loved them Dad, I just couldn't get past my addictions and my episodes. But I loved them...one night I caught some miserable asshole trying to fuck my six-month-old

Angie. I beat him to a bloody pulp. Sandy threw me out that night and I never heard whether the piece of shit died or what. But I never heard anything more.

So now I had a 6-year-old daughter and a 6-month-old daughter and no place to go, no money and no life. We were homeless for about 6 months, ended up in Yuma, AZ and it was the lowest point of my life. So low, that I had no choice but to find help however I could. I got into a drug program that helped not only me but helped the 2 girls also. They provided a place to stay, supervision, food, and medical help. The girls were finally getting the care they needed. Frankly I was just going through the motions of the treatments, I still was doing drugs and making bad decisions, but then life changed for me. I met a volunteer worker named Shaila and we hit it off and she really helped me, and I found myself wanting to get better...for her. And it worked and I started to actually get better! And Shaila and I fell in love, and we lived together with the girls. Life was starting to make sense. Oh, I still had relapses and bad days, but I was getting help and medication that was really making a difference. Also, I felt like I wanted to get better.

Shaila got pregnant and we had another little girl, and we named her Laila...after her mom. So now I had 3 girls, one 8, one 3, and a newborn. Life was great and I was doing pretty good. I still had bad days and periods that were tough, but with Shaila helping me and loving me, life seemed right. And for four years it was a great life. I had been clean for almost a year. I still struggled with my personality issues but the meds I was taking were helping tremendously. I wish I had called you and mom, but I was afraid...afraid it might make me step backwards.

Then, one-night Shaila had gotten a call to go into the center and help a patient. The miserable son-of-a-bitch murdered her while she tried to help him. I came apart, my world was at its end. I knew then that god or whatever force controls this planet, didn't want me to be happy...my destiny was to be shit. I stayed at Shaila's for a while, but I was back on drugs and off my meds and I was a total mess.

I took her car and came back to Palm Springs about a month ago, for one reason...to get off this earth and go to wherever you go when you know that the right path is death. But I knew the three girls would need a home and good people to give them a good life...you and Mom. But when Mom... Dad, I still didn't give it a second thought...I want you to take the girls. I know you'll give them everything they need, and you'll raise them right! You did me...it just that I was a hopeless case.

Please raise the girls...Daq is angry, confused and has seen too much for any 13-year-old to have seen...she's going to be mean and stubborn and difficult. But Dad, she needs you...the love, the understanding and discipline that you tried to give to me, but I was too gone to accept it.

Now Angie...at 8 years old is smart beyond belief...I wonder if she really is mine, there's a chance she's not...but I raised her and I love her...that makes her mine. She's quiet and helpful and I think is probably more stable than Daq...by a long shot. But she needs love and support and more than anything else, guidance.

Laila is 5, just turned 5...she is quiet to the point of no words at all. I don't think she is comprehending what is going on and is blocking everything out...help her, bring her back...if she is anything like her mother, she will be amazing.

I love you Dad...I'm so sorry about Mom. I know you loved her more than anything in the world and she felt the same about you. I'm sorry.

Try to explain to the girls about me someday...but for now, just love them.

Goodbye Dad. And Thank You.

Bobby

Tears had fallen over most of the letter by the time Alex had read it. He sat and physically shook from a restrained lament. After about ten minutes, he folded the letter up and stuck in in his back pocket.

He opened the door to the conference room and stepped into the hallway. Officer

Chen and detective Halloran moved across the hallway and slowed down to a stop, looking down at the floor. They had been trained to identify emotions in people and with Alex they immediately spotted a bereaved person, easily a truly broken and distressed individual.

"We're very sorry Mr. Barton."

"Thank You. Are we finished here?"

"If you have anything else to tell, perhaps about the letter?"

Alex shook his head, "The letter was very personal, and I would prefer not to share it. It would not give you anything that would help you." He knew this was a lie, but it was an intimate decision, one he knew his son would appreciate.

Detective Halloran nodded.

"What is my next step?"

"Oh, there's paperwork to fill out. Wouldn't be America if there wasn't a ton of paperwork." Officer Chen looked at Alex and started to apologize but Alex cut her off with a smile and a comment of "How true!"

Chapter Six

Officer Chen was correct, there was a ton of paperwork. But Alex plowed through it and at around 3PM he stood in the vestibule of the local mortuary talking with an associate. The body of Bobby had finally gotten released to Alex and he was making his final arrangements. He had decided that he wanted his son cremated and the ashes put into an urn. He also said he wanted to take the urn with him, he knew it would be Faith's wishes that she could be with him, side by side, even now.

"Would you like to view the body before cremation?" The mortuary associate asked.

Alex looked at him and then to the floor. "I don't know. I haven't seen him for nearly thirteen years. I don't know how to feel."

"If I may Mr. Barton. I think you'd regret not taking this final chance to view your son, regardless of how long it has been, or circumstances involved. I've seen both sides and I definitely believe that those that did view, never regretted it." He looked at Alex and saw the indecision he was having. "I will give you some time to think about it."

"No, you're right. I would regret it, and I know if my wife was here, she would tell me the same thing and I also know she would want to see him and have the chance to say goodbye. I will view the body."

"Follow me." He led Alex into a viewing room where his son lay on a beautifully appointed and cushioned table. Bobby was fully clothed in khaki pants and a brightly colored Hawaiian style shirt. Alex walked up close to the table and felt the fabric of the shirt. "If you have something else you would like to dress him in before the procedure…"

"No, this is perfect. He loved these bright colored shirts, even as a small kid, he loved them."

"These were the clothes he was wearing when he was brought to us. We cleaned and pressed them before putting them back on. I think he looks good."

"I do too, thank you for all you have done."

"Certainly. I'll leave you alone. Take as long as you want and when you're ready just come to my office."

"Thank You."

As the door closed and Alex was alone with his son, a myriad of emotions swept over him. He felt a sadness at the loss of his son, but also at the circumstances that surrounded his life. He felt sorry for himself and for his wife for never having had the privilege and joy to raise a son to manhood. He felt an emptiness of the ultimate finality. He was feeling guilty at not being able to do more. And...he felt...anger. He started speaking out loud to his son. "Oh Bobby! Why didn't you let us help you! If we were doing something wrong, we could have figured it out, we could have figured something out. You didn't need to run, you didn't need to hide, you didn't need to stay out of our lives. Out of my life! You were my son, my flesh and blood! I would have done anything to help you, even given my life! But dammit...you had to do it your way, had to put in that crazy, mixed-up mind of yours that you knew what was best for me, and your mother...when it wasn't...it wasn't! We could have worked it out, we could have gotten you better, we could've been a family. And then you tell me in a letter that you didn't think it could work now, especially since mom had died...how dare you assume to know how I was going to feel!" His voice was rising.

Now the emotions turned to tears...his voice went to a whisper.

"Now look what you've done! I've lost Faith...and now you...and I didn't even know you were here! Damn you! We had the right to know! We had the right to know...we had the right to know...we had the right..."

Alex cried uncontrollably. He spoke in a louder voice, "We had the right! We could have helped! But you wouldn't let us, you ran away from us! You just wouldn't let us." He clenched his fists as he stood crying. He slammed his fists into his thighs. He became lightheaded and dizzy. He knelt on the floor with only one knee on the lush carpet. He stayed that way until he stopped crying and felt completely drained of any strength he had. He felt as if he could lay his head down and sleep.

The associate watched from his monitor view of the room, ready to help if needed, as Alex knelt on the floor. He watched as Alex stood and dragged a chair over to where his son lay.

He sat quietly as he remembered his son as a child and how happy they had been for the first few years of his life. It was easily the happiest time of his life. He then took his son's hand into his and for the next half hour just talked to him about his mom and everything that had happened in their life without him. There were more tears, some laughter...and some closure.

He stood, laid his son's hand back at his side, took a deep breath, leaned down and kissed his son on the forehead. "Goodbye Bobby. I'm glad we got this opportunity to talk. Rest well my dear son, till I see you again, and please, say hi to your mother for me and tell her I love and miss her. And don't forget that I love you too! And don't worry about your girls...I got this! I promise."

He left the viewing room, went to the associate's office, and made the final arrangements.

Chapter Seven

It was nearing 4:00PM that fateful Monday when he called the Child services representative. Officer Chen had given him the phone number and the name of the representative.

"Jennifer Grey."

"Yes. Ms. Grey, my name is Alex Barton and I'm calling about the three girls that were picked up last night at the (almost said suicide) homeless camp where my son died."

"Yes, Mr. Barton I'm very sorry for your loss. I am with the girls now and would like to meet with you today if that's possible?"

"Absolutely. Are they OK?"

"Well..."

"Never mind. That was a stupid question. Just tell me when...and where."

"How about here, in my office at 5:00? Do you know where we are located?"

"Yes, On Indian Canyon?"

"That's right. My office is on the second floor, room 212. See you at 5:00?"

"Yes. Thank You."

Alex hung up and got to his car. He was emotionally drained and thought it might do him well to sleep for a while, before meeting his three grandchildren.
'Jesus...three grandkids!' that thought suddenly impacted him way harder than he had anticipated. Of course, he hadn't really thought about it, until now.

He drove to a small park located on Indian Canyon Drive. He pulled into a shaded parking place, left the car running, closed his eyes and tried to think about all that had happened on this day. But sleep overcame him, and he fell asleep with his chin resting on his chest. A noise awoke him about forty minutes later. It was his cell phone. He looked at the screen and saw it was his neighbor Burt calling.

"Hi Burt."

"Hi Alex. Thought I'd call and let you know I just took Ellie out about a half hour ago and she's all set." He hesitated, "But, you know the real reason I called, don't you? Is everything OK?"

Alex smiled thinking of his friend and next-door neighbor. He remembered back nearly ten years ago when he and Faith had first met their new neighbors. There had been a flurry of activity when they first moved in, but just a day after the frenzy had let up, they came to the front door and introduced themselves. *'Hi, we're your new neighbors. Sorry for all the confusion over the past couple of days. I'm Burt, and this is my partner, Ernie.'* The two men stood for a few seconds as if expecting a reaction. Alex spoke first, *'Really, Bert and Ernie?'* Then Burt again spoke, *'That's right! You officially now live next door to Burt and Ernie; however, I spell Burt with a u and not an e.'*

'Well Burt and Ernie...it's nice to have you in the neighborhood...in the neighborhood!' Alex sang that last part. Everyone laughed, and Faith said, *'Come in and we can celebrate with a drink and hopefully get him to stop singing!'* And from that day forward they became some of our best friends. Friends that saw me through some tough times, friends that help however they can, friends that have helped get me through the loss of my love, and now will be here to help me through this crisis.

"Another day in the continuing saga of life with Alex..." Alex's voice constricted. "I can't go into details yet Burt, cuz I don't really know any, also, I don't think I have ever had a day like this in my life...and you know my life and some of the crap I have gone through...and this one is the weirdest one yet!"

"How can we help? You know we're here and will do whatever."

"I know that my friend, and thanks, it means a lot! Just take care of the animals till I get back, and I really don't know when that will be."

***

He looked at the time and realized he had about fifteen minutes to get to Jennifer Grey's office. He got out of the car and walked around a little in hopes that would clear his head from his nap. He realized he hadn't had anything to eat since early morning, and wished he had a piece of toast. He smiled at this thought, this had always been a joke between Faith and him. She had once said to him that his fix-all for everything was...a piece of toast. *'You could be holding your bitten off leg, and you would try and fix it by eating toast!'*

He said out loud, "God, I miss you, Faith." Then thought to himself, *'She'd know what to do.'*

He drove to child services and parked his car, chewed four Altoids, then put two more in his mouth to suck on, and three more in his pocket just in case. Walked into the building entrance and found room 212. He laid his hand on the doorknob, closed his eyes, and turned the knob.

Life was about to drastically change for Alex Barton.

Chapter Eight

"Ms. Grey?"

"Yes, Mr. Barton?"

"Yes, nice to meet you." He extended his hand, and they shook. She looked about Alex's age, maybe a bit younger and Alex could tell by her eyes she was someone who cared. Over the years of selling and working with people to solve their heating and air conditioning problems, he had gotten pretty good at reading people, and he sensed that this was more than a job for her, this appeared to be a passion.

"Please call me Jennifer."

"Thank You. Well Jennifer, you're probably as confused as I am shocked with this whole situation. For the last thirteen years I have assumed my son and infant granddaughter had been living as someone else never to return or they had been dead. Now I have back the thirteen-year-old granddaughter, a son who has been alive this whole time and just died only a few miles from my house, and two new granddaughters I never knew about. So far, one helluva a day with still more to go."

"Mr. Barton, I can't even imagine."

"Alex, please call me Alex. Where do we start?"

"Well, I have had an extensive conversation with the police that you spoke with this morning. I have also seen the reports...but I would like to have another conversation with you about your son and possibly the letter he wrote to you that you told the police you would rather not share?"

"Yea, I've kind of re-thought that and I have the letter with me. I thought that you may want to read it." He handed the letter over to her and sat back in the chair. "Go ahead and read and then we can talk." He watched her as she read through the letter, she took her time, and he could see she was analyzing all the details. After she was done, she laid the letter down and looked at Alex who then spoke, "I don't know if you are now under any type of obligation to report anything to the police."

"Technically, if I learn about a possible crime, I am supposed to report it. But without getting into a rather hazy area, let's say I use my own judgement. With what I read; I will tell you that I think this letter will be better off in the police report. They will be able to close the books on this quickly and really there is nothing incriminating, with the possible exception of the beating he gave to the person trying to rape his daughter. The police may try to contact the Denver police and share this information, just in case. But this will help clear up a lot of loose ends that cops need to close…and it will certainly help you with the three girls."

"How will it help me with the girls?"

"Well, that's what we need to talk about. I have arranged a foster home for the girls tonight and..."

"Whoa...foster home? They're coming home with me! You read the letter, and I have just made a promise to my son today. I don't care what it takes or what I must do, but they're coming home with me! I'm adopting them, whatever you want to call it, I'll sign anything, do anything, but...they're coming home with me!"

Jennifer smiled and said, "OK...glad to hear you say that! And I love your conviction. I'll help you through the process, I promise."

"Thank you."

"Now, I think the girls will be getting some food right about now so if you would like, we could talk now. That be OK with you? Then you can meet your grandchildren." She smiled a smile that was warm and reassuring, a smile that said, *'You can trust me.'*

***

They talked for over an hour. Alex told her the same story he had told the police, only in more detail. They talked about the letter, again in much detail, and they talked about him and Faith and their decisions. Somehow, Alex felt comfortable telling her details, in fact it was the first time since Faith's death that he had given many of these details, and it felt cathartic.

"Alex, there is no way that any of this is your or Faith's fault. I feel secure in thinking that you know that, but with what you are about to undertake, you need to believe it at all times, and draw on it when you really need it. You get me?"

Alex smiled and nodded. "I do. Thank you, that's good advice and probably advice I'll need to be reminded of. Should we meet my girls?"

"Before we do...you need to hear what I've been able to ascertain since yesterday. My, workup of each child?"

"Yea, of course. You're absolutely right."

"OK, first let's talk Daiquiri. Here is a young girl, she just turned thirteen about a month ago, that has seen way more bad life than she has seen good. Although the last mother was a good influence on her, when she died it had a profound repercussion on Daq. I think that she now believes that being good, or even good itself in this world, is a death sentence, and not worth the effort. She's very confused, she's scared, she's bitter, she's looking for direction in her life. And that is what scares me. I believe she has someone that has come into her life that is not good, in fact is the polar opposite of good."

"What do you mean?"

"Based on a conversation I had with her today, I believe she might be mixed up with a kid…person…man…" She hesitated a few seconds, then looked Alex in the eyes, "a miserable piece of shit that the world would be way better off without!"

"You have my attention."

"His name is Jimmy. Jimmy Baxter…Braxster…something like that, lives in the indigent area. I've never met him, but he has been a name around here for a little while. He's bad business. A known addict that will do anything for a fix, or just to make some money. He's sold drugs, he's stolen, robbed, assaulted, lied, and done just about anything to help himself find another score."

"How is he hooked with Daq?"

"His name came up when we examined Daq this morning. It's procedural that we do a medical exam and when we did, we found some bruising and blood in her vaginal area...along with semen."

Alex took a rapid deep breath and rolled his head and eyes to the ceiling, as his body tensed up into a taunt coil.

"Easy. That won't help this situation." She watched as Alex relaxed some and started to focus back to her. "She needs your help...not your anger."

"Easier said than done."

"I know. Now the really frightening part of all this..."

"That wasn't the frightening part!"

"No! I think he is planning to start selling her out...sex trafficking, or pimping, based on some information she gave to me."

"Oh my God! At her age...how can this even...what kind of perverted..."

"Listen, this is tough to hear, but it's necessary to hear. She is right at a time when she is supposed to start learning about her body and all its workings, and a very intimate, and complex subject called sex. She will draw conclusions and images of what sex will be like in her lifetime. And she's going to need direction and understanding, and a proper outlook and vision of what sex actually is, and how it will relate to her and her life. If she continues the path she is on, can you imagine what her perspective, or philosophy will be about sex? And she will look to you for that roadmap, even if she tells you and the rest of the world that talking to you about anything like that, would be the grossest thing she could think of. But you will be it!"

"Wow, and I thought the biggest problem would be helping her through her first menstrual period."

Jennifer laughed, "Well, I hate to tell you this...I don't think she has had her first period yet."

They both gave a short laugh. Alex sat silently staring into nothing, as a million different thoughts ran through his mind. Jennifer just watched him in silence also. Finally, he looked up at her and said, "My son says I'm the right guy...and I told him today he was correct...I have to believe that I am."

She smiled slightly and nodded. "And you won't kill Jimmy?"

"As long as he leaves us alone, but no promises."

She let it go but realized that Jimmy may well not leave them alone. But that would be a discussion for another day.

"OK, let's talk about Angie, who is eight...going on fifty. This little girl is highly intelligent with a mind that absorbs knowledge and retains it at a rate that I have not seen before except in autistic children. However, I don't think she's autistic. I believe she just has a brain that works that way. When I said to her that we would be getting her somewhere that would help her in the future...her response was 'you should be careful making statements that could become litigious in the future.'"

"Great, an eight-year-old that has a better vocabulary than I do."

"Better than most do! She has a gifted mind, we tested her, and you may very well have a prodigy on your hands. She will need to be challenged throughout her life, most gifted children do, and among everything else that you'll have to do, that will fall on you also. She will need stability, discipline, structure and most of all, support in her needs to expand her unquenchable thirst for knowledge. Oh, she also needs to know how to be a human being. Social skills, becoming an adult, interactions with others...and of course the woman things...but you should have that nutted before too long."

Alex just looked at her with a slight smile. Jennifer smiled back.

"But seriously, she will be a challenge, in a much different way that Daq, but still a challenge."

Still smiling, he looked at Jennifer, and with arms slightly raised he said, "Next!"

"Right! Now I need to get serious. Not that anything I have said so far has not been serious, but this little girl, Laila, is terrified. Her world has come apart in front of her eyes without the luxury of having any knowledge of what the real world is. As an infant she was loved and nurtured and before she knew about anything, it was ripped out from under her. And now she has no idea what has happened or will happen. And all the recent things in her life have been so traumatic that she has withdrew completely. She could almost be considered a zombie, just walking through life doing whatever comes next and following a group. She needs love, security, structure, and encouragement. Things I feel confident you can provide." She sat silent for a few seconds then looked deeply into Alexs eyes. "I've done this job for a long time. I love it and it means everything to me. I feel I've gotten pretty damn good at reading people. And I feel very confident in you, you seem to have the passion and commitment and...love...that this situation is going to need. But you will need help...and don't ever think you won't, or don't ever think you'll be weak if you need it. And for god's sake...get away from the situation periodically. If you don't, it will drive you crazy and eventually you'll fail. Understand?"

Alex stared into her eyes, nodded, and said, "Thank You. Will you be part of that 'help that will be needed'?"

"Of course. I'll help if I can, however I can, even if it is to refer you to someone else."

"Good."

"Ready to meet your girls?"

After a deep breath, he looked at Jennifer and said, "Yep. Let's shoot this fucker!" Then quickly realized that that probably wasn't a very acceptable way of saying OK. "Sorry, that's a movie line that my wife and I used to…"

"Ed Wood. Martin Landau playing Bela Lugosi…the octopus scene!"

"Wow! That is impressive! Not many people would have known that."

"I think it is a very appropriate quote." She gave a humorous chuff and said, "Let's have the girls come in…one at time at first."

Alex nodded.

Chapter Nine

The three girls sat in the waiting room just down the hall from Jennifer's office. They were all quiet with anticipation. Laila sat on Daq's lap while Angie sat in a chair facing them.

"Do you remember him at all Daq?"

She shook her head. "He's probably an asshole."

"Why?"

"I don't know... cuz Dad took off when he lived with him? I don't know...just probably." She smiled down at Laila who was looking up at her while sucking her thumb."

"I hope he's nice." Angie looked down at the floor. She felt like crying but she gritted her teeth and stopped herself.

Daq saw her and said, "Ang...it's gunna be OK. I'm not gunna let nothing happen to you guys. If we don't like it there, then we're outa there...I'm gunna be making money now and we can be OK."

Angie started to cry as much as she fought against it, "I don't want you to make money in a bad way. And not with him."

Daq remembered the first and only time Jimmy had met Angie, he had bullied her and made fun of her. Then she remembered what he had said about some guy wanting a fun poke with your little sister. She swallowed hard and looked at the floor. "Let's not worry about it now."

Right then Jennifer Grey walked in and smiled at the girls. "OK, it's time to meet your grandfather. I've been talking to him for a while, and I think you guys are really going to like him. And he's excited to meet you! So, I think it would be best if you met him one at a time before you go with him to his home."

"You mean we're going home with him!" Daq blurted out.

"Looks like it." She smiled at Daq and said, "Let's have you meet him first. He says he remembers holding you in his arms when you were just a baby."

"He's probably some old perv."

"Daq...you said you'd give him a chance. We've checked him out thoroughly. He seems very nice and wants to help you, and he has a nice home that you'll be able to live in. Give him a chance. OK?"

Daq handed Laila off to Angie and headed out the door. They slowly walked toward her office and Jennifer then opened the door and ushered Daq into the room. She looked up at Alex who had stood as soon as she entered the room. She stared at him.

"Hello Daquiri, I'm Alex, your grandfather. You look way different than you did the last time I saw you. You were only a few months old. I..."

"You look like my dad."

Alex smiled and nodded, "Happens with father and son sometimes." He slowly lost his smile and said, "I'm so sorry about your dad. He loved you so much, but his illness just refused to let him live any longer."

"What would you know about it."

Jennifer started to say something, and Alex held a hand up and she stopped.

"You're right. I don't know much about it..."

"That's cuz you were never around."

"I know that. Every day of my life I know that. But he didn't want me around and made sure I didn't know where he was. We tried everything to find him, but he didn't want to be found. And that broke my heart. He was my son, and I loved him more than anyone could know."

"Probably still you were an asshole. That why you don't have a wife also? She doesn't want to be found either?"

Alex gritted his teeth. "No, she also had an illness that refused to let her live any longer. It was a different kind of illness, but it still took her away from me. She died around six months ago. We can talk more about her later…and you kind of look like her, especially in your eyes." He sat down and looked straight on into Daq's face. "Daq, I know this sucks for you. And you're probably scared and pissed off at everything and everyone right now. I know I would be! But I want you to be part of my family…no…our family, right now, starting tonight. I'll need your help, but I know damn well we can do this! What'd ya say…give it shot?"

"You don't love me."

"The hell I don't!" His answer was quick and firm. "I have loved you since the very first time I held you in my arms when you were just a few months old. My heart opened a spot up just for you and let you in...and you've never left and never will. Don't you ever forget that!" He stood and moved toward her. She immediately pulled back, and he stopped. He gently laid his hand against the side of her face, "Never, ever forget that! And, unless I am very much mistaken, it's about to open two new spots also." He smiled at her as she looked up to him with eyes that were filling with tears.

"I better get back with Lai...she'll be wondering." She looked at Alex as she left and just nodded her head to him as he smiled at her.

Jennifer put an arm around Daq as they walked back to the waiting room but wisely said nothing. She opened the door and Angie sat holding Laila. Laila slid off her lap and went to Daq who lifted her up and together they sat down. Angie stood and Jennifer said, "Let's meet your grandpa."

Angie stood and moved to Jennifer and took her outstretched hand. When they stepped into the office, Alex stood and smiled at Angie. She stood wide-eyed looking back at him with an expressionless, almost analytical stare.

"You look like my dad."

Alex smiled and said, "Yea...Daq said the same thing. That's what happens with Father and Son. It is really nice to finally meet you. My name is Alex...I'm your grandpa...and...I'm looking forward to having you live with me along with your sisters so we can make a family. Would you like that?"

"It might have appeal. But based on what I have learned about you, you've never raised any girls. You didn't, did you?"

"No. I had a sister growing up and was married to a woman for thirty+ years...does that count?"

"Nope. You need more than just familiarity with the species."

"I think with your help, I'm going to do fine." He smiled at her and found himself staring.

"What! Are you laughing at me?"

"Absolutely not! I find you captivating. I enthusiastically look forward to our time together. I know I will learn a lot from you and with your help, I know we can put together a family filled with fun. Will you help me?"

She looked directly into his eyes for a second. Then said, "You look serious enough, maybe even determined. I'll help how I can. Right now, I'm worried about Daq though."

"Me too."

She looked into his eyes again, then smiled slightly and nodded her head. "I suppose it's time for...what are we supposed to call you?"

"Uhhh...I don't really know. Technically I'm your grandpa, but I'll be working as your dad. So..."

"Well, I guess we'll work on it."

"That's a deal."

Jennifer was smiling broadly at this exchange. She held out her hand and said, "Shall we get Laila?"

Angie nodded. And they headed out the door. When the door closed behind them, she looked at Jennifer and said, "I like him."

"And he likes you." She opened the waiting room door and Angie went in and sat next to Daq and Laila. Jennifer looked at Laila sitting on Daq's lap and said, "Come on sweetheart, let's go meet your new...she stopped herself."

"Her what!" Daq snapped. "He's nothing to us!"

"Stop it Daq!" Angie said. "I liked him, he reminded me of Dad. I want to give this a try! Don't mess it up before we even start."

Jennifer jumped in, "Daq, she's right. Give this a chance. It will never work if you shut down already. OK?" She lifted Laila up into her arms and carried her out into the hall toward her office.

When the door closed Daq glowered at Angie. "Jesus Ang don't give in already. We don't know a damn thing about this guy. Except he hasn't even been around for our dad. And you're ready to curl up in his lap!"

"I'm willing to give him a chance! Daq...I want a house again. I want a bed. I want food on a table. Not stuck in a homeless camp trying to sleep and eat in a car and with everyone all around us. Especially the likes of that asshole Jimmy!"

"Watch your mouth. And Jimmy's not bad, he's just trying to help us make it out here."

"Oh baloney! That worthless imbecile is about himself and that's it! And I know he's hitting you...isn't he?!"

"Oh, just shut up...and forget about it!" She flopped down into her chair and turned away from Angie. But as she sat and brooded, her mind again went to the conversation she had with Jimmy, the one where he said *'You'll get used to the pain...and you're having a fun poke with a different guy this week...and you'll do what I tell you, whenever I say...'* Then he slapped my face hard and said he'd do that more if I didn't do what he wanted.

Right about then Jennifer entered the office holding Laila in her arms and faced Alex. "She's black!" Alex blurted out. And as soon as the words had tumbled out of his mouth without his brain knowing anything about it...he realized just how stupid, how condescending, how racist, and how completely obvious it sounded. He looked at Jennifer, who, by the way, was also *'black'*, as she held Laila with a look on her face that said, *'I really can't believe you just said that.'* Rather chagrined, he said, "As you can obviously tell, I have keen observation powers."

She set the child down and looked at him with a slight smirk on her face, "Yes, I've just recently become aware of that talent."

"Hello baby girl!" He carefully walked up to the frightened child sucking her thumb and trembling slightly. "I'm your grandpa but you can call me Pops." He squatted down and gently laid his hand on her arm and smiled. "Honey, I know you're scared, confused and a little lost right now, but I promise I'm here to take care of you and protect you and give you a home to live in with your sisters. We're going to be a family. You can be as quiet as you want for as long as you want. I know you need to see for sure everything is OK, and I'm very confident that you will. But until that happens, you just do what makes you comfortable and secure. Leave the rest to me." He slowly leaned forward and kissed her forehead. As he leaned back away from her, he noticed she was staring at him. He looked at Jennifer and said, "If she was talking, I'm pretty sure she would tell me I look like her dad." He held out his arms in the typical adult way to say, *'would you like to come to me and allow me to pick you up?'* She did, and Alex picked up her up and looked at Jennifer. "Shall we gather the troops and head for home?" Jennifer nodded and smiled. "Oh, and I'm sorry about the comment…I'm not…"

Jennifer grinned, "I know you're not. I also have keen powers of observation." Jennifer smiled a warm and seemingly all-knowing smile. The five of them sat for a while longer and talked.

Chapter Ten

After getting the three girls into the SUV along with what belongings they had, Alex sat in the driver's seat and said out loud, "I could use some food and some ice cream!" He started the car, backed out of the parking spot and headed into downtown Palm Springs on Palm Canyon drive. He parked on the street near Sammy G's Italian restaurant and announced that this was one of his favorite restaurants and they had a great selection of gelato and ice cream. He asked for a table outside and the four of them were seated near a large fountain that was decorated with lights and misters all around it. The girls all seemed somewhat taken back by the busy restaurant, the number of people, the lights, the mist machines, and the music. Everyone sat quietly looking at each other when Alex said, "What kind of ice cream does everyone like?" No answers. "You like the traditional? Vanilla, chocolate, strawberry? Or do you like something fancier?" Still no answers. "OK, my favorite is Belgian chocolate gelato. So, I'm going to order a dish of that, and I will share with Laila. But I'm also going to get an order of lasagna because I haven't eaten today. Now you two need to order something. You can order off the menu or just tell the server what you like, and they will help you pick. Angie looked at the menu and then looked at Alex and said in a low voice, "I think I want the chocolate peanut butter cup gelato."

"Great Choice!" He purposely boomed his voice. "Daq, how about you?"

"What the fuck are you trying to do?!"

"Trying to get you to order some ice cream...what do you think I'm trying to do?"

"Trying to get us to like you cuz you're buying us ice cream."

"That's probably a little true. Daq, after we're done here, all of us are starting a whole new life. And that's scary, for you guys and for me. I know you didn't predict that you'd be living with me...did you? I know I didn't. Do you think I got up this morning thinking I would be bringing home three little girls? Let me correct that...two little girls and one teenager. I'm scared shitless, cuz I don't know what I'm doing any more than you do."

"Probably cuz you fucked up so bad with my dad and your own wife."

He pushed down the anger that he felt right then and looked Daq directly in the eyes. "You want to believe that...go ahead. You want to hurt me by saying stuff like that...go ahead. But understand this! You three are now my daughters. Oh, I know you're my granddaughters, but now you are also daughters! And as a father of three daughters, it is my job to cloth, feed, protect, and keep you in good health. It is also my job to teach, guide, and help you through this journey called life, all the while loving you without question. That is my mission, that is my job, and not one that I am sure I know how to do! But, like it or not, by God, we all are going to strive to make it happen!" He stared at Daq. She stared back and finally said,

"I always liked rocky road."

Alex smiled, "Just like your dad."

Chapter Eleven

The Trip home was a relatively quiet ride. Alex had asked a few questions, but the answers were abbreviated and obtuse. He decided to remain quiet till they arrived at the house. As he drove through the guarded gate and waved to the guard, the three girls just stared. Finally, Angie said, "This isn't like an internment camp, is it?"

Alex laughed, (although he was amazed that an eight-year-old would know about an internment camp) "No, nothing quite that nefarious. This is called a gated community, where not just anyone can get in unless you live here."

Daq chimed in, "How does it know if you live here?"

"There is a little gizmo on the front of the car that the gate can read and lets you in."

"A transponder." Angie said matter of factually.

Again, Alex smiled at the young girl's knowledge. "Yes, a transponder. Very good."

Daq asked, "Are there walls all around the houses?"

"Yes, walls all around the entire complex and of course privacy walls between houses."

"Jesus, we're in prison!"

Alex laughed, "You're not in prison...it just gives a little added security to the homeowners living here."

As the garage door opened Alex slowly pulled into the garage. He tapped the horn lightly, which was the signal for Maurice (if he was in the garage) to jump up on the shelf nearest the door to the utility room. He didn't jump onto the shelf, so Alex continued into the garage at a slow pace.

He shut off the car and got out and went to the passenger side of the car and opened the front door. "Daq...here we are. Help me, by helping them to get settled. OK?" She nodded. Alex went to the back door, held out his arms to Laila, which she readily allowed him to pick her up. "Angie, we're here. Can you grab your stuff and Laila's, and we'll go in the house and get settled in." He went to the back door, pushed the button to close the garage door, which seemed to fascinate the girls, and entered the utility room. Old Maurice stood on top of the dryer as he always did when Alex got home waiting for his head scratch and scritches under his chin. When he saw the three girls, he jumped off the dryer and ran into the hallway with his back bowed and fur standing up. "No, it's OK Maury, they belong here." Not completely convinced yet, he went under the bed in the master bedroom.

Now that brought out Ellie. Ellie came down the hallway from the kitchen and came face to face with the three girls. She stopped for a few seconds, then realized that here stood three friends she had never met before. She ran to the girls, tail wagging so fast it was almost invisible. She jumped up on Daq and Angie and then barked at Alex to set the other one down, which he did, and she jumped all over Laila also. The three girls all smiled and laughed at the antics of the excited and energetic White Terrier. "Girls, meet Ellie! She is what keeps this house moving. I have never met anyone that she didn't love, and you guys will take that to a new level. She is now a dog with four...five counting old Maurice people to play with and love. Maurice will take a little more time, but he will come around."

He settled the girls into where they would sleep tonight, Daq in the room by the utility room, by herself. The other two girls would be together in what was now Alex's office. The sofa folded out into a hide a bed that Angie and Laila would be able to sleep on for tonight. But promises were made to all three that shopping would be taking place over the next few days.

After a little clean-up and hygiene, Angie and Laila laid down on the sofa bed. The time was pushing ten o'clock and he knew they had to be getting tired. "Ok ladies. Time to sleep, and tomorrow we will go shopping and buy some things to make this place into yours." He tucked in Laila, kissed her forehead, and whispered to her. "You be as quiet as you want. I'm here to take care of you now. And Pops loves you." He then went to the other side of the bed and kissed Angie on the forehead also, "I don't know if you feel you're too old for that, but I wanted to do that at least for tonight."

She smiled at him and said, "I'm not too old."

He said, "Sleep well girls, I'll leave a light on in the bathroom and your door open a little bit so if you need to use the bathroom you can find it. Goodnight."

He then knocked on Daq's door and waited a few seconds and entered. She was lying on the bed just staring at the ceiling. "Bit different, isn't it? Everything that has happened over the last twenty-four hours?"

"You'll never know."

"Yea...I get that. Listen, sleep tonight. There are some clean t-shirts in the top drawer of the dresser that you can wear as PJs for tonight. I think you'll enjoy the bed, the room, the peace and quiet, and the rest that you need. Tomorrow we can talk about logistics...

"What's that mean?"

"How we're all going to live together and stay together in a new house and environment. The nuts and bolts of our new lives. Sleep, you'll feel better in the morning." He reached out with an open hand to touch her face, and she jerked her head away. He looked into the face of this thirteen-year-old that had gone through more than most adults will ever see in a lifetime. He also saw the bruising on her face and remembered the conversation with Jennifer about Jimmy. He felt an instant upsurge of anger, but immediately repressed it. Slowly he laid his hand against her bruised face and gently held it there, and whispered, "I won't ever hurt you." He stood and left the room and closed her door but left it ajar so a little of the light could come in. "Goodnight Daquiri, and...I do love you."

Chapter Twelve

Daq got up off the bed after Alex had gone and peeked through the crack of the ajar door. He wasn't in sight, and she heard him in the kitchen. She quickly went to the dresser and pulled out a T-shirt. Obviously, this was a collection of T-shirts that his wife used to wear because they were a medium size and mostly were girly type colors and sayings. She pulled out a light pink shirt with *'Wine...the stuff of Champions'* printed on it, quickly stripped down to her bra and panties and slipped on the T-shirt. She crawled into the bed, and he was right about it being comfortable, it was soft and kind of smooshy, and cuddly. As soon as she laid down her eyes began to droop, and sleep was creeping up fast. She thought about the day she had had, honestly the worst ever, even for her. And then she thought of Friday, Jimmy was expecting her around 3 in the afternoon. How was she going to pull that off? She knew that Jimmy was her ticket to eventually make enough money to take care of her sisters and they could live by themselves somewhere. That was a good thing, a necessary thing. But then she thought about the conversation she had with Jimmy yesterday and the slap and threat. He'd probably hate the idea that she was here now and how it would affect his plans, and what he would do about it. What about her sisters? Were they going to get brought into Jimmy's world? She didn't like that idea but still, the idea of the money and getting away from everyone was a top priority, but she also knew she had to protect her sisters. She'd find a way to get to him on Friday. If she didn't, he would find her, and when he did, he'd slap her around and hit her to teach her a lesson. And as much as she wanted to believe that this grandpa guy would protect her like he says, he'd be too old and weak and stupid to deal with the likes of Jimmy. It would be nice if this Alex would be the way out, but she doubted that. Her way was going to be the best, but how was she going to handle all this? But she'd have to think about all of it tomorrow, because right now she had to sleep.

Chapter Thirteen

With the girls down and sleeping, at least he thought they were, he decided to relax and unwind before going to bed. He deserved that. He poured a double bourbon on the rocks and sat down in the living room. He sat where he could look out onto the street and at 10:30 the streets were bare except for the rustling of branches and the streetlights dimly illuminating their surroundings. It had a ghostly look and feel, which Alex thought was appropriate for the circumstances. His mind started going over all that had happened during what would have to be the strangest day of his life, so far. Old Maurice was curled on his lap and Ellie was stretched out on the cushion behind his neck.

His mind flitted to one subject to another...His son, Faith, the girls, the road ahead, what Jennifer had said, how he was going to tackle all this, and oh, even the conversation he had had with his employer. In less than twenty-four hours he had gone from a single widower with a dog and a cat and a job...to a single father of three girls ages 13, 8, and 5 with no job but still had the cat and dog. He took a healthy pull on the bourbon as his mind raced on.

"Mr. Barton?"

Alex jumped at the sound. He turned quickly and saw Angie standing in the entry to the great room. "Whoa, you scared me almost to death. I'm not used to having others in the house." Standing still, she just stared in his direction. He set down his bourbon. "What's wrong Angie? Is something bothering you? Can't sleep?"

"No, I just wanted to talk for a second."

"Well, come on in and sit. You can sit with me or in the other chair."

She came into the room and sat in the other chair next to the chair Alex was in. As soon as she sat down Ellie jumped off the back of Alex's chair and was in Angie's lap, wagging vigorously and bestowing kisses on her new friend. Angie giggled at this and tried to calm the dog down, without much success.

"She really likes you! I think you've got a forever friend." He smiled at the two of them and said, "Ellie, calm down." He raised his hand in a gesture that said, *relax.*

She did and curled up in Angie's lap.
"What's on your mind Angie?"

"Laila really likes you and I think she will start to trust you. Please don't do anything that will hurt her or make her mistrust you. I mean if you're not going to keep us like you've been saying, then say it now. We've had enough fallacious promises. I mean we all loved our dad, but he was very unreliable a lot of times and…he was not well." She started to cry.

"Angie. I meant what I said. In fact, I made a promise to my son and to my wife today, that I would do this. And I want to do this! And I believe that both of them are watching me and will make me keep my promise and it's a promise I want to keep! Angie, it may not seem like it yet, it's only been hours, but this is meant to be. Honey, this is real. It's going to take work…but it is real. And it's OK about how you feel about your dad. He was a great son, father and man, but the illness he had took him over and I want you to remember the good about him."

"Daq doesn't trust you and thinks you're going to be mean, and probable try to take advantage of us, like boss us around, make us do all your work, be kinda like slaves. And, you know, what she calls sex stuff."

"Nothing could be farther from the truth. Angie, I want this to be a house that works together. Let's talk about when you lived with Shaila? Was that good?"

Angie nodded, "That was the best I remember."

"Did she boss you around, make you into slaves?

"No."

"Did she let you do whatever you wanted?"

"No, she had house rules. But she wasn't mean or bossy...she just watched out for us."

"And that's my goal. My job is to make this house safe, healthy and happy for everyone living here. And you can only do that if everyone works together."

"OK, I'll help...but we need to talk about Daq. Mr. Barton, she needs..."

"Please, call me something else, I hate Mr. Barton...sounds like I won't give you coal for the fire."

She smiled broadly, "OK, no Scrooge. We called our dad...Pop. But it might be a little early to call you that."

"No, it's not." Again, he was impressed by her knowledge by knowing about 'A Christmas Carol.'

"OK. She may be in trouble...I mean real trouble. She's running around with this jerk of a guy who I think is planning on making money with her by making her have sex with other guys. And I know she doesn't like it but she says she is going to do it for the money so we can have extra money, and we can live somewhere by ourselves. And now even with you here she thinks she needs the money to get away from you." She paused and took a breath. "I think she's going to run away cuz she's supposed to meet this Jimmy jerk-head sometime soon."

"Did she tell you this?"

"No. But trust me when I tell you to heed my word."

"How come?"

"Because sometimes my brain...tells me things."

"You mean like voices?"

She smiled at that, "No...I'm not schizophrenic...or just plain crazy. I think that my brain is highly attuned to...sensory perception...and at times, important times, it doesn't just think something, it tells me something. I know that sounds like the same thing, but it's not."

"Tell me how it's not."

"I feel like the rest of the world is still and silent when that message from my brain comes through. Like it's the only thing my mind was computing at that time. You know how sometimes someone is telling you something or you're thinking about that something, but you're aware of other things and thoughts. Like right now I'll bet you are thinking about Daq, and about that Jimmy, and probably about me and if I'm some kind of weirdo, but still the main thing is what I'm saying to you. Well, when my brain tells me something, not just thinks something...really tells me something, then

I hear or feel nothing else, just what I'm being told. That's how I know it's something important...it's not a voice, it's a thought that overpowers all other thoughts."

"Wow. You have an amazing mind young lady. I only hope I can help you develop it the way...it is intended."

She stared at Alex for a few seconds, then smiled. "I'm thinking that I won't worry about that, at least not now."

"Good. So, tell me what you're thinking about Daq running away?"

"That she's supposed to meet Jimmy and that she is both afraid to miss the meeting cuz of what he'll do to her and that she wants to be sure not to ruin her chances on making money."

"Do you know when they're to meet? And where?"

"No. But Daq always met him in the afternoon. And I know she walked from where we were parked when she was with him, so I would say his hang-out is fairly close to the homeless camp we were in. I'd wager that she will be around here till she gets a chance to sneak off and go meet him. Is there a bus stop somewhere close around here?"

"About a mile and a half from here."

"I think that's what she'll do. Wait until she can sneak away, catch a bus, and stay with Jimmy, for how long I don't know. She doesn't like leaving us, Laila and I, for very long, but now that you're in the picture, I don't know what she'll do."

"OK. Thanks Angie, it means a lot to me that you trusted me this quickly with the information about Daq…and about you. You told me what I need to do about Daq and Laila, but what about you? What do you need?"

"Just someone to believe in me. I know that with my labyrinthine brain, it's difficult to believe me, understand me, and most of all help, or support me. I need someone to do all that and still like me."

"Got it. I already believe in you, and I will support and help you all I can. Understand you? That will take time to get to know you. Which I will do, but…with your enhanced mind don't try to toy with me, don't try to outsmart me and don't use your mind against me. Fair enough? And as for liking you? Already done...as soon as I first laid eyes on you."

"That was a good answer. I think we'll be able to work together very well." She smiled a broad grin at Alex, stood, and moved to Alex and they embraced in an extended hug. He helped her back to the bedroom, kissed her goodnight again, and whispered to her, "Remember, I ain't perfect."

He went back to his bourbon and chair and thought about Daq and what he should do. Soon the day and the bourbon made him very sleepy. He got up and went to the bedroom. As he readied for bed, he thought to himself. *'At least I'll be able to sleep in tomorrow.'*

And that...was the last time he ever had that naïve of a thought again.

Part Two

Perpetuation

Chapter One

At 4:22 AM the next morning, Alex was awoken by Ellie loudly barking from the end of the bed. This caused old Maurice to scramble up to the top of the bed with his back hunched and hissing at the unknown. The barking scared Laila who had woken up Angie to go potty and was now crying loudly in the hallway next to the master bedroom. Alex jerked the door open in a tank top and boxer briefs, and snapped, "What the hell are you doing!?" This caused Laila to cry harder and louder and for Angie to cower a bit and retreat toward their bedroom.

Now Ellie was barking loudly and more urgently. "Shut up Ellie!" Ellie quieted but did not stop. "God dammit Ellie...Quiet!" Now Angie started to cry. "Angie, don't you start." He went back into the bedroom and sat on a chair next to the bed. He glanced at the picture of Faith and him, then put his head in his hands.

"So. That's the way you handle things huh?"

"Daquiri...not now."

"Sure. Let's just ignore that you couldn't even handle a five-year-old getting up to go to the bathroom. And we're supposed to blindly trust that you're the one to take care of us." She rolled her eyes and went back to her bed.

Alex sat collecting himself for a few minutes and realized that she was right. Not the best start to a whole new life. He stood, slipped on a pair of running shorts, and went to the closed door to where Angie and Laila were no doubt cringing at what had just happened. He opened the door slowly and peeked his head in. "Sorry girls, I just got woken up and taken by surprise which caused me to yell. I'm sorry…I promise I'll get better." He looked at Angie who sat looking at the floor with tears in her eyes. He entered the room and sat down next to her, and she turned away, but he put his arm gently around her and said, "Honey, you don't need to be afraid of me, I just got surprised, and I was dead to world asleep. You know? I haven't changed since we talked, and remember, I ain't perfect." He kissed her on top of the head, and she relinquished to the hug he was offering. He looked at Laila and said, "Sorry little girl.

Pops yelled and I scared you. I'm sorry. Do you need to go potty?"

"She wet her pants."

"Oh..."

"I'll get her cleaned up."

"Nope! I got this." Alex stood and went to his bathroom in the master bedroom and came out with a box of wet ones and a dry towel "Does she have dry, clean underwear?"

Angie nodded and pointed to a bag lying on the floor. He stood and reached for it, opened it up and dug around till he came up with a pair of panties with little roses printed all over them. He sat down next to Laila, stood her up, turned her back against his chest and began to take off her wet panties.

"Don't you think I should do that?"

"Nope! I'm going into Dad mode!"

"You mean in 'Pops' mode?"

"Whatever! Get used to it! I may not always be the sharpest knife in the drawer, but I am here to be your dad or pops or poops, but I'm going to do it!" He nodded and smirked at Angie. She smiled and nodded back.

He slid her wet panties off and to the ground. He then slipped her feet out of them and began to clean her with a wet one. First, he cleaned her bare butt, then slid the wet one down her legs and cleaned her legs inside and out and even cleaned her private area. Right then Daq burst into the room.

"What are you doing?!"

Alex took the dry towel and dried off Laila and helped her slip on her dry panties. "There. Is that better? Do you have to go potty again?" She just stared at him. "Yes" ...he nodded. Or "No" ...he shook his head. "Yes...or...no?" She looked at him and shook her head. He smiled, "Good girl! Now hop into bed and let's see if we can get some sleep before breakfast. "How about you Angie? You got to go?" She stared at him. "Yes" ...he nodded or "No" ... She smiled and nodded. He smiled back and tipped his head toward the bathroom, "Go." And she did. When the door to the bathroom closed, he stood and went to

Daq. "Get this straight! I am not a perv, I am not a child molester, I am not a pedophile. None of you need to worry about me being interested in any type of 'sex thing' with you girls! And I will be damned if I am going to have you insinuating that I might. Are you hearing me? Not everybody in this world is a creep that would do the things you're telling these two girls I conceivably could do to them. Damn it Daq! Did you believe that of your dad? Did you!"

She shook her head. "No."

"Then why me? Am I that much different than Bobby, I mean your dad?"

Again, she shook her head. "No."

"Then let's get off this! No more…agreed?"

This time she nodded. "OK."

"Cuz if you keep it up, you'll need to worry that I'll tie a rock around your ankle and throw you in the river!" As soon as he said it, he regretted it. It was too early for her to understand his sense of humor.

She looked straight into his eyes and said, "What River?"

Alex suddenly realized that she was giving him the same line that his Bobby had given to him many times many years ago when he had made the same joking threat to him.

"Don't worry...I'll find one." He said, reliving the past he had once had with his son.

"Yea...Good luck with that. You probably couldn't even find the rock." Just like Bobby had answered. She turned and went to the bedroom.

Everyone ended up back in bed and slept till nearly eight o'clock.

Chapter Two

The next few days were very enlightening as the girl's gathered knowledge of Alex and vice versa. Conversations were guarded and concise, but an occasional smile or question gave Alex a little hope.

When Alex got up and put on shorts and a T-shirt on this Friday morning, he smelled the distinct aroma of onions being fried on the stove top. He walked into the kitchen area and there sat Angie and Laila at the island watching Daq cook breakfast. Ellie and Maurice were standing next to him somewhat perplexed about the drastic change in routine. As he let Ellie out into the backyard he said, "Morning ladies."

Angie spoke first, "Morning."

Laila said nothing as Ellie raced back into the kitchen and jumped on Maurice. As the two of them wrestled, Alex began to prepare Ellie's food, looked at Angie and said, "Want to learn how to feed her?" She nodded and got off her chair and watched the process.

"I suppose you'll be mad about me getting stuff out of your refrigerator for breakfast."

Alex looked at Daq and was about to say something about her remark but decided against it. Instead, he walked around the island, leaned over the skillet and inhaled. "It smells delicious." He investigated the pan and saw onions and peppers (red and green) sautéing and a bowl of diced potatoes ready to go into the pan. She also had a bowl full of eggs that were beaten, spiced and ready to become scrambled eggs. "Wow! Quite the feast." She didn't say anything, just scraped the potatoes off the cutting board into the pan with onions and peppers. She then got another pan out and added olive oil and sprinkled a good amount of a spice she had found in the spice cupboard and started heating the pan slowly, as she stirred the potatoes.

Alex watched her intently as he saw a side of Daq he hadn't seen in their short history. This was the first time she moved with confidence, with purpose, and with a positive energy he hadn't seen. She noticed him watching her, "What!?"

"Nothing! Just watching you work. You're good at this."

"At what?"

"Cooking! You seem to have a talent."

Her mood changed from confrontational to subdued. "I like it. It's something I can do that feels like I'm doing something good, and something that people will not look down their nose at me. Shaila was teaching me."

"Well, I'm sure not going to look down my nose at this! My nose loves it! I can't wait to taste it. I do get to taste it don't I?"

"Yes, I'll give you some." She turned to keep working at her task and Alex detected a slight smile.

She finished up her breakfast and served her two sisters, who hungrily devoured their breakfast. But Alex could tell that Daq seemed most interested in his reaction. So, when she put the plate in front of him, he made sure he did his evaluation of the first meal she ever cooked for him, as professional, serious, and well thought out, not rushed. She coyly watched him, trying to make out like it didn't really matter to her, as Alex smelled the food and took his fork and lifted a small portion of potatoes and scrambled eggs to his mouth. As he chewed the forkful of food, Daq no longer was being coy about watching him, she intently watched as he chewed and swallowed. After swallowing he smacked his lips a few times, looked at the ceiling and then turned to Daq. In a calm and businesslike voice, he said, "I don't think I've ever had better. This is amazingly delicious! Well done, Daq! I will give you an excellent review."

And there it was…the smile Alex was hoping he would see. A smile that said she was proud of her talent and even more proud of the fact that it had impressed him. Right then, old Maurice jumped up on the counter next to Daq, sniffed her face, and rubbed the side of his face against hers.

"Is he allowed up here...where we cook?"

"Sadly yes. Faith and I spoiled him for many years and nothing about that has changed. However, we...uh...I, keep him away from the food. But more importantly, it appears he has accepted you as his buddy. That's big for him, he generally takes his time with new people. And, by the way, he's asking to be fed and it looks like he might be OK with you doing it. Want to give it a shot?"

"Let me get everyone served first, then, sure I'll feed him." She gave the two girls the remaining potatoes and eggs, then looked at Alex for directions of the feeding. As they moved down the hallway to the utility room Daq looked at Alex and said, "When did your wife die?"

"A little over six months ago."

"You kinda talk like she's still here sometimes."

"Yea. It's hard to let go sometimes."

"Sounds like you guys were bff."

"We were...100%." As they came to the end of the hallway Alex turned left into the master bedroom and brought out the picture of him and Faith. He showed Daq the picture and said, "You remind me of her. And that is the biggest compliment of all!" He smiled down at the picture and the memories and put it back on the nightstand. He moved back to Daq who was now in the utility room with Maurice. He showed her the routine of feeding Maurice and told her about kitty city and some of the idiosyncrasies of Old Maurice. Then he mustered the courage to say, "Daq. I need to talk to you about something."

"What!" Her defenses went up immediately.

"I just want to talk about something that Jennifer from child services told me. And about the medical exam you got while you were there."

"Listen. I don't need you, or anybody else to tell me what to do. What I do, who I see, and what I do with who I see is none of your goddamn business!"

Alex felt a strong wave of anger well up inside him. "WRONG!" He calmed himself and his voice. "Let's get that straight right now! If you think for one second that I'm going to let you hang with the likes of this Jimmy shithead or anybody remotely like him, then you don't know me! It's my job to protect you from shit like that..." He realized his was voice was raising again.

"You don't even know me! Or anyone else I know...and that includes your own son. I have been with you exactly three days and now you're the know all to everything I do! You couldn't manage that with your own kid and now I'm just supposed to jump up and say YES SIR...well, bullshit!" She went into her bedroom and slammed the door. "Leave me the fuck alone!"

Alex stood looking at the door and absorbing what had just happened. As his anger dissipated, he started to realize that the entire situation had gotten out of hand and Daq obviously didn't understand what he was trying to do. He started to go into her room to see if he could settle this down, then thought better of it. After thirty years of marriage, he had learned that when there is that much anger in any discussion or event, you're best to let time pass and anger subside. He turned and walked back into the kitchen. Angie was at the sink scraping dishes and putting them into the dishwasher. Her back was to Alex and Alex didn't say anything.

"She's right you know." Angie kept her back to Alex. "Talking to her like you did is going to drive her away."

"I just wanted to talk to her. But she blew up in a matter of seconds, and then there was no talking to her."

"You think that was entirely her fault?"

Alex looked at the back of the busy Angie, and even though he didn't necessarily like what she was saying, he was in awe of her intelligence and ability to think through situations so rapidly, and her ability to articulate what she was saying and thinking. "No, it wasn't. And you're right. I jumped her...even though I had best intentions, I approached it all wrong. Funny thing is that if I was making a sales call, I would have never started the conversation with a negative about the client, even if my intentions were to help. So...I know better. Thanks for helping me out." She continued to work at the dishes and said nothing more.

Alex looked at Laila who was still sitting at the kitchen bar just watching the happenings around her. She was silent and somber. He moved to her and put his arm around her. "Sorry about all the noise sweetie, it will get better, I promise." Right then he heard Angie singing and humming while she worked at the sink. He recognized what she was singing as 'come on down to my boat baby' a one hit wonder by a pop group called 'Every mother's Son' from 1967. He smiled and suddenly remembered back to a time when his son Bobby and he would sing that together while doing the dishes when Bobby was still at home. He picked up Laila in his arms and went to Angie's side, looked down at her and started singing. *'Come on down to my boat baby, come on down where we can play. Come on down to my boat baby, come on down we'll sail away.'*

Angie, smiled broadly and said, "You know that song?"

"You learned it from your dad, didn't you?"

"Yea."

"Who do you think taught him?" Alex remembered his older brother who was born in 1951 and had taught him all about 60's music. Alex had never forgotten it and to this day the music of that era has always been his favorite.

They sang a few minutes longer as he helped with the dishes. Laila, who was now sitting on the countertop next to Alex as he and Angie sang and danced, watched with a smile on her face. Alex noticed but said nothing, not wanting to make her conscientious and perhaps retreat away from her momentary happy place. But he had noticed, and it felt good.

Suddenly Angie got very quiet and stared down into the sink.

"What's going on kiddo." Alex whispered to her.

She looked up into his face and said, "Daq's gone."

Chapter Three

Daquiri slammed the bedroom door and waited to see if Alex would come back in.

When he didn't, she sat on the bed, eyes filled with tears and visibly shaken at the exchange she had just had.

'Goddamn him! I thought he really liked my cooking, but it was just another bullshit scheme to get me under his thumb. He's not my dad, so he's not going to tell me who I can see or who I can't. I know he's got some bullshit reason for wanting us, what it is I don't know. But I'll find out. Angie and Laila are giving in to him, but I'm not! When I find out I will get us all out of here. But I need to have something set up...and him telling me I can't see the people I need to see is not going to happen. Even child services think they can spread shit about me?! Why can't anybody stay out of my business. I don't need or want any help from anybody! Everybody, just leave me alone!'

She sat on the bed, angry...frustrated...confused...and scared. She thought about Jimmy.

'I know he's mean and slaps me sometimes, but at least he treats me like I'm a grown-up person. Not like everyone else...like I'm a baby that doesn't know anything and has to

stay in a circle of grown-up protection. You have to do this...you have to do that...you have to obey all our rules...you can't be a real person; you have to be what I want you to be! I hate where I am now, but I'll bet that Jimmy will know what to do and how to get me out of this. I just need to figure out how to get to him. He'll agree with me, and he'll want to help me, so this will be perfect. I'll get out of here and show up at his place early. He'll like that...it will show him I'm serious about helping him so I can make money. He says that getting a poke from guys actually will be fun after a while (cuz it really hurts right now) and that I'll be able to make enough money to take care of myself and the girls. We can live with him, till we can get our own place, and I'm sure once we are working together, he'll take good care of us and be a lot nicer.'

She opened the bedroom window quietly and slipped out. She went down the street away from the house looking for a place to get over the wall. She knew trying to get out the gate would be a problem, since she thought of the community as essentially a prison. She found an area that was right up against the wall with a small tree and various bushes and most importantly...no houses...so no having to worry about someone seeing her and turning her in to the prison guards.

She climbed into the tree and grabbed the top of the cider block wall and pulled herself up and over. Now to find a way to get to Jimmy, maybe there's a bus stop around here someplace, that would work.

Chapter Four

"Do you know anything else?" Alex asked Angie. She shook her head. He patted her on the back, grabbed Laila off the counter and set her down on the floor. "Watch Laila for a few minutes. OK?"

Angie nodded. "I'll bet you anything she's going to Jimmy."

"And you don't know where he lives?"

"I don't. But it's close to the homeless camp."

"OK. How would she get anywhere from here? She doesn't have a phone. Does she have money for a bus?"

"Some, but not much. But she does have bus passes, Jimmy gave her some of those."

Alex nodded and went to Daq's bedroom. Sure enough, she was gone, and the window was open. Alex thought about what the next step should be. Call the police? No, too many questions and there would probably be an inquiry. Jennifer Grey? Not a bad idea except he'd lost the kid she gave him exactly three days ago. Not a glowing review. He remembered something Jennifer had said in passing about Jimmy living in the indigent area.

He got on his cell phone and called his neighbor Burt, he used to work for the city of Palm Springs and might know the area.

"Hi Burt."

"Alex, I been worried about you. What's going on?"

"I'll tell you all about it. But right now, I need a big favor. Can you please come over and watch my two new daughters while I make an emergency run?"

"What!?"

"I know. Can you come over right now and I'll try to explain, but I'm in a helluva hurry."

"OK. Be there in about twenty seconds."

"Thanks."

Twenty seconds later the doorbell rang, and Alex opened it, and Burt stood there, with a ready-for-duty look on his face.

"Thanks Burt!" Alex was holding Laila and Angie stood behind him. "Let me introduce you to Angie standing back here, and Laila in my arms. These are my two granddaughters, who now live with me. I need you to watch them till I get back. I'm going to get my other granddaughter who is thirteen and has run away and I need to get to her."

"Of course. You go and find her and bring her back safely. I'll stay here with these two till you get back."

"Thanks Burt. By the way, do you know where an area in town is called the indigent area? Out by the airport?"

"Yea. Do you think she's there?"

"Maybe."

"Well, get her the hell out of there. Not a safe place for anybody, but a thirteen-year-old? Not good! You know where the homeless camp is by the airport?"

"Yes." It's behind that camp about two miles east. Take Ramone from the airport east about two miles then turn on a street, don't know a name, that takes you into the desert behind and you'll see it, about a mile into the desert a deserted area where there used to be some small houses, if you can call them that, a bad element hangs out in there."

"I actually think I know where you're talking about. I had a job out that way a few years ago, I thought the city was going to tear that down."

"Not in the city. County problem and it just never seems to get taken care of."

"OK. Thanks again Burt."

"Be Safe! And get her out of there!"

Alex went to his bedroom and put on some jeans and a t-shirt, grabbed the cash off the dresser, his wallet, and then to the utility door. He jumped into the car, backed out and headed to the airport. His thought was to stop at the homeless camp and ask a few questions. He also knew that there is a bus stop by the airport which is the closest to the indigent area. His idea was to ask around at the homeless camp about Jimmy and Daq and then as quickly as he could get to where Jimmy lived. If he couldn't find Daq within the next couple of hours, he knew he'd have to call the police. Not to mention what this Jimmy would do to her.

As he neared the Airport, he came across the bus stop. He stopped and got out and there were a couple sitting on the bench and one person who appeared to be a homeless person standing outside of the enclosure. He went inside the enclosure and asked the couple if they had seen a young girl get off the bus, he gave a brief description of her. They both shook their heads and when Alex asked if he could give them his cell number and if they saw her prior to their leaving would they give him a call. They agreed and pleasantly wished him well.

He stepped outside the enclosure and went to the homeless person.

"Excuse me. Have you seen a young girl around here today?"

"You got a few dollars to spare man?"

"Yea. But I need some answers. Did you see the girl?"

"Maybe."

"That's not an answer. I need yes or no."

"No."

"You know a guy named Jimmy? Baxter or something like that?"

"Braxton. Yea, I know Jimmy."

"Know where he lives?"

"Yea."

"Can you tell me…exactly?"

"Jimmy wouldn't like that. He'd come after me."

"How would he know it was you. I sure ain't going to tell him. Hell, I don't even know your name."

"Still…kinda dangerous for me."

"I seriously doubt that, but will this help?" He held out a fifty-dollar bill.

The man reached for it and Alex pulled it away. "Not till I get directions...and it damn well better be the right information. If it's not, I'll find you and get my fifty back...one way or another. And I'm familiar with these parts so don't think I will just let it go, cuz this is damn important to me and the girl I'm talking about could get hurt."

"I'll give it to ya straight. He lives in the in the indigent area."

"That I know...where is it."

The man gave him directions and after a number of questions Alex knew where he was going and where Jimmy lived when he got there. He drove to the location and parked away from the area and walked to where Jimmy lived. He stayed out of sight and waited. He had figured that he had beaten Daq here, she had a long ride to get to the bus stop.

The area had three small, dilapidated houses, if you could call them that, set back into the desert. There was no running water, no electricity, basically nothing but broken-down walls and roofs.

Alex watched the house identified as Jimmy's for some time but saw no signs of life at all. As he waited another man started to walk towards him, but Alex held up a hand and said, "Get Lost!" Alex had seen a picture of Jimmy from Jennifer and knew this wasn't him. The man obeyed. Right then he saw someone walking toward Jimmy's shack and he immediately recognized her as Daq. He started to move to intercept her when an old beat-up pickup drove to her from behind and stopped. She got in and went to Jimmy's and then went in.

Alex moved quickly to the front door, which consisted of a rotting wood door with no handle. He knocked and swung the door open. Jimmy and Daq turned and saw him standing in the doorway, "Who the fuck are you!?" Jimmy snarled at him.

"What the hell are you doing!" Daq yelled. "Why are you here! And how did you find me?"

"Who is this old fart, Daq?"

"That's my grandfather."

"Well, best you be on your way grandpa. You ain't wanted here."

Alex gave Jimmy an admonitory glance. "Daq, you're coming with me, right now."

"The fuck I am. I'm staying with Jimmy. I'm not living with you so that you can ruin my life anyway you feel is right for you. I want my own life and Jimmy is willing to give that to me. So, get out!"

"Not a chance! You're coming with me, right now! If you think for even a second that I would leave you here in this shithole with this scumbag, you got a whole lotta learning to do about me!"

Jimmy took that opportunity to jump in. "Hey old man! Didn't you hear what the lady said? Out! Or do you need some help?" Right then a large brawler walked in and stood beside him in a rather threatening manner. Alex smiled.

"Listen…JIMMY…you better be prepared to kill me, because that is only way, I will be stopped from taking my daughter back home! And if you think that you and your gladiator friend here have the stones for that...go for it."

"Pretty big talk from an old man like you."

Now Alex Barton stood 5'11" and weighed 190lbs. Perhaps a little more than he wanted around his waist, but in pretty good shape. He had been an athlete in high school, playing football and track. When he graduated, he went into the Navy and shortly after enlisting an officer noticed his ability to defend himself and got him into the boxing program. Alex spent the next three years boxing for the Navy and never lost a match. After the Navy he tried his hand at boxing professionally for a few years but hated the schedule, the atmosphere, and the seedy side of the boxing world, but learned a lot about the pugilistic sport.

Over the years, he kept up with his training and boxing to stay in shape. Over the past six months, he trained even more to keep his mind off the loss of Faith.

"You stay the hell away from me or I'll have Jimmy kick your ass!" Daq screamed at him.

"Get the message old man?"

With lightning quick speed, Alex threw a left jab into the left eye of Jimmy sending him backwards and holding his now bleeding eye. Before the big brawler had any opportunity to react, Alex crossed a right-hand punch into his face. Alex then circled around both opponents and as the brawler turned around to pursue, Alex put two left jabs into his nose and followed quickly with straight on right hand punch that exploded the brawler's nose into a cascade of blood. He screamed and fell to the floor holding his broken nose with both hands. Alex turned to Jimmy, who was holding his eye and standing in complete disbelief at what he was seeing, then Alex threw two more left hand jabs into his face. This caused Jimmy to turn his back to Alex who then pushed him against a wall and with a powerful right hand delivered a calamitous punch into his kidneys that sent Jimmy to the floor. He then spun around and saw that the brawler was still lying on the ground holding his nose and looking at Alex with eyes filled with fear. "Stay down!" Alex snarled at him.

He then turned to Daq, his face still contorted into an angry sneer and moved to her and grabbed the back of her shirt. "We're getting in the car! You need me to help you?" She shook her head as she looked at the face of a man that was saying he didn't want the wrong answer. "Then let's go...right now!" She quickly strode out the door holding a small cloth bag, with Alex closely behind her. He pointed to where the car was parked, and they walked together towards the car.

"You know you didn't..."

"Not now Daquiri...NOT NOW!"

They were silent all the way back to the house.

Chapter Five

Jimmy awoke from his punch to the kidneys short of breath and in excruciating pain in his lower back. He rolled onto his back and lay looking at the stained and cracked ceiling for what seemed an eternity. He finally looked to his left and saw his bodyguard brawler sitting on his butt with his shirt rolled up into a ball and holding it against his bleeding nose.

"Fuck, I wasn't expecting that." Jimmy croaked.

"You weren't! I thought this was a cakewalk, just taking care of some old cupcake dude. Now look! He busted my fucking nose!"

"Quit bitching, You're getting paid."

"Not enough! You gunna take care of the bill for my nose?"

Jimmy just shook his head as he rose from the floor. The pain seared through him as he attempted to straighten up. Looking around, he muttered to himself *'Daq's gone, and there goes my cash cow. That asshole comes in blows the whole deal. But I ain't done yet. I still got a chance to get her back, but if that don't work then I got a guy who buys girls like that. All I gotta do is get him interested, which I know he will be, sell her and I get the cash.'* He smiled at the thought, then said out loud, "Oh this ain't over grandpa! Not by a long shot."

Chapter Six

When Daq got to the house she immediately got out of the car and went quickly into her room. She slammed the door and stuck the small bag under the bed. She lay on the bed and looked at the ceiling and began to cry. *'Everything got ruined today! How the hell did that old man beat up Jimmy and his other big dude? Just my luck that he probably signed a deal with the devil to give him superpowers. I mean, he beat the shit out of them. And he looked like he was going to do the same to me.'*

'Now I'm screwed! Jimmy probably won't ever talk to me again and he'll get someone else to take my place. He was the only friend I had, the only one who was willing to let me be something other than a snot-nosed kid. Now I'm probably stuck in this house with that want-to-be hot-shot that wants to control my life. And probably will beat me if I do anything he doesn't like, now that he thinks he has the power over me.'

She started to cry harder, and a feeling of overwhelming sadness hit her as she rolled over to her side and cried into her pillow. *'I want my daddy back. I want Shaila to not be dead...I don't want to be here!'*

She cried until she fell asleep.

Chapter Seven

Alex walked into the great room where Burt and Ernie were sitting with Angie and Laila. Laila was sitting on Ernie's lap and Angie was sitting alongside Burt. Alex viewed the dynamics of the four and quietly thought to himself that the way it was right now is how he would have predicted it would be.

Ernie was a quiet man, reflective and reserved, but mastered an intellectual and dry sense of humor. There was also something about him that exuded strength, but Alex couldn't quite put his finger on it, but it had a definite intensity of confidence. His age was approximately the same as Alex and you could tell that he was a man who would give whatever was needed to help a friend or loved one. He would naturally be perfect for the quiet and introverted Laila. As she sat next to him and he read a story to her, Alex smiled and felt good about the future for her.

Burt was more the outgoing and vivacious of the two. Quick witted and always ready with a comment, conclusion, solution, or anecdote...but with a vast knowledge of many subjects. He would have naturally been the one that Angie would have morphed to and based on the two of them having a serious discussion as Alex walked in, that is exactly what had happened. Burt had been retired for quite a few years and Alex estimated his age to be in the mid-seventies, but with an abundance of energy.

Burt saw Alex first and immediately stood and moved toward him with a look of question and hope in his eyes.

"I found her and she's back here. In her room."

"Thank God. Is she coming out?"

"I don't think so." Right then Angie came alongside Alex and looked up. "She's fine Ang...just very upset and mad at me."

Angie pursed her lips and said, "I figured that would happen. She's going to blame you for everything."

Alex got down to one knee, gave her a hug and whispered, "I know she will and I'm going to need your help on this one." She hugged him back and Alex felt a wave of warm emotions go through him. He smiled at her as he stood. "Could you take Laila and go to your room so that I can talk to Burt and Ernie.

"OK. Can we go see Daq?"

"I wouldn't for a while, let's let her rest and reflect."

When the two girls went into their room, Alex poured Burt and Ernie drinks of their choice, himself a double bourbon on the rocks and sat down and told them the entire detail of his last week.

The three men sat in silence for a few minutes, then Ernie said, "Well nothing we can come up with will top that!"

Alex laughed, which caused a contagious laugh from all three. With offers to help anyway they could Burt and Ernie left and went home. It was midafternoon by then and Alex went to Daq's bedroom door, "Daq. Can I talk to you please?" There was no answer, so he quietly opened the door and peeked in. He saw that she was asleep on the bed and retrieved a throw blanket out of his room and covered her even though the temperature outside was over 100 degrees, the air conditioner was blowing on her. He closed the door and went back to the living room and sat down. He was reflecting on what had happened when Angie and Laila came to his side. "Hi girls…kind of a weird day huh? I'm sorry about that. But I hope it will get better, I really do hope."

Angie looked at him and said, "We're not easy. But don't give up, especially on Daq, she's going down a bad route. But she loves us, and we love her, and she takes care of us. So please help her." She took a deep breath to avoid the tears she felt coming.

"I won't give up. I made a promise, remember? And I'll stick to it." Then as lightly as he could, "You guys must be getting hungry, let's start an early dinner. Maybe we can convince Daq to join us after a while."

Chapter Eight

Alex knocked on Daq's door. When he heard nothing, he knocked again and said, "Daq, I'm coming in." He slowly opened the door, and she was lying on the bed with her back to the door. "Daquiri, can we talk?" Nothing. He gently laid his hand on her shoulder, and she immediately pulled away. "OK. I know you're mad at me, but you need to hear this. Daq, it is my job to protect you. And that is what I did today, and I'll do it again if necessary. I want to talk to you. You need to understand the situation we're in, it's the only way we can work this out. Will you please talk to me?"

"Fuck you." She said in a low guttural voice.

He gritted his teeth and looked up to the ceiling. "Not quite what I had in mind. Alright. You want to play it that way? Then you leave me no choice than to play that way also. So, until you're ready to talk, you're to stay in this house, no going anywhere. And your two sisters are worried about you and want to see you. I expect you to be civil to them, even if you're not civil to me. Understand?" No response. "And, if you talk to me, all this can go away and we can work something out, I promise."

He closed the door and stood for a moment wondering what his next move would be. He shook his head and wandered out toward the great room. Angie and Laila were sitting on the couch, and he sat down and talked to Angie. "Listen, Daq isn't talking to me, and she is still very upset, so I need you to help with making sure she is OK. So, will you go in and see her, make sure she gets nourishment and try to convince her to talk to me? I'm worried and she's not willing to even look at me. And quite frankly I don't know what to do...and I'm scared, scared she's going to do something, I don't know, escape, run away, hook up with that Jimmy..."

"I'll see what I can do."

And she was true to her word. She spent time with Daq, took her food and talked with her behind the closed doors of her bedroom. On Sunday, Daq actually came out of the room and sat with the girls in the great room and ate dinner and watched TV. But she wouldn't give Alex an inch, wouldn't talk and wouldn't even look at him. This both hurt and worried Alex, because he really didn't know what the correct procedure would be in this situation. She was in a very fragile state, and he knew that a misguided attempt may make it worse. He decided to let it ride for a while and see if time would help heal the position. He called Jennifer Grey, and she was a great help in talking to him and advising him on steps to take.

The next week had no major setbacks but no major advances either. Laila was still not talking and was still the stand-off little girl that Alex had hoped would have come around by now. He loved the smiles he would get from time to time and some small interactions, but still no words. He wondered if the trouble with Daq was affecting her.

Angie seemed to be the one accepting the new home with a certain amount of verve. Alex chalked that up to her intellectual abilities. She had assessed the situation and calculated the good and bad and had resolved that the good outweighed the bad and it would benefit all three of them to adapt and create the most advantageous environment they could. He felt also that she had analyzed him, and that she had been able to see him for what he was...sincere about taking care of this new family. She also knew that his efforts with Daq were well intended, even though misguided at times. She would continue to help council him on that subject. Alex was more than appreciative of her support and efforts to bring everyone together. Plus, he liked her immensely, she was exceptional and just a damn great kid. Daq was another story, she was cold, distant, angry, and blamed all that had happened on Alex. She had barricaded herself off from Alex and he had noticed she was starting to do the same with Laila and Angie. She was not budging on her position and Alex was at his wits end trying to figure how to get her to break down and talk. He was considering professional help and had Jennifer helping with that process.

And, unbeknownst to Alex, Daq had been in communication with Jimmy. The canvas bag she had brought home from Jimmys contained two items, one of which was a burner cell phone. She had called him a few times and he was also feeding her misinformation about her situation and encouraging the behavior she was showing.

***

On Monday the 28th, Alex was up early and after his morning routine with the pets he went to Daq's room and knocked on the door. "Daq? Would you fix breakfast this morning? I have some work I need to get done and I know Angie and Laila would love to have you come out and be with them."

She looked up from her bed and scowled at him. Then turned away and said, "Yea, I'll fix them breakfast."

"Thank You! I know it will mean a lot to them, also to me."

"I ain't doing it for you. Just them."

"Daq, why can't we talk? I want this war between us to stop, I just…"

"Will you get out of my room! I want to get dressed."

He sighed deeply. "Fine." He closed her door and went to the great room and sat down. As he thought about his ordeal with Daq, his phone rang. The screen read 'work'. He realized that he had missed another Monday morning sales meeting, which he hadn't even given any thought of going to it. But he realized the time had come to confront his work and his future when it came to his now new family, and his employment. Frankley he was surprised that it had taken them this long to call.

"Hello."

"Alex, this is Tom. You weren't at the sales meeting again this morning."

Alex remained silent.

"I think it's time we talked."

Again, Alex said nothing.

Alex? Are you still there?"

"Yes."

"I've talked with our manager, and he has spoken with the head office, and we would like to meet with you, today if possible."

"When today?"

"11:00 AM?"

"Where?"

"Here in the boss's office."

"I'll be there, unless something comes up that I can't, then I will call you."

"Alex, it will…"

"See you at 11:00." And he hung up. He thought about what he had to do to get ready for this meeting. He called Burt and Ernie and confirmed that they would sit with the girls while he had the meeting. He then went to the kitchen and saw all three girls sitting at the table eating breakfast.

"Save any for me?"

Daq didn't respond or even look at him.

Then Angie spoke," Sorry Pops, we didn't, but I'll share with you." She smiled sweetly up at him.

"Oh, thanks kiddo, but I'm OK." He patted her on the cheek. Then knelt next to Laila and said, "Hello pretty girl. Did you like breakfast?" Still no words but an affectionate look in her eyes made him feel better. Daq glared at both girls. He said, "I'm going into the office today for a meeting at 11:00, so Burt and Ernie are coming over to keep you company, and I shouldn't be too long. I thought maybe when I get home, we could all go for a walk around the neighborhood, and since it will be another hot day today, we could go to the clubhouse and take a swim in the pool. Sound good?!"

Angie, very excited, said, "You mean we can use the swimming pool!?"

"Yes, you can! Just never alone...you always must have an adult with you. No exceptions to that."

"Ohhh, that's so cool! Hey Lai, want to go swimming today? Laila smiled at her sister in an obvious affirmative reaction.

"Great! It's a date! How about you Daq? I'd love to have you come."

"No thanks." Daq sarcastically growled.

Alex, now getting more irritated as time went on at her attitude, quickly shot back with, "OK! But remember, you go nowhere." He went into the master bedroom and got ready for his meeting. As he sat getting ready, *'I think you just made it worse...keep your mouth shut!'*

Chapter Nine

When Burt and Ernie arrived around 10:30, Alex explained the day and thanked them again. When he arrived for his meeting, Tom met him at the door and very coolly escorted him to the boss's office. Alex went in and sat down. He had his portfolio that contained all the information and notes he had done prior to the meeting. Tom said nothing as they sat and waited. Alex smiled at the tactic that was presenting itself, *'Ah, the old intimidation routine where the big boss makes you wait for his entrance and your immediate boss just stares you down.'* Right then the door opened and in walked William Perkins, the manager of the Palm Springs division and operation. Behind him followed two other gentlemen dressed in impeccable suits and looking very corporate and concerned. *'Wow, intimidation factor two! Bring in the corporate big dogs. I must have enough of a case that they are a little worried. Good to know.'*

Mr. Perkins started the conversation as he sat in his chair and the other two pulled up two other side chairs, faced them toward Alex, then sat down. "Alex, thank you for coming in this morning. I don't know if you remember Mr. Jacobson, our west coast VP and sales Manager. Alex glanced at him as he nodded towards Alex.

"We've met a couple times." Alex said and turned his attention back to Mr. Perkins.

"And next to him is Mr. Wilson, one of our corporate attorneys."

Alex glanced at him, and he didn't make any acknowledgement whatsoever. So, he turned his attention back to Mr. Perkins. "Alex, it appears that we have a problem that needs to be addressed."

"Mr. Perkins. Am I still employed?"

The attorney chimed in. "As of right now, yes."

"But I will bet that is about to end abruptly. In fact, I would be very surprised if you don't have termination papers with you that you want me to sign that says I'm being fired for insubordination."

The VP then started to speak, when Alex's phone rang, and he held up a finger to the VP indicating that he needed to be quiet. "Excuse me." He looked at his phone and saw the name Burt on the screen. "Hi Burt, what's up?"

"Daquiri took off again. Slipped out the window in her room. Ernie is out after her and has caught up to her, but she is refusing to come back with him."

Alex stood up, "Goddammit!" He took a big breath and exhaled slowly, then calmly said, "Find out where she is, tell Ernie to keep her there no matter what it takes, and I'll be there shortly. Text me where she is as soon as you know."

"OK. Sorry about this."

"Not your fault."

Alex hung up and put his phone into his pocket. Turned to the group sitting in the office and said, "Sorry to have to bring this intimidation party to a close, I have a family emergency to attend to. Let me conclude the conversation by saying that I recorded the conversation with Tom a week or two ago when I asked to be excused from the sales meeting. The entire conversation is on my phone, and I think you all would be surprised at that conversation, you know, the conversation where I informed Tom here, that my son died and I wouldn't be at the sales meeting and he eloquently said to me, you know how important these sales meetings are! And before Mr. hot shot attorney here informs me that it would be inadmissible, I will tell you that inadmissible does not mean that it won't be brought up or heard about. So, I think you can figure out what that means." He picked up his portfolio, and pulled out a file folder and laid it on Mr. Perkins' desk. "This is a proposal I drew up for a severance package, it basically says my current base salary is $60,000. Per year, plus commissions. The proposal states that you pay me the base salary for one year, no commissions and no benefits and I will sign a one year non-compete agreement and gag order because of this company's realignment. Thank You for the time gentlemen, and I will expect an answer within forty-eight hours."

He picked up his portfolio and headed to the door, when Tom stood and angrily said, "Now just a minute Alex!"

Alex looked at him as if he were the most pathetic individual on earth and simply said, "Tom, just shut up." He opened the office door and walked out. As he walked to his car, he received a text from Burt. *'Bus stop near here on Vista Chino.'* He knew exactly where that was, started his car and headed that way.

When he arrived, Daq was standing in front of Ernie screaming in his face. Ernie held his ground, and she was not able to get around him. When Alex approached, he heard her yell at Ernie, "Keep your faggot hands off me!" He didn't budge or blink, just stood stoically in front of her almost daring her to try and go around him.

"Daquiri! Don't you dare talk to my friends that way! Now get in the car!" Alex was trying hard to quell his anger, but he wasn't doing very well at it. This felt like the last straw. All week she had been rude, mean, foul, and completely unresponsive to anything he had tried to do for her. He was trying to make her realize that he was offering her a better life, a safe life in a home with family and love. But she was the one choosing to ignore what she had in front of her and instead, pissing all over it. Alex had lost his patience and now was just plain mad.

"Fuck you! I'm not going anywhere with you!"

"Oh yes you are..." He moved toward her with a look she recognized as the same look as when he had fought with Jimmy. Ernie stepped in front of him as he pointed his finger at her, "If you need help into the car,

I will be glad to accommodate you." She moved past him and got into the back seat of the car and slammed the door. Alex looked at Ernie, "Ernie, I am so sorry she said that to you. I can't apologize enough. I don't know where she came up with that…"

"Alex. Stop." Ernie smiled, "She's a very troubled teenager who is lashing out and what better way to get me to give up and walk away. Only I fooled her. I've been called much worse. And…I know you, that wouldn't come from you. So, don't give it another thought, glad I could help. And don't give up on her." He got into his car and left.

Alex turned to his car and walked to the driver's side and got in behind the wheel. "Daq. This has to stop. We're not getting anywhere together. Please talk to me, let's try to work out something where we can live together."

"Leave me alone and let me go be with Jimmy." She started to cry.

"Goddammit! I will not allow that to ever happen!" Alex lost his temper. "Why in the name of hell would you want to go live with that piece of shit, in that stinking shithole he lives in. Can't you see what he's doing?"

"He loves me and wants to help me."

"To what! Be a whore!" Alex quickly realized his temper had gotten the best of this conversation and he gritted his teeth and started to calm down. As she cried harder, he spoke in a subdued voice. "Daq, I'm sorry...I didn't mean that. I'm just very upset, and frankly, confused...I'm just trying to..."

"Just leave me alone." Her sobbing reply came.

"I'm sorry for losing my temper, but I will never leave you alone. I will do whatever it takes to make you safe." Alex said in a deferential voice.

Daq whispered to herself, "That's what I'm afraid of."

Chapter Ten

When they arrived back home Daq immediately got out of the car, went to her room. She grabbed a towel off the floor she had left there from her shower earlier and cried into it to muffle the sound. After a few minutes of crying, she took a deep breath and reached under the bed and pulled out the sack she brought back from Jimmy's and pulled out the burner phone. She arranged her position on the floor so that she could see the door if it opened. She also turned on her clock radio and played music to help drown out her voice. She called Jimmy.

"Hello."

"Jimmy. It's Daq." She cried into the phone.

"What happened? I thought you said you could make here today."

"He caught me again. The son-of-a-bitch. He's never going to let me go."

"Well Jesus Christ! I can't just keep waiting for you Daq. If you can't figure out a way to get out of his prison, then fuck it! I want to help ya, but I can't keep waiting. You just fucked this up for the last time!"

"Jimmy..."

"No Daq! I'm done! This fucking asshole you live with now is not going to stop. He is just too much of a problem to deal with, I mean he already beat the shit out of me and now you can't get out from under his thumb. No, I'm done. You can keep what's in the bag you got, but keep out of my life, you just ain't worth it. I don't want you around anymore! Got it! Stay the fuck out of my life! You're nothing but bad luck and not worth the trouble!"

"No…Jimmy…"

He hung up. Daq sat and began to cry uncontrollably. In her mind, life had just dealt her the final blow. She had always thought that this was the way she could be in charge of her life. Take care of her sisters the way dad would have wanted, make her own money and be with someone who really loved her. She'd never get this chance again. She sat and cried in the towel as sadness and despair overtook her every thought.

Now Jimmy was laughing as he thought about her. He had already contacted the guy he knew who was interested in girls like Daq that he could bring into his stable of young girls he sold for sex. He was a sex-trafficker/drug dealer that worked in Los

Angeles, San Diego, and in the Coachella valley. He was a connected dealer that had girls in different places and was always on the lookout for more. He also would get girls to sell to the big-league traffickers, if he could find the right ones. Jimmy was confident that he would be interested in Daq and that he could put together a sweet deal for himself. And as an added bonus, he would garner the satisfaction of knowing that he had fucked up the life of old gramps and his snot-nosed little bitch. *'Payback can be a bitch old man!'*

***

Alex followed Daq and when the door slammed in his face, he went into the living room and sat down. Burt looked at him and started to say something, but Angie came to Alex and sat next to him. He could feel her trepidation, and he put his arm around her and whispered, "It'll be alright, it's just going to take some time." But he felt the ambiguity in his statement as he looked at Laila sitting in the chair sucking her thumb and still not saying anything, but the tears in her eyes speaking volumes. He closed his eyes and knew he needed help.

Burt saw the scene and he and Ernie both got up to leave. He laid a hand on Alex's shoulder, "We're here if you need us."

"I know…and you'll never know how much that means."

They left through the front door and closed it. Alex pulled Angie closer and made room for her in the chair and then motioned to Laila to come over to him. "Come on Lai…come be with us." Angie lifted her head and nodded at her, and she came over and Alex enveloped her in a hug and sat her on his lap. She laid her head on his chest and the three just sat in a silent embrace.

As they sat in their curative hug, Daq had come out into the hallway with the intention of talking to Alex. When she saw the three of them in an embrace, she felt a hopelessness and loneliness that made her start to cry again, and she retreated to her room.

Chapter Eleven

The next day at 9:00 AM, William Perkins called Alex.

"Hello."

"Good morning, Alex, I hope that all is going well for you."

Alex had to smile at that comment given the current circumstance he was dealing with. "As good as can be expected."

"Listen Alex, I've spoken with Tom a little more about your situation and I want to apologize for our lack of understanding. We were not aware of your situation; in fact, we knew nothing about a son."

"It was a very private matter that we didn't talk about."

"I understand; however, I don't think I have the whole picture. And if I am not totally out of line, I would like to know more...not intricate details...just a better understanding. But if you're not comfortable..."

"No, you're right. I do need to be a little more intricate with you."

Mr. Perkins listened as Alex explained the current position he was in with a little history about his son and his death and the three daughters that are now in his custody.

Alex finished by saying, "And now, we're just trying to become a family."

Mr. Perkins let out a breath and said, "Well we had no idea. I apologize for our lack of compassion. If there is anything we can do, please ask…and I mean that."

Alex felt a bit of warmth from the conversation. "Thank you, I appreciate your kindness."

"We'd like you to stay. You can have time off for the family if needed. However, if you feel you must leave, corporate is asking for a two year non-compete, and no more than a $36,000. Payout for one year only."

Alex, thought for a moment. He had run the numbers many times in his head on what would be a feasible separation package. "Could you make it happen that I get paid $2000.00 per month for the entire two years of the non-compete agreement?"

A pause. "Yes. I can make that happen. Is that what you want to have happen?"

"I believe that it will be the best for both parties."

"Then that is what I will do. And if during the next two years you ever want to come back to work, just let me know."

"I appreciate that Mr. Perkins. Get me the necessary papers and I will sign them."

"I'll get them drawn up and mailed to you within a few days. Thank You and good luck Alex."

Alex hung up feeling much better about his status with the company and his future. One less thing... (Forrest Gump). Now he could concentrate on his family or whatever this was right now. Right then Angie and Laila came out of their room, and they agreed on something to eat, then to take Ellie for a walk and perhaps swimming in the afternoon. But there was Daq.

Alex went to her door and knocked, when he heard nothing, he knocked again and said, "Daq, I'm coming in." He slowly opened the door.

"Get out. I don't want you here." She sat on her bed looking away from the door.

"Daquiri, you can't keep doing this. This is ruining any chances we have. Your sisters are being affected by your refusal to cooperate."

"They seem fine!" She spit the words out like a bitter pill. And right then, she knew what she needed to do.

"Daq! Talk to me, for god's sake let's work something out..."

"Just leave me alone. I'll work it out on my own. I promise." Her voice and demeanor had mellowed.

"OK, but please, let me in on it. I want to know how to proceed. We can't keep doing this. OK?"

"OK."

"We're having something to eat, then going out for a walk, then maybe swimming this afternoon. Join us?"

"No, just let me think about everything today. Then tomorrow you, or we, can figure this out."

"Sounds good. Can Angie bring you some breakfast. I know she's worried about you."

"Sure."

He left and headed back to the kitchen feeling a little more hopeful about the situation. Perhaps she had evaluated her situation and concluded that she needs to be more cooperative. He went into the kitchen and helped prepare some breakfast and told Angie to take some into Daq. Which she heartily agreed to.

When she got to Daq's with breakfast, Daq asked her to bring Laila in also. Angie called Laila and told her to come into Daq's room and the three sisters stayed in her room for over an hour. Alex looked at that as a positive and was certain not to bother them.

When they finally came out Laila was smiling and obviously happy with her time spent with her sister. However, Angie had a different look in her eyes.

"What's up kiddo?"

"I don't know. She was fine, but something seemed different."

"There has been a lot going on and I think she is resigning herself, so she is probably just a little different than she has been, but

I think she's heading in the right direction. You agree?"

"I don't know; I hope so."

Alex silently thought, *'Me too.'*

The three of them readied to go out and after a final ask to Daq about going along, and her refusal, they went out for a long walk and then to the pool and swam most of the very warm afternoon. Alex was very pleased to see Laila enjoy herself in the pool. She was all smiles with Angie and Alex as she played, still no words, but a more relaxed and happier little girl.

When they arrived back home, they found Daq in the kitchen looking through cupboards. "Hi Daq! Cooking dinner for us tonight?" Alex said, in his most cheery and nonchalant voice.

"If that's OK." Reserved but not surly.

"Sure is! But I think Lai needs a little nap before dinner."

Daq looked at her sister and nodded, "I'll put her down, then dinner around 6:00?"

"Perfect. Glad you're doing this, it's nice to have you out here with us! Oh, by the way,

Burt and Ernie are taking Ang and Lai downtown tomorrow, so maybe you and I could spend some time together?"

She nodded and smiled then took Laila's hand and went into her own bedroom where she put Laila down on her bed for a nap. Then sat down on the floor and silently cried until she also fell asleep.

Chapter Twelve

The next morning around 10:30, Burt and Ernie came to the house. Angie and Laila were ready and eager to go. As they started to leave out the front door, when Daq came around the corner from the hallway and went to each girl and gave them a hug and a kiss. "Goodbye sisters!" She smiled and waved to them as they left.

Alex got a very positive and warm vibe. "That was nice Daq. Glad to see you getting out of your room and more involved. Maybe we could have lunch together today?"

"Maybe. I'm busy writing things down that you and I can talk about, so I will let you know when I'm ready. OK?"

"Sure. Sounds good. If I can help, let me know that also." He reached out to pull her into a hug and she pulled away. "Daq, I'm not going to hurt you, I just wanted to give you a little hug."

She smiled and moved in and allowed Alex a small hug that she did not reciprocate. She then turned and went to her room, and for the next four hours just sat and reflected on her young life...or the confusion, heartbreak, disappointments, violence, and turmoil that made up her thirteen years of life. And she thought about her future. *'Living with this man that claims he wants to be a father to us and give us a great life, but really wants to control us so he can play the part of the big man, Mr. important, and I know there has to be a catch...there always is, and I'm not falling for it, not this time, not ever again. Oh, and how he hates Jimmy; he won't even let me have a friend. A friend that wants to help me, let me be my own person. And now he is even stealing away my two sisters, they use to need me and rely on me and now...so fine, I'm not needed or wanted, and I can't get away, he has a way of always finding me and forcefully bringing me back. So, I'm done! No one will even miss me, I'm better off dead. It's better than living like this.'*

***

Alex thought about checking with her around 1:30 but didn't, thinking it might give her time to devise a meaningful talk with him. At 2:30 PM he had still heard nothing when his phone rang. He looked at the screen and saw Burt's name appear. "Hi Burt!"

"ALEX! It's me, Angie. Find Daq! She's in trouble and needs you...RIGHT NOW!"

"What's going on? What are you talking about...!"

"FIND HER! Hurry and find her right now! HURRY!!"

Alex threw down the phone and sprinted down the hallway to Daq's room. The door was open slightly and he looked around quickly to see if he could spot her. He started into the master bedroom when he heard something fall in the garage, he turned and threw open the door and what he saw made his heart stop for a few seconds and then begin to pound so rapidly that he thought sure it would break through his chest, and he gasped at any bits of oxygen he could get into his lungs. Standing next to the car in the garage was Daq, holding to her temple the second item from the canvas sack that Jimmy had given her...a .22 caliber pistol. He froze in place, raised his hands up in front of himself, took a ragged breath and said,

"Daq...please...don't..." She closed her eyes, choked back a sob, and straightened the gun out against her head. Alex could see the added tension she was putting on the trigger. "Daq! No, please no...don't do this. This is wrong, you can't kill yourself! Your life has just started. I beg you...please talk to me!"

"Why?!" She opened her eyes. The gun tilted upward. "You don't give a shit about me. Nobody does! Not You, not my sisters anymore, not Jimmy, not even your neighbor friends. I'm just somebody to push around, to get slapped down whenever someone wants. I won't be missed...maybe I can be with my dad." She started crying.

"Daq, please. What you're saying isn't true. Your sisters not only love you, but they also need you! And Daq, you couldn't be more wrong about me...I love you more than you'll ever know."

"Bullshit!" Again, she straightened the gun to her head.

"NO! Daq, please listen to me." He cupped his hands over his mouth and nose and took a breath. He raised his eyes to the heavens, then lowered them to meet her eyes. "Please, you need to listen to me. Daq, please, just for a few seconds, listen to me. Take the gun away from your head for just a few seconds and look at me. Please! Open your eyes and look into my eyes. Please!

She opened her eyes and tears streamed down her face, she slightly moved the gun from her temple and pointed it to the ceiling. "What?"

Alex again raised his hands to his face and looked to the heavens as if asking for divine intervention. "Daq, please you need to let me tell you about your father, and about me..."

THUNK!

Old Maurice landed on top of the car right next to Daq. She screamed and jerked her head towards Maurice. Alex, using all his boxing skills, quickly shot out his arms and grabbed the gun that Daq was holding and lifted it towards the ceiling. The gun went off and the bullet lodged in the rafters above the car. Old Maurice jumped off the top of the car at the sound of the gunshot and scampered through his kitty door into the house. Alex pulled the gun free from Daq's hand and laid it on a counter directly behind her.

Daq screamed loudly as Alex enveloped her in an embrace. "No...I don't want to be here...let me go!" Alex held the embrace, a hug that refused to yield, a hug that encompassed love, fear and regret. She pushed and pulled and tried to get out of the lock of this immovable hug. She cried and screamed and finally relinquished and gave into the warmth and comfort of it. She cried softly into the chest of Alex and raised her arms to embrace him also. The two adhered to each other saying nothing more than a few whimpers. This lasted a number of minutes.

Finally, Alex spoke, "Daq, I want you to climb inside of me, put yourself inside my heart and never leave. You are part of me and if I have never let you know that, then I am the dumbest shit to ever walk this earth." He loosened his hug but then picked her up like she was a three-year-old and laid her against his chest. She responded by wrapping her arms and legs around him and not letting go. He turned and walked into the house with her in this position. He went into the master bedroom and sat on the couch next to the bed. When he sat, Daq still refused to let go of the grip she had on him. After a few minutes she slid off his lap and sat next to him with an arm around him and her head leaning on his shoulder. He held his embrace on her.

"Daq, I am so sorry that I drove you to this. I'm sorry I'm not a better father or grandfather...I guess I have no experience and obviously no brains either. I would have had a hole in my heart for the rest of my life if..."

"It's not just you. It's a whole bunch of things. I just feel like I'm better off dead."

"I know that now. But this world needs you! We all need you! And this world, that feels like it has pissed on you, has so many things to offer that you don't know about. So many! There are bad things sure! But you can't allow the bad to win, especially since you haven't gotten the chance to see the good. But there is good Daq...believe me, I promise you, there is good. You just have to stick around to see it. And you must allow your heart to know how I feel about you...you need to understand that my life without you now would be ruined, incomplete, meaningless. If I haven't done things right so far, I promise I will, but I couldn't deal without you! Please tell me you understand!"

She sobbed violently and nodded while burying her face in his chest.

Alex tightly hugged her. "Let's rest now. I can see you're exhausted, and I want you to sleep, but remember I will be here while you sleep and when you wake. I promise. And I want no more talk about dying or better off dead...understand?"

She nodded. Right then the front door burst open, and Angie ran in screaming, "Daq! Daq, where are you?!"

"Angie, we're in here." Alex yelled.

She rounded the corner of the master bedroom and fell into Daq's arms and started to cry. "Don't you ever leave us! Never...you hear me! I don't ever want you to leave us."

Alex locked his gaze onto Daq's and simply tilted his head and nodded with a slight smile. Daq kissed her sister. "I'm here Ang. I'm here. I'm sorry."

Laila came into the room and Alex said, "You want to come give your big sister a hug?" She nodded and Daq held out an arm and she cuddled down into her sister's hug. "Why don't the three of you stay in here for a while." He went to the doors and closed them leaving the three in a jumbled pile on the sofa. He went to the living room and saw that Burt and Ernie were sitting in the chairs. He came in and they both jumped up, and he said, "She was attempting to commit suicide when Angie called.

"Oh shit!" Ernie looked at Alex, "Is she OK?"

"I was able to stop her. She's OK now. But that was the most frightening thing I have ever gone through."

"Thank God she's alright." Burt said. "You need to get her some help!"

"I'm going to talk with Jennifer Grey again. She's the case worker I dealt with when this all started. I liked her a lot and she seemed to know a lot about everything. I think she'll be a good start."

"If we can help just let us know."

"Will do, and thanks you guys. You're a blessing." They gathered themselves and started to leave the house, both hugging Alex, but Alex said, "Please stay a while." They both sat back down.

***

As evening crept in Alex never bothered the girls but would occasionally go to the master bedroom door and listen, happily hearing talking, some laughing, and at times just sleeping sounds. At 6:30 he knocked on the door and slowly opened the door and the girls looked up at him.

"Anyone getting hungry?" All three nodded. "How about Pizza? I can have it delivered here in about thirty minutes. Everybody OK with that?" Again, all three nodded their approval. "Why don't you all get washed up and ready to eat. Daq, can you help me get the table ready?"

She looked at him a little suspiciously, but then nodded. "I'm not going to try again."

"And Thank God for that but having you with me right now is important to me and it just feels right. OK?"

When the pizza arrived, everyone sat at the table and ate, talked, and laughed. Afterwards everyone helped clean-up and then Daq got the other two ready for bed. When they were down, she went to Alex and said, "The girls are down. And I just wanted to say I'm sorry about today. And I meant it when I said I won't do that again. But I was wondering if I could sleep on the couch in your room tonight. I just feel like..."

"I was hoping you'd say that. I wanted you to sleep in my room also. I don't feel like being alone either. You ready to hit the rack right now?" Her sleepy eyes told the story, but she said, "Yes...I'm really tired." They went to the master bedroom, and he made up the couch for her and when she lay down, he tucked her in, just like he did every night with Laila and Angie. He kissed her forehead, and she held on to his arm. When he realized that she wasn't going to let go, he sat down next to her and positioned himself in such a way that she could hold onto his hand. She fell asleep quickly, and after a full thirty minutes, Alex quietly got up and went to the living room. He had a bourbon and silently cried over the emotional day he had just had. After an hour, he quietly went to bed and fell asleep watching Daq sleep and sweetly snore.

Chapter Thirteen

At 2:00 AM, Alex woke from a dream where he had not been able to stop Daquiri from her suicide. He quickly looked to his right and saw her peacefully sleeping on the couch just a few feet from him. He closed his eyes and shook his head to get rid of the terrible image the dream had left with him. As he laid back down and his head lay against the pillow, he heard. "Hi Alex." He opened his eyes and looked to his left, and there, sitting cross-legged on the bed, was Faith.

Alex raised up in a bewildered state and whispered, "Oh my god, Faith? Is that really you?"

"Yes, it is. You looked a little haggard, so I made special arrangements to visit."

"Can I touch you?"

"No, unfortunately it doesn't work that way. This is kinda like a dream-state where you and I can talk but no one else can hear us or see us, and we can't touch." She looked over at Daq and smiled, "I still remember holding her when she was a baby, and looking at her makes me a little jealous that I can't do it now."

"God, I miss you."

"I miss you too Alex, and I want you to know that I see you every day. So, I know you're going through some tough times right now and I want to see if I can help." She smiled at him, "So, you're a father again?"

"Yea, to three little girls. And Faith, I don't have a clue what I'm doing. But they're our grandkids and I'll be damned if I let them go anywhere but here with me. But I need help figuring out how to raise a family, especially girls. I mean, Jesus, this is like being in a foreign country. And, oh...sorry about using the name Jesus..."

She laughed at that, "Listen, we don't have a lot of time before I have to go, so I want you to pay attention."

"That's my Faith!"

"You're falling into the trap of solving everything yourself. Mr. fix it all. You have a young family now, a family that needs direction and purpose. And you're getting in their way by trying to solve every detail of their lives yourself. You need to understand that you're not omnipotent, you have to let them find their way and your job is to direct them."

"I think that Daq and I made some good headway today, even though it took a serious situation to do it."

"For now, yes. But Alex, she needs you to help her find her way. Don't tell her what it is but let her find it. And for God's sake, help her to understand what Jimmy is and why she should stay away! You need to help her know about him and, you need to inform her about sex, and I mean all about it."

"Oh great...me, explaining to a thirteen-year-old about sex! "

"Hey, that was always a special thing for you and me, and we were pretty good at it...make her understand that and why we were good at it."

"I wish you were here with me Faith."

"I know, but that wasn't the way it was supposed to go. And now you must make the most of your life because you have been given a huge responsibility, but one that you are qualified for, and one you can accomplish." She paused for a few seconds and smiled, "Do you remember when Ellie first came into our lives, what a hellion she was?"

"I sure do, I thought for sure she was spawned from the devil."

"And for the first couple of weeks I thought you were going to have a heart attack. And that was because you weren't letting her find her own way, you were trying to make her into what you thought she should be."

"And you made me research dogs and I learned how to be a pack leader."

"Right! And you learned how to work with her so that she was happy but fit into our life. It's not any different now, you must do the same thing, but with one huge difference...children are not dogs, they have a sense of understanding that must be nurtured. If you tell a dog to stay, they instinctively understand that, but a child needs to understand the why of any of your directions, because they do have the ability to reason."

"So, treat them like dogs...only dogs that are able to reason."

"You got this Alex. Remember, this isn't about you...it's about them, you're just the teacher, the pack leader." Do your job and don't let yourself get in the way of that!

"Thanks Faith. I love you so much. I sometimes don't know how I get through my days."

"I love you and always will. We both will have our memories to remember and cherish, but I also want you to remember that you are still alive...you must live your life…don't worry about me…I'm good here. Live your life!"

Alex opened his eyes and Faith was gone. He glanced to his right and saw that Daq was still sleeping on the sofa. But Ellie was sitting right next to him looking into his face. "Did you see Faith?" He scratched her under the chin, and she continued her solemn look into his face. "What? Do you think she was right about teaching the girls the way I trained you?" Then she laid her head across his chest and slowly wagged her tail. He petted her for a few minutes then quietly got up and slipped past Daq, noticing that old Maurice was curled up next to her sleeping against her stomach. Ellie went back to sleeping on the bed in her normal spot. He went into the bathroom and took care of his morning duties and then got Ellie up, who wanted to get old Maurice up also, but was waylaid quickly when she could have an early breakfast. Angie and Laila got up and Alex fixed them a quick breakfast and told them to go into the living room and watch TV because he was going to talk to Daq. Angie understood and nodded her approval.

Alex went back into the bedroom and found Daq awake and petting old Maurice. "Morning you two." He scratched Maurice on top of his head and touched Daq on the side of her face. She didn't pull away this time. "Daq. Why don't you take care of feeding Maurice and getting yourself ready for the day and I will make some toast and yogurt, and we can have breakfast in here after you're all done. I really want to talk with you today, but the difference is that it will be a talk…not just me talking and you listening, but us together talking about how we feel. Will that be, OK?"

She looked at him somewhat suspiciously.

"I promise I won't pontificate this time."

"Does that mean you won't babble on about how much you know and how stupid I am?"

He smiled and said, "That's exactly what it means. And…I do not think you're stupid."

"OK." A slight smile.

She picked up Maurice and walked into the hallway where Ellie was waiting, she put the cat down and the wrestling match started as she went into the bathroom. When she came out, she fed the cat and met Alex who had toast and yogurt, in the bedroom. She sat on the couch, and after closing the door, he sat on the bed as he handed her the meager breakfast he had made.

"You know Daq, I should have done this when all this started a few weeks ago. But I was so wrapped up in what I thought I should do, what I thought I must do for you to become the perfect hero that saves the three damsels in distress, that I forgot about the real you, about your life and losses, about you as a big sister and what you thought about when you looked to the future. In short, I only thought about me. And Daquiri, I am so sorry about that. I don't blame you for being upset and even for trying to escape. I was wrong and selfish, and I want to make that right. So please, tell me about you…and how you feel about all things, past, present, and future." He shifted up on the bed so that his back was against the headboard, he then patted the left side to him and said, "Come join me up here. Sit next to me." She gave him a mistrustful look. "Daq, we already had this discussion about my being a perv…don't worry, I just want us to be close for this discussion. OK?"

She rolled her eyes and nodded and crawled up on the bed next to him. Ellie immediately jumped up and curled up next to Alex on his right side and old Maurice curled up on Daq's left side.

Alex looked at her and simply said, "Tell me about you."

"What do ya mean?"

"Just what I said, I want to know about you and your feelings since the time you can remember. I didn't know you after the first year of your life. And I think it's important to know how you have felt over the years that I didn't know you. So, tell me your story…everything! What you remember, what you felt, what about your father, what did you really feel about the way your life was going?"

"Shit, I don't know…I can't remember over half of it."

"Well, start with the first thing you do remember."

Daq sat for a moment then started talking. And for the next two hours, Alex listened and only spoke to encourage, probe, or respond to her conversation. There were tears, laughter, remembrance, regret and fear, but Alex listened to all of it and did not one time pass judgement, anger or reproach.

When she finished, she looked at Alex and said, "So now what? You going to send me to a school for depraved, weird, and troubled girls."

Alex laughed and put his arm around her, "No…but I am going to make you sit through a little history about me. And I want you to know about your grandmother, my wife…my Faith…my love." And for the better part of an hour Alex talked about his life with Faith and the love they shared. He shared with her the pain and loss he went through when she died. She asked a few questions about her and finally said, "She sounds a lot like Shaila was with Dad."

"Yea…I got that connection also. I'm sorry I never got to meet her. She sounds great and I would have liked to hear the rest of the story if she had lived.

"Me too."

"One more thing we need to talk about."

"What?"

"Sex."

She pulled back again.

"No...goddammit Daq, get this through your head...I"

"I know, I know...you're not a perv!"

"Exactly...

"OK...OK...I get it. What about sex?"

"You tell me...everything you know about it."

She looked at him with an appraising look and a little embarrassment.

He quickly replied, "No, it's OK...I want you to tell me what you know, and it's not anything to be embarrassed about, it's important. So please tell me."

"Well, Jimmy says that sex is when a man gets a boner, you know, his thingie gets hard and bigger, and then sticks it into a girl's pussy, you know, down here. Then he moves it up and down until it squirts out a bunch of creamy stuff called jiz. Then it's over." She just looked down at her feet and didn't look up at Alex.

Alex took a large, deep breath and let it out very slowly trying to control the disgust and overwhelming rage that he felt. He thought to himself that he wished he had stayed in that little run-down shack and beat that miserable little piece of shit into a bloody pile of gel. He knew he had to be cool right now that this conversation could turn confrontational very quickly. "Well, technically that is a very infantile and simplistic description of how sex is done. However, it would have the same results if I handed you the keys to my car and said start the engine and drive down the street. There are a few details needed to accomplish the task properly. You understand what I'm saying?"

She nodded, "I'd have to know how to step on the gas and steer the car."

"That's right. And it's no different with sex. There are things to learn about that also. But that's for another time, when you're a little older."

"But I've already had sex."

" No. Daq, you haven't. What Jimmy did was a selfish, self-serving, despicable…" Alex stopped himself and took another deep breath. "Listen, you probably won't want to hear this Daq, but you're young, too young to even worry about sex. As your body grows, you'll learn more about how it works and when sex will become important to you. You'll know, just let life happen naturally. Just know that you and your body is all yours, and no one else can make decisions about it. And, as questions come up, talk to me. I know I'm an old dude that just came into your life, but please understand I want only the best for you and, believe it or not, I actually know quite a few things. Being old means you've been through a lot, and you learn a lot, and my job is to pass that knowledge on to you, so please, always ask me for help with anything! OK?"

She nodded. But never made eye contact.

"As a matter of fact, there is something I want to ask you."

She sighed and looked away.

"No, Daq this isn't bad. Don't always assume I'm talking about bad stuff. This is a condition that girls about your age go through and if you don't know about it, well, it can be scary."

"What?"

"Have you had your period yet?"

"My what?"

Alex nodded and told her about the monthly happening that women go through. That led to additional questions, and they talked for another half hour. After the conversation came to an end Alex told her what it meant to him to have her with him. She acknowledged the conversation, but Alex did not feel that she was completely on board. That worried him because she could easily slip back into the depression that had led to an attempted suicide. He made up his mind at that second to call Jennifer Grey at child services. He had had an instant connection with her, and he felt he would be able to talk with her about this and she would understand, listen, and work with him to help devise a plan to work with the girls, especially Daq.

***

When he called, he was surprised when she answered the phone. "Hello, this is Jennifer Grey, how may I help you?"

"Hi Jennifer, this is Alex. I, uhh, would like to talk...there is something..."

"Alex, what's wrong? Just talk to me, that's why I'm here."

"Sorry. You're right, I would like your help and expertise again. Now more than ever before. But I don't want this to become a situation that causes any interference from police or government. So, I want to tell you everything that has happened over the past few weeks and have you help, but not...do you see where I'm going?"

"I believe so, however I can't give you any guarantees on my position, but I will tell you this, after you confide in me I will give you the straight truth when you are finished, and if my hands are tied as to what I have to do I will tell you that and at that point you can retract the entire conversation. However, if I deem it appropriate, I may be able to help you in only my capacity and no other agency has to know about it. Fair enough?"

"Yes. And as a side note, I trust you implicitly. I can't really say why…but I do."

"Thank you, Alex. Now tell me what's going on."

And Alex told her every detail of the past three weeks, with the suicide attempt taking center stage. He expanded on the conversation and his feelings about it that he had had with Daq just hours before. Jennifer set a time to meet Alex face to face.

Chapter Fourteen

Jennifer sat in the back of the cozy restaurant on Palm Canyon Drive reviewing her notes about Alex and the three girls. When she saw Alex, she waved and got his attention. He walked back to the table and smiled warmly at her, and she felt a small ardent emotion as he held out his hand to shake hers.

Jennifer was about 5'7" tall and was dressed in a flowered blouse and gray skirt.

At age 60 she was a very beautiful woman with chocolate brown skin that was silky and showed very few wrinkles. Her dark hair had a few wisps of grey that gave her a rather seductive look, along with a trim body that had definite signs of someone who took care of herself. She had been single for a little over four years since her husband had decided that life in the arms of a much younger woman would be preferable.

"Jennifer, I want you to know how much this means to me. The fact that you're doing this without involving anyone else is, very important to me."

"Well, to be clear. I am doing this officially. I am evaluating your situation and helping however I can at your request. That is what is going to be in my report. The suicide attempt will be listed as a cry for help and the specifics will not include the word suicide, but if I am ever questioned about it, I have it in writing that this was your statement that you gave to me as your children's services care worker."

"Understood. I really appreciate it."

She looked into his eyes as she smiled and said, "I'm happy to help. I've been somewhat intrigued by your case, or situation is a more non-sterile way of putting it. I have seen very few like this. And your conviction and allegiance, I've found impressive. So, I'm happy to help if I can. But this is serious."

Alex stared back with a warm look of corroboration and affection. "I know it is."

Slightly embarrassed, she proceeded. "OK, let's get to it. I would like to talk to Daq first and foremost. I would like to hear her version. And hopefully she will open up and talk to me, which I'm good at making happen. Then I want to have an open dialogue with her whenever she wants or whenever you suggest it. Do you have any problems with that?"

"No, absolutely not. I think it is perfect, and for a while if she could meet with you maybe every week for a while that would be even better. And maybe even if you could come over to the house sometimes and have dinner, lunch, or game night...just something that always isn't me. I think that, and you, would be great for all the girls. And listen, if I'm getting too needy or taking advantage of your willingness to help, just tell me! And I'll happily pay for your time when you meet with Daq, or..."

"OK Stop. I'm helping because I want to, and I may be able to provide another adult figure in their lives with your approval and lead. So don't insult me with money again or I'll bitch slap you into submission. However, I will take you up on the homecooked meals and game nights. That sounds great for someone single and who works too much." She smiled broadly at Alex as he pretended to be guarding against getting bitch slapped.

They talked for another hour and Alex shared everything that had happened in his newfound family right up to meeting her in the restaurant. He also explained an idea he had for bringing the girls into a family setting starting Friday September 1st. She was riveted by his explanation of his new idea and forcing the idea of a collaborative family. He looked at her, "I like you; I feel comfortable around you, and more than that, I trust you. So, I think this will work out great, but please let me know if I am taking advantage."

"Thank You, I feel the same about you, so, no worries. One thing bothers me though."

"What's that?"

"Jimmy Braxton. He's an evil little son-of-a-bitch. And he will not take kindly to having you beat the shit out of him. He could become vindictive and that scares me. I've heard stories about him and his buddies and some of them are pretty ugly. Be on the alert!"

"I think we probably heard the last of him. Hopefully he got the message not to mess with Daq anymore."

"I hope so."

***

Jimmy and his henchman sat at the makeshift table in his little hovel that he called home and headquarters. Across from them sat a well-dressed Chad Renquist also known as the 'snake' because of the cobra tattoo on his chest. The snake striking with open jaws and large fangs. It started on his chest and ran up his neck with his Adams apple serving as the movement for the tongue and fangs of the snake. Jimmy glanced at the henchman sitting with Chad and could immediately tell that Chad was a big player in this business.

Now Chad was a sex and drug trafficker that did business mainly in the Los Angeles area but also supplied girls to other small-time traffickers in San Diego and even into the Coachella valley. He had a stable of young girls that were either homeless or drug addicts. The girls' ages were the youngest at 10 years old to the oldest that was 24. Most of the girls lived in a run-down, and very small storage unit that Chad had purchased a few years back in the outskirts of Los Angles. There were two girls per unit, unless you were special then you got to have a unit all to yourself. Each unit had a portable toilet and cots that served as their bed. He kept most of the girls on drugs, he found that keeping them quiet and compliant was much easier that way. He had heating and air conditioning in the units to help maintain their health and keep them happy. He also made sure that the girls were rotated periodically, having one girl in one place for too long was not good. Other girls that lived independently had rules to follow and they knew better than to break them. All of their life consisted of appointments made by Chad and his associates for sex, drug smuggling and even violence and murder.

When Jimmy approached him about Daq he was interested especially after seeing the picture of her and realizing that she had not yet been working. He knew he could get extra money for a few months by advertising her as a near virgin. Men who liked young teenage girls would pay extra for someone who was not...overly used. Also, she might be a candidate for selling to one of the big trafficking organizations or cartels. Young and pretty made for better bargaining. He had connections that would be interested, he had sold and provided them with many girls over the years and found that it was a profitable venture and an efficient way to keep his own inventory fresh and new. This process had also kept him well connected and informed in the world of drugs, sex and human trafficking.

So, Chad had been generous to Jimmy, a $1000.00 payment and 3 months of free meth and a free session with any of his girls, once per month for a year...but, Jimmy had to deliver her to him. So, Jimmy now knew he had to kidnap Daq away from old grandpa. That wouldn't be easy but for a grand, and free meth, he'd figure it out.

So, between Jimmy and his few henchmen and a few of Chad's enforcers, they planned a way to kidnap Daq from her safe haven that the old man called home. Jimmy couldn't help but smile when he thought of how he was going to be responsible for ruining her life and by doing that, ruining the life of the old bastard that had bested him.

Part Three
Parlay

Chapter One

The Bet

Friday, September 1st

At 7:00 AM the sound system in the Barton house started playing 'Good morning Starshine'. The sound did not play in the bedrooms but in all other rooms and hallway. Alex waited in the kitchen as the three girls stumbled out wondering what was going on. Angie and Laila seemed pleased with the music, and both smiled as they entered the room where Alex stood smiling at them.

"Good morning, ladies!"

Both smiled broadly and Angie said, "Morning Pops, this is new."

"Yes, it is! Once all three of you are up and fed and ready for the day, we are going to have a family meeting, and I will try and explain everything."

Right then Daq came up the hallway with old Maurice trailing behind her, "What the hell is with the music?"

Alex laughed and said, "Kinda figured you would be the one to hate being disturbed.

However, I am making breakfast and after breakfast we all meet at the kitchen table for our first family, around the kitchen table meeting. I have something to say and an offer to make. OK?"

"I guess." Daq said as the other two nodded.

"Great! Breakfast in ten minutes!"

Alex went about cooking breakfast and when all three girls were back at the table, he served up a meal of scrambled eggs, hash browns and juice. They small talked as they ate and when everyone was finished, Alex cleared the table and had all three sit down.

"OK girls. What I want to talk about today is, all of us. I've always said that I want us to be a family, and I haven't done a very good job of making that happen. And for that and all the mistakes I have made I apologize. But I want to remedy that and what I am thinking is that none of us really know how to do that. I do know that when Shaila was alive you all had a good family vibe going together. Right?"

Daq and Angie nodded their heads. Laila continued to suck her thumb.

"So, I am proposing that we make a bet. A thirty-day bet starting today. 'Thirty days hath September.' As of right now we start acting like a family and we continue to do that for thirty days. And if at the end of the thirty days you're not happy and it's not working...then you can leave with no questions asked. Plus, I will give you $5,000.00 to get started on your new life. Now Daq, a lot of this bet rests on you because you're the big sister and these two couldn't leave without you, but I'm going to let you three figure that out.

Daq chimed in, "So, if after 30 days I say I want out you're just going to say OK and here's $5,000.00?

"That's correct."

"Even if I want to go live with Jimmy?"

"Yes."

"And if I take Ang and Lai with me that's OK?"

"Yes."

"Bullshit!"

"No, no bullshit. Daq, I don't want to live like this for the next ten years. I'm willing to let all of you go if we can't make it as a family because if we're all un-happy…what's the point? At least this way we all can say we gave it our best try and it didn't work so it's time we went our separate ways. I do this in my business all the time and it is a great way to leave bad business or business that is not working behind and move on. But, I am very cocky…I'm betting you're going to want to stay."

Then Angie joined in, "What if me and Laila want to stay but Daq doesn't? Can Daq leave without us?"

"Yes, as long as you all agree."

Daq side glanced Angie but then joined in, "I still think you're lying. This just sounds too easy to be true."

"You're right, there is a codicil."

"What's that mean?"

Angie quickly spoke, "An addition to the original proposal."

Daq rolled her eyes, "And here we go."

Alex smiled, "In order to know whether you want to be in this family and whether it will work or not, we must first be a family. So, starting today we will become a wolfpack.

"A what?"

"A wolfpack. I've studied wolves a lot, because I wanted to know how to train Ellie, and I can tell you that they have a great family structure. They work as a team in all aspects of their lives. Hunting, traveling, relaxation, home and protection, and even entertainment. Everyone has a place and is expected to do their job and be a productive part of the family. If we four were wolves, the two youngest would be expected to learn and follow the leads of the older two and to do what they were told in the way they are taught. You, Daq, as the oldest of the siblings in the pack would be expected to work with the younger and be sure they are safe and succeeding in learning proper technique. You also would act as a positive support and nurturing partner in the family."

"And what about you?"

"I'm the pack leader."

"What does that mean?"

"That means I'm in charge of the family. In a wolfpack the pack leader sets the rules and makes sure they are enforced. For example, when they move to another location or they are hunting, the pack leader is the front man, he leads the way and every one of the others must follow and obey him, if they don't, then they are disciplined. If a pup is told to stay and he/she strays away, then they are disciplined. A pack leader knows his job is to teach and protect and he can only do that if the pack is disciplined to follow his lead and direction."

Daq started to say something and the look on her face said it was going to be combative.

"Daq, let me finish. Now in the wolf world, explanations are not necessary for discipline or teaching, because animals have instincts, and instincts tell the animal that what is happening is a normal and natural thing. But we as humans need to understand. And that is the big difference between our wolfpack and an animal wolfpack."

Alex looked at Daq.

"If you and I were walking together and you got ahead of me and I said to you, '*hey, don't walk ahead of me, you have to stay behind me*'. What would be the first question that would come to your mind? And be nice about your answer." He smiled at her.

She smiled back and said, "OK. I guess it would be...why? Why can't I walk in front of you?"

"Exactly! Because humans have a reasonable and categorical need to know why. Where an animal does not. They instinctively know that their job is to obey the pack leader. Now, if I answered your question of why by saying that there were hidden bombs where we are walking, and I want to be in front because I know where they lay, and I will protect us from stepping on one. Would that answer be sufficient for you to understand why I don't want you to walk in front of me?"

She nodded. But Alex noted a small look of impressment on her face.

"So, in our wolfpack, I promise to always explain my actions and decisions, and you all, have the right to understand or question my explanation."

Angie chimed in, "So, if we need more information about your explanation, you will grant us that?"

"Absolutely."

"What if we don't agree?"

"Then we will talk about it till we are all satisfied."

"What if we think there is a better way."

"Tell me and if we all agree, then we will do it your way."

Angie nodded and smiled. Daq furrowed her brow and said, "Really? If I don't agree with you, I can do it my way?"

"I didn't say that. I said we will discuss it and together come up with a conclusion."

"What if we can't agree?"

"Daq, there's always going to be exceptions and bumps in the road, but we must have a direction, and I think this is a good start. Don't you?"

"Maybe."

"Good! Let's talk about what each of our positions and jobs will be. But first, I want you to watch a video that I have recorded on our DVR from one of the animal stations that shows an actual working wolfpack. Then we can sit down and discuss this further."

After the video was completed for the next hour, they discussed, as a family, school and schedules, entertainment, hobbies, activities, and acceptable behavior versus non-acceptable behavior. But they all understood that for this bet to be made correctly, they all had to conform to the rules of the wager. As they broke up from the family meeting, Alex crossed his fingers.

He looked at the three girls and said, "OK! We have a plan. For the next 30 days...We are a family! We will all have our jobs to do and starting tomorrow...we do them." He looked at Laila and whispered to her, "Part of being a family means you must talk to us. I know you're not ready to do that yet, but that really is something that we all want you to do. So, could you try to start talking soon? You think you could do that, please."

Still sucking her thumb, she looked up into his face and nodded. Alex smiled a hopeful grin; a good start to the 30-day bet. "OK family...Let's shoot this fucker!" He saw that the three girls were staring at him, and he went through the explanation of the movie quote but added that the language used wasn't very nice, but it was a perfect fit on many occasions.

Chapter Two

Progress

The next morning, as the music played, the three girls appeared in the kitchen. Alex was cooking breakfast with Ellie acting as the welcoming committee. Angie and Laila were first to appear. "Good morning, Angie and Laila! Have a seat and I will get you some breakfast. We're having oatmeal and toast, and apple slices on the side this morning.

"Oatmeal?" Angie wrinkled her nose.

"Ahhhh...not just oatmeal...Pop's famous oatmeal! Organic Irish steel cut oats, butter, brown sugar with a hint of vanilla, and a dollop of maple syrup. You're gunna love it!" He watched as they both did indeed, seem to love it.

Daq came down the hallway with old Maurice following close. She had a look of disgust on her face at the mention of oatmeal, but she didn't say anything. Old Maurice jumped up onto the island counter and greeted Alex, then jumped down and the morning wrestling match between dog and cat began. Everyone watched for a few minutes then Maurice went to his dish and Daq lifted him up on the dryer and fed him. She then sat down and ate some oatmeal which she loved but wouldn't admit and talked with her sisters. Alex let them talk and didn't interrupt. He watched as the three interacted and laughed.

When he saw that the conversation was about over, he sat down at the table and said, "OK girls, the first step we need to take on our trip to becoming a full-fledged family is...our jobs around the house."

Daq rolled her eyes.

"Daquiri, that's not a good first day start. I want you to fully apply yourself to this family try-out and even try to enjoy it. If you don't, this won't work and then the bet is off." She looked at him and nodded.

"OK. Let's start with you. I want you in charge of all the outdoor work. Every day you will pull weeds, water, pick up debris, and trim the bushes and trees. Also, I want a ditch dug in the back from one end of the yard to the other..." He looked up at Daq who had a look of horror on her face. "Daq! I'm kidding...just throwing in a little humor."

"Very little." But she did smile at the joke.

"Fair enough. Your job is two-fold, first, you will be the house chef, except for breakfast, that will be mine. Lunch will be as needed because of school, outings, work etc.so don't worry much about lunch. But all dinners are yours, except Thursday nights, which will be family dine out night. First Thursday will be Daq's choice of restaurant, second Thursday will be Angie's, third will be Laila, when she starts talking." He looked at Laila and winked at her. She smiled. "Fourth will be mine and any fifth Thursdays will be open forum and when we all agree that's where we will go...So Daq, you will do the grocery shopping and be in charge of cooking and serving the evening dinner. Second, you're in charge of old Maurice. Feeding twice a day and litter box clean-up." She showed no animosity over her apparent duties.

"Cleanup of breakfast will be Daq and Angie and cleanup of dinner will be Angie and Laila, of course I will help on all clean up when needed or if someone needs being spelled. Your bedrooms are your responsibility. You can decorate anyway you want, re-arrange any way you want but I want it to be tasteful, clean, and presentable, including making your beds. On Thursdays before family dinner out night, we will collectively clean the entire house including vacuuming, dusting, mopping the floors, cleaning all the counters, and cleaning the toilets. Laila on that day will be in charge of all the dusting in the house. And don't you worry Lai, Pops will teach you how."

"Now for me. I oversee my room and bathroom completely, that won't even be part of the Thursday family clean day. And Ellie is my responsibility. I also will take care of the outside and the garage." He looked at all three and said, "I think that's about all. If any other little jobs come up, we can figure out who will take care of them. But for now, I think this is a good baseline to start with. What do you all think?"

"I think we're doing most of the work." Daq smirked at him.

Alex thought about how to answer that for a few seconds before answering. "OK. Let's talk about my assignments so you understand more about the itinerary of the household duties. First, outside. Once a week I clean the entire outside of the house, which includes using the gas-powered blower to clean all areas around the house...sidewalks, front porch, back patio and even the yard debris. Then I trim any bushes that need it, pick up all the debris including from the blower and getting it into the green can. Which brings me to another assignment, getting the garbage can, the recycling can, and the green waste can out every Tuesday morning before 7:30 AM. Also, I generally must use the blower a couple times a week because of the wind and the amount of dirt it blows in. Now all of that, and given the estival nature of our extreme heat, makes it a rather arduous task. But I'm willing to trade." He looked at all three who were silent. "OK, let's talk garage..."

"No. I think I get it." Daq quipped. "But I do have a question. Around 5:00 AM I hear thumping coming from the garage. Is that you?

"Yes, that's when I work out now, but I will move the bag farther away from the wall to your room and I will be quieter. Sorry if I have woken you up, I will try to be better and not so noisy. OK?

"No problem...in fact I think it's kinda woke you do that." She smiled at him with a look of being somewhat impressed.

"Thanks...it's important to me. So, everyone OK with the schedule?" All three nodded

"Great. I do want to tell all of you why I am taking complete care of my bedroom. That room was Faith and I's respite, it was always just us in that room, and I want to keep it that way."

"Because of the sex you guys had?"

"NO!" He realized he spit that our angrily. He tempered himself. "No Daq, it was way more than that. You and I will talk more about sex a little later. But I want you to understand that our bedroom was where we slept, talked, laughed, danced, and enjoyed each other's company. That room was ours and ours alone and for as long as possible I want to keep it that way. OK? Everyone OK with that?" He waited for an answer.

Daq responded first, "OK." And nodded.

Angie replied, "OK with me Pops."

"Good...so now I think..."

"OK Pops."

Alex whirled around and looked at Laila who no longer was sucking her thumb. She smiled up at his astonished face. "Welcome to the family!" He cried and reached down and swept her into his arms. "I am so proud of you and so happy to hear your voice!" He kissed her long and firmly on the forehead. "I love you baby girl."

"Love you too."

That brought tears and blessedly the two sisters came over in celebration and he lowered her down while they hugged and squealed with delight and adoration.

Chapter Three

School

The girls were familiar with school. They had attended in Yuma under Shaila's guidance. But the anticipation of a new school without Shaila and their dad was more than a little intimidating. So, Alex made sure he was part of the enrollment and introductions of teachers and faculty. He carefully explained to everyone the situations surrounding the children.

The main objective for Daq in Alex's mind was for her to start living a typical thirteen-year-old life. Not an easy task for someone that had gone through her tribulations. But Alex was determined to make it happen and first on his list was to talk to her about sex.

Angie was faced with some problems of her own. She was a highly intelligent eight-year-old with an IQ much higher than most people in the world. But again, Alex was determined to give her a childhood to match her age. So, much of the discussion with her was how to keep her active in a class of children that were far behind her level of learning. The teachers had said they would work with her to stay in the class and not become the brainiac kid that everyone would hate. But would help her stay challenged by working with her on special projects. Alex also would help with keeping her challenged and interested in new endeavors. A word of the day would be a breakfast topic. 'Finishing the story', a great and imaginative game, would be another way to keep her thinking and being creative. Officer Chen had offered to have her come to the station and learn more about police proceedings and how the justice system works including a few cold cases for her to look at and work theories. Jennifer Grey said she had some programs to work with her also, and Alex thought it would be worth the effort to get with her for some help. And...seeing her again was something to look forward to.

Now Laila was a little different. She had seen a lot and went through a lot, but young enough to move ahead without a lot of baggage. Not that baggage wasn't there, but a new environment and new people were going to immediately help her to move ahead. So, kindergarten was a good move for her. Alex went with her to the kindergarten and spent a few hours with her in the classroom with the teachers and she met a few other students, and everything went well. When they went home Alex asked her if she had a good time and she replied, "Yes, I liked playing with the other girls."

Alex felt somewhat buoyant after the school visits, and after the family discussions between himself and the girls. It felt as if some normalcy was coming into the girls' lives.

Dare he say that things were looking up? Was this group coming together?

Chapter Four

Jimmy's Back

It was time for Jimmy to make his move. Chad 'the snake' had paid a visit to Jimmy. He wanted to get this new girl into his care quickly as he was down his best money maker. A fifteen-year-old girl that was particularly popular with many of his steady customers. In fact, many paid extra just to request her. She had become very sick with chest pains and a horrible deep cough. She was feverish to the point of delirium and hallucinations. Her speech was slurred, and she made no sense when she tried to talk. She laid down on her cot and writhed in pain as her cough and fever overtook her. Chad being the wonderful and caring person he was, told her to rest and gave her the night off. She was dead the next morning.

When Chad learned of this, he drove her body to a remote spot in the desert in the Coachella valley and tucked her away in some brittlebush. She was really a nobody from nowhere and probably wouldn't be missed. And if the body was ever found, or what would be left of it, there really wouldn't be much to go on. Pretty safe bet. And since he was in the vicinity of Jimmy, it was a good time to get this Daq girl into his fold. Daquiri would become a perfect fit for him, young, cute, not well used, he could make her his next cash cow, at least for a while. So, he sought out Jimmy to get her in the next few days, he even increased his offer to him of an additional three months of free meth. He could even use a couple of his henchmen if needed.

Jimmy accepted the offer and took him up on the addition of the two henchmen to help. The two henchmen were called Sampson and Hombre. Now Sampson was big, strong and mean and nothing much else and so was Hombre, but Hombre had one thing that was of particular interest to Jimmy. He had a cousin who ran a landscape business and had a transponder to get through the gate at the old man's community. They could have Hombre's cousin take them along on a job and then they could go and scout out the old man's house and from there they could devise a plan on how to kidnap Daq and get her away from the old man. So, on Thursday, September 6th, Sampson and Hombre came into the community disguised as landscape workers and not only investigated Alex's house but the entire neighborhood. When they had the necessary information, they called Chad and devised a plan on how to coordinate a kidnapping of Daq. And as a bonus he told them to get the little black girl and bring her as well, if possible, without screwing up the whole deal. There was a pretty good market for 5-year-olds in the sex business and it paid big bucks. She'd need some breaking in of course, but he'd be able to handle that job, might even take him a few months. He smiled an evil smirk and the cobra on his throat opened its fangs wider as he swallowed.

Chapter Five

September 10th

The Talk

With school starting the next day, Alex felt he needed to have his talk with Daq. So, Angie and Laila went over to Burt and Ernie's to spend the afternoon with them. Alex summoned Daq and they sat in the living room. Daq's posture was apprehensive, but she sat down and looked at Alex with a glint of curiosity and significance. She said nothing. Alex started, "Daquiri, I want you to understand about sex. Sex is a technical term for two people having sexual relations together for enjoyment and being together. And what I want to add right now, is that what you and Jimmy did was not a kind act of enjoyment or love. It was the act of a selfish son of a bitch that thinks of only himself and no one else…excuse my language. Did you enjoy or even like what he did?"

"No."

Of course you didn't, you weren't ready and didn't know that he stole something from you that every teenager should have the privilege to go through."

"What do you mean?"

"Everybody deserves that first feeling of attraction, where you see that one person that makes you feel different than you did with everyone else…that first smile at each other…the first time you talk…the first time you touch or hold hands…your first kiss." He looked at her and saw a look of interest in her eyes. "I remember the first time I started to notice that I was attracted to girls. I believe it was the 5th grade and I found myself acting differently around girls than I did around boys. And some girls I liked more than others and I wanted to do things around them that they liked, that made them laugh, and that went on for about a year. Then I found the one girl that I really liked, and I wanted to be around her and talk to her, make her laugh, and I really wanted her to like me the same way I liked her. But she never really liked me the same way. But as time went on a new girl came to our school and my attentions turned to her and I started acting the same way around her as I did with the other girl and that went on for a few months, but then…someone told me that she really liked me…and BOOM, that's all I needed to hear, I was all about her!" Alex looked at Daq who had a warm smile on her face. "I would walk her home after school, and we would talk and laugh…I would carry her books for her too."

"You what?"

"Carried her books for her. See, back in my day at school we had books to study, and we were expected to take the books home to study and bring them back the next day. Well, the gentlemanly thing to do was to carry the lady's books for her, you know being the big strong boys that we were. She was the first girl I held hands with, she was the first girl I danced with, and I even kissed her...on the cheek. I found that I thought about her all the time."

"Then came summer, and we parted ways promising we would see each other at school next year. But the summer brought new adventures, hanging out with friends, going to summer parties, and lo and behold...new girls. And I found myself wanting to be with another girl I met at a party. And she was a whole year older than me, and she taught me about kissing on the lips. And perhaps a few other things."

"Like having sex?"

"No...no. What I'm trying to tell you Daq that it's not about sex...not at your age. The fun is growing up and learning." He looked at Daq who seemed like she was starting to understand. "I had other girl friends in high school, but then...I met one that stood out above all the other girls, and I found that I didn't want to be with anyone else. That was my first connection with falling in love. I couldn't wait to see her, to kiss her, to feel her in my arms. And we had fun together. We talked and laughed and enjoyed seeing movies, dancing, hiking, picnic lunches, parties, and talking on the phone.

And...yes, we had sex. The summer before our senior year, we did have sex. But to us...it was making love. It was sweet, exciting and we were horribly clumsy at it, but it was thoroughly enjoyable. And when I met your grandmother Faith, the world changed completely. I loved her more than anything and I never wanted to be without her..."

He couldn't talk over the lump in his throat, and he looked at Daq through tear filled eyes, and she was smiling. "And Daiquiri...that's what I want for you. Now is not the time to be thinking about sex. And I will never forgive Jimmy for doing what he did to you and what he was trying to do to you. Never! You deserve to learn like I did, like kids still do...even though it's changed since my day. But learning about what someone is thinking when they smile at you, when they touch you, when they hold your hand. And making love should be something reserved for a special person. Someone that means something to you...and when you're ready, when you're older and have experienced all the things I have talked about."

"How will I know?"

"You'll know. As your body grows and as your experience grows, you'll know when the time is right. But do not rush it, experience the wonderful ride to get there. You understand where I'm going with this?"

"I think so. What I had was not really sex. I should just forget about Jimmy and start, kinda like...over."

"Yes...and enjoy the ride, believe me it is worth it. There will be happy and sad, exciting and boring, but you will never forget the experience. And...I'm here for you. Any questions, any thoughts, anything...talk to me, I probably can help. OK? And Daq, forget about Jimmy. I know it happened but believe when I tell you you'll much happier in life forgetting about him and everything that happened, trust me on this."

"OK. But Alex?"

"Yes? Can't you at least call me Pops?"

"What about...uhh...like Burt and Ernie?"

"Sometimes, men find out that they like being with other men, and sometimes women like being with other women...and there's nothing wrong with that...but you'll know that too if it happens with you, your body will tell you. Is that a good enough answer, at least for now?"

She smiled, "Yea, thanks...Pops."

Chapter Six

Attempt

September 15th

After five days the girls all seemed to be adjusting and for the most part, enjoying school. Daq had already found another girl that seemed to like the same stuff that she did. They seemed to be getting along famously. That was a favorable development. It was a worry that she might have a hard time developing relationships with others because of her past. She did say that some of the kids were trying to bully her, but that wasn't a big deal, she could handle herself, she told Alex. There were no tell-tale effects on her day-to-day interactions with her sisters or Alex. All were positive signs that her school experience was going well.

Angie, as everyone had figured was way ahead of the rest of her class. But she was enjoying the comradery of the other kids and learning how to fit in with others. Jennifer Grey saw her once a week with advanced education and Alex was coming up with ideas for her gifted intelligence all the time. He had come up with the word of the day from Ang, at breakfast every morning. He also had discovered a mystery game that introduced very difficult scenarios that the players had to figure out how to solve. She also was working with Officer Chen who had helped her at the time of her father's death. Once a week they would get together, and she would have Angie look at old cases from the police files (nothing gruesome) and try to solve the cases. So, Angie was getting plenty of stimulation while interacting with her classmates.

Now Laila, who was now a very prolific talker, had become a very precocious child. Perhaps her silence had allowed her to observe the world differently and by doing that learned a different scope of life, both good and bad. Her kindergarten teachers had said she was happy and outgoing but could be a bit manipulative and imperious.

So, after one week of school, Alex had learned a lot and was feeling optimistic. This particular Friday afternoon the girls were home from school and each doing something of their choice. Daq was reading a cookbook, her new house job as chef seemed to really be a motivation for her. She loved to create meals and was interested in learning about ingredients. She sat reading on the front porch which had a small patio area with two chairs, and a table between them, along with a bench, as she kept an eye on Laila who was playing in the front yard with Ellie. Alex was inside working with Angie on a mystery challenge of 'Finish the story'.

Daq glanced up as a car stopped in front of the house and two men got out, the larger of the two waved at Daq and the other started talking to Laila. Daq stood up, waved cautiously, and started toward the two men. She noticed that the one man had his hand on Laila's shoulder and was almost pushing her toward the car. Ellie was letting him know that she didn't approve. At only fourteen pounds, she felt much bigger and was certainly expressive.

"Hey! What are you doing?!"

The bigger man said in a calming voice, "Oh don't worry. He just loves kids."

"Well tell him to let go of her."

"Hombre..." He just waved his hand back and forth. The other man let go of her. Laila moved away and Ellie stayed right with her, still expressing her dis-pleasure. "We just wanted to ask a question or two. We're working here in the neighborhood, and we are kind of lost so we were hoping you could help us. Would you look at our directions and help us find our way?" Daq was close to him now. "I have the directions over here." He pointed to the car. "Would you help us?"

"No, she won't." Alex strode toward them. When he got to Daq he pulled her away and stood facing the substantial frame. "Daq, get your sister and then come over here with me!" She obeyed and retrieved Laila with Ellie close in tow, still growling and barking.

"Now you and your little killer of a dog don't sound very friendly." He was visibly agitated by the fact that Alex had come out of the house. (Damn dog!)

"We can be, but we're very cautious till we know what's going on."

"Are you accusing us of something?"

"No accusations have been made. I just don't let strangers get too close with my daughters, especially to lay hands on them. You know, safety precautions."

"So, you think we need to be precautioned?" He moved closer to Alex and put his face directly into his. "I don't think I like that." He moved even closer to Alex's face.

Alex stood his ground and didn't budge an inch. He stared directly into the eyes of this unwanted stranger and said, "I don't recall asking what you think. So, your thoughts are of no matter to me." They stood nose to nose for a few seconds when Burt and Ernie came up the sidewalk toward the house. The stranger backed away slowly continuing to stare at Alex, then said, "Let's go!" The two got into the car and drove away. Angie came out of the house and stood by Alex. And of course, Ellie had to put in her two cents in by barking at the moving car.

Burt looked at Alex and said, "What the hell was that?"

Daq said, "Just a couple of creeps that work around here somewhere. Wanted me to show them where they were supposed to go."

Alex glanced at Burt with a demur look. "Probably nothing, just a misunderstanding and the one guy took exception."

"OK. Well, we're heading to the club house for Friday fish fry, you guys care to join us?"

"That would be up to Daq. She is the chef, and we live by her schedule of food service. What do you say Chef?"

"Yea, we could do that."

"Yes Chef! Can you give us a few minutes and we will go get ready."

"Can do, we'll wait right here." Both Burt and Ernie smiled with gratification of the progress being made in the Barton household.

The three girls and Alex headed for the house. Angie and Laila leading the way. Alex put his arm around Daq. "Have you heard from Jimmy, or do you know if he has tried to contact you?"

"No...nothing. Why? You think those two were with Jimmy?"

"Probably not, but worth thinking about. Keep a watchful eye out, just in case."

"OK. Pops?"

"Yes?"

"You're a pretty tough old dude. That why you keep working out every day?"

"I just like to keep in some semblance of shape, and other reasons..." His mind thought of Faith.

"Well, I think it's fire."

"Fire?"

"Cool." She giggled.

"So, fire is cool?" Alex just smiled.

They all quickly got ready to go and headed out the door. "Well girls, let's shoot this fucker!" They all snickered as they went to meet Burt and Ernie.

Chapter Seven

The Snake

Chad sat and listened to the story that Sampson and Hombre told him of the trials they had had with Alex. He said nothing, just glowered at the two men telling their story. Jimmy sat next to him and quietly waited to see what the Snake's take on their story was, and what his next move would be. He thought to himself that maybe now Chad will understand why he had had so much trouble with the old man. That old dude was a tough son of a bitch, and you just don't mess with his kids. Let's see what his plan will be to deal with him.

"So, let me get this straight. You had a chance to get the two girls into the car but before you could the old man came out and foiled your plan. That about right?'

Sampson and Hombre nodded their heads. They weren't feeling very confident right now. Sampson said, "We didn't plan on the damn dog being so loud."

"And instead of nicely just backing away to re-group for another time, you had to play tough guy and get in the old man's face and show him how mean and nasty you were?"

Silence.

"Dumb son of a bitch! And you Hombre! You felt it was necessary to put your hands on the little girl? Why didn't you show her your dick while you were at it!"

"Well..."

"Shut the fuck up! You dumb assholes! All you've managed to do was get the old man's suspicions up and now he'll be on guard more than ever!" He shook his head and stood up and walked around. "Fuck! That was a great opportunity, and you guys couldn't put it together, so you make it ten times worse."

"We'll do better next time, I promise."

"Well, that ought to make it all better! Why don't you two just go out and stand in front of his house and wait for the perfect time! I'm sure he wouldn't recognize you!"

He glared at the two of them and put his hands in the air as he turned away from them. "OK, we need to start over for the perfect time to grab them up. Jimmy, do you have anyone that could get by as a landscape worker who isn't as dumb as these two lumps of shit? Someone who will just watch and listen and learn then report back to us?"

Jimmy thought for a minute, "Well it can't be my bodyguard, he's already been seen. But I think he has a buddy that might be interested, for a price of course. He's smaller and Hispanic, but pretty smart. His name is Armando, he might be perfect."

"Let's get him over here as soon as possible and see if he's willing to do as I tell him."

***

Armando showed up at Jimmy's hangout around 6PM. After Chad settled on a price with him, he devised a plan for surveillance. He felt confident that Armando would do as he says and do a pretty good job of it.

So, he got his landscape company to put him on the truck when they went into the gated community, and he was to act as a worker but also as a sales rep for the company going to houses to see if they needed a landscape company. Of course, his territory would be right around Alex's house. His mission was to find out about schedules, times that the kids were away from Alex or when Alex would be out.

Armando was smart and a little devious and quite frankly enjoyed the challenge. He was a man of all trades, most not legal, but had a charm and ability to scam people. He was also smart and did his homework. When he worked, he knew all about the job, what was expected of him and everything about the people involved. Perfect for what Chad was looking for. He was being paid well for his time and was promised a nice bonus, both cash and the use of Chad's girls.

Chad had made arrangements in Los Angeles for his business there, to be run by a trusted friend so he could spend some time here. He wouldn't stay with Jimmy, so he got a hotel in downtown Palm Springs. He was tired, he had been out doing some reconnaissance work with Jimmy. It was time for him to relax a bit but knew he had to be alert. He had supplied Armando with a burner cell phone and wanted daily updates on his progress. He contacted an associate, or pimp, that he had connections with that was in the Coachella valley and got a girl to stay with him to take up time. She was eleven, a little older than he liked but she was the youngest the pimp had. She'd do.

Chapter Eight

Moving along

The week of September 18th went...well, you could only say 'kinda normal', but very bewildering. First, the week started by Alex getting the girls off to school and as he came home, he noticed a neighbor woman sitting in her courtyard out front. She looked familiar, but he couldn't quite place her. He knew the house she was sitting in front of was a rental property, so it didn't surprise him that he didn't remember seeing this lady before. But it worked on his mind that she looked very familiar and quite frankly it was a bit of an exasperation.

Meanwhile, Daq was at school and sat in a classroom for her history class. She had done well in school and at home since her attempt, she seemed willing to accept things, become more involved with the sisters, and even with Alex. There were still disagreements and arguments but with Alex's commitment to making her understand the why of decisions made her more amiable and she seemed much more adaptable.

She looked out the window which had a view of the street that went by the school, and she noticed a rather familiar face on the street walking by. As she stared, it suddenly came to her who it was, it was Marcie from the homeless camp she and her sisters had lived in. Marcie had been living with her mom close to where Daq and the girls lived. They had gotten to know each other and were friends, or at least as close as you could living in a homeless camp. Marcie looked terrible. She was dirty, skinny and had bruises up and down her arms. Daq raised her hand and stood up. "Mrs. Jamison? I need to go outside for a minute right now, I see a friend of mine who looks like she is in trouble."

She started moving to the door when Mrs. Jamison said, "Daq, please be telling me the truth. Because if you're not, everyone who knows you will be disappointed. Go ahead."

"Thank you. I'm telling the truth, I promise."

She ran out the front doors and onto the street and yelled down the street, "Marcie! Marcie, wait up. It's Daq."

Marcie stopped and looked back and saw Daq running toward her. She smiled broadly and waved. When the two met they embraced.

"Daq. I thought you were gone forever. I'm so glad to see you. What happened? And are you in school now? Where are you living? And you look…amazing."

"A lot has happened, and I'll tell you about it, but right now I got to get back to school before I get in trouble. Come with me and I'll see if I can get you to stay with me."

"I don't want to go into school, I mean I'm dirty and smelly, and look at you."

"OK. Let me talk to my teacher and I'll see if Alex can come to pick us up. Where's your mom?"

"I haven't seen my mom for over two weeks. I'm living by myself right now. Who's Alex?"

"He's my grandpa, and we're all living with him right now. Come on, I will tell you all about it. But I want to hear more about your mom, cuz does that mean your living by yourself in your car?"

Marcie nodded and started to cry. Daq put her arm around her and said, "Come on, it'll be OK."

They went back to the school and went back to the classroom. Daq opened the door and asked Mrs. Jamison to come out into the hallway. She came out and Daq explained the situation. She took both girls to the office and allowed Daq to call her father about this situation.

After she called Alex, he agreed to come and pick up the girls. He arranged it with the school, and they worked with him to get Daq all the info she needed to complete her school day at home.

While they waited for Alex, Marcie started telling Daq about the last two weeks. "Mom was going out almost every night, but she always came back, sometimes not till morning, but this time she hasn't come back at all. I'm scared she's hurt or worse. Or maybe, she found someone or something that is more important to her and she just plain doesn't want to come back and doesn't care about me."

"Oh, I doubt that, Marcie. I'm sure there's a good explanation, but I'm worried she might be sick or something and can't get to you. Alex will be able to help. He's good at this and...actually, he's pretty dope all around."

"Sounds like you're starting to like him. After you first met him, he was like poison to you, at least that one time we talked after you moved away. What's going on?"

"Oh, I don't know. We've got a deal that if I don't like living with him at the end of September, I can move out and he won't bug me about it. So, I'm trying to stay nice so that I can move out, if I want to."

"You think you'll want to?"

"Probably." (*Deep down...maybe, but maybe not...*)

Right then Alex drove up and got out of the car and walked toward the office where they were sitting. When Daq saw him, she smiled and suddenly felt better and knew he would help with this situation.

"Hi Daq." He put his arm around her shoulders and gave her a little hug. "Thanks for calling. I'm glad you did." She looked up at him and smiled and nodded. "This must be Marcie." He extended his hand, and she really didn't know what to do. He saw her concern and changed his hand into a fist for a fit bump and she understood that and reciprocated. "Daq tells me you've got some stuff going on?" She nodded. "Well, let's see if we can help." Marcie started to cry, Alex set his hand on her shoulder, and she then moved in and put her arms around him. He looked at one of the women in the office with an apprehensive look and she smiled and nodded as if to say, 'it's OK you can hug back'. Alex put his arm around her and whispered, "We're going to work this out. OK?" He motioned to Daq to come to her aid, and she did. She gave Marcie a hug and led her to the car. Alex thanked the staff and gathered up Daq's stuff and went to the car.

Alex got in and Daq and Marcie were seated in the back seat. "We need to stop and get Laila from school, then we can head home for a while before we go out to where Marcie is living now."

"Why do we have to go out there?" Daq asked.

"To see if her mother is back and if she isn't, then collect whatever Marcie needs to stay with us for a while."

"You'd let me do that?" Marcie quietly spoke.

"Of course. I would insist." He smiled at her while looking at her in the rear-view mirror.

The august feeling Daq had right then about Alex gave her a new realization about her feelings towards him.

Chapter Nine

Daq's Friend

After Marcie had taken a shower and Daq had fixed dinner for everyone they drove out to the homeless camp, Alex again saw the woman in the rental house sitting out on her front patio in dark glasses and a hat. *'Damn, who is that! I know I've seen her before...but where?'* As quick as the thought came into his head it left. Now he had to concentrate on Marcie and her predicament. He thought about Jimmy and wondered if he'd gotten his claws into her yet. He knew he would have to approach that subject carefully both for her but also for Daq. He didn't want Daq to become tired of him constantly bringing up Jimmy.

When they arrived at the camp, Marcie led them to the car she was living in, and Alex was a bit taken back. It was a small two-door coupe with a back side window broken out. Inside the upholstery was torn and dirty with a blanket and pillow. There were fast food wrappers and cups all over and one bottle of water that was half gone. It was 6PM and it was hot.

"You been staying here by yourself? Your mom hasn't been around at all?"

"Not for the last couple of weeks, but even when I knew she was here, she didn't sleep here much. She spent a lot of time in bars and wouldn't come back till morning. Sometimes she would take me to the bar with her, but she always dropped me off back here, at least whoever she was with did."

"Anybody else been around to talk to you or take care of you, or want to take care of you?"

She was looking at Alex when he asked that question but dropped her eyes to the ground when she answered, "Nope. Just me."

He looked at her for a few seconds then said, "OK. You guys stay here, I want to ask a few questions around. When he left, Daq asked Marcie, "Have you really not talked to anyone else? What about Jimmy? Has he been around trying to get you to come with him?"

"No." She answered but not with a lot of conviction. Daq looked at her with a little suspicion. "You know what I love most about where you live now? How cool it is inside. I only got to have air conditioning sometimes if mom took me to the bar. Man, to have it all the time, that's really rad. And you're grandpa! He seems really...nice."

"Yea, I guess so. I'm getting to like him more. But I'm not ready to say I will stay at the end of the month. We'll see."

Alex came back and said, "Well, I talked with some of the neighbors here and nobody has seen her either. One lady over there has been keeping an eye out for you, so I thanked her."

"Did ya give her some money?"

"Yea, twenty bucks. Why?"

"She talks a big story, but she's just looking for hand-outs. Don't trust anything she says."

"Well, good to know for the future. Anyway, let's get home."

"Do I get to go with you? Or did you..." Marcie sheepishly asked.

"I picked up a few things out of your car that I think are yours, so you've got something to wear. But tomorrow we'll go buy you something that will work a lot better. So, the answer to your question is...yes. You're coming home with us and staying with us for as long as needed. Daq can fill you in on everything about living in our house. OK?" She smiled a huge smile that answered the question immediately, then she began to cry. Daq walked side by side with her on the way to the car, but before getting there, Daq turned and looked at Alex with gratitude and admiration in her eyes. Alex smiled back at her with a sense of euphoria. But a bit of disturbance surrounded him with Marcie.

Later that evening after everybody got settled. Alex walked by Daq's door and heard the two girls giggling and whispering. He smiled, that sounded a bit more normal.

Chapter Ten

The Neighbor

Alex had finished his workout and was about to take a walk/run around the neighborhood when he spotted the familiar face, but still couldn't place it, sitting outside in the front yard in the patio area. "Good morning."

The woman looked up and didn't say anything, just gave a slight nod.

"Are you new around the neighborhood? I just live up the street and I can't say I have seen you before. That certainly doesn't mean you haven't been here; I've been known to be completely un-observant." He laughed lightly and smiled.

She stood up and walked in her front door, shut it, then set the dead bolt. *'Well, I certainly observed that!'* He thought to himself as he moved down the street to continue his walk.

When he got back home it was close to the time of picking up Laila at kindergarten. So, he showered and got dressed and thought he would stop by the local coffee shop and have a vanilla latte' which was always one of his favorites when he was a working stiff. He had a little over an hour before picking her up and that would be ample time to get a coffee and sit in the outside area and enjoy downtown Palm Springs.

He moved to the front door and opened it and there stood the lady from down the street. "Oh, hi there. Can I help you with something?"

"I'm Virginia Belson. I'm sure you recognized me and are looking for something from me. Perhaps a story, or a picture, or an autograph or just a story to tell your buddies. I apologize for being rude this morning, but this type of thing does get old after a while. So, tell me what you're after and let's get it over with."

"Uhh, I'm sorry but none of what you just said means anything to me. Frankly you looked familiar, and it was aggravating that I couldn't place your face, so I thought if I introduced myself that would help me remember. I was in sales for years and I hate it when I don't remember someone that I may have worked with. That was it."

"Oh, I'm very sorry. I meant no disrespect. I am sorry, it's just that this happens…never mind, but I do sincerely apologize." She turned to walk away.

"Excuse me, but you still look very familiar. Have we met before?"

She turned towards him and said, "Ever see the movie, 'Helen in Love'?"

He thought for a second, "Yes…oh my god! You were Helen's sister in that movie! And I remember thinking that you were suburb in that part, I even said you stole the show!"

"Thank You." She smiled warmly at him.

"Can you come in for a minute? I'd love to talk a little more. You were up for an academy award for best supporting actress. You got screwed. In my humble opinion."

"Thank you again. I kinda felt the same way." She quietly gave a soft laugh. "I could come in for a few minutes, but I have an agent coming over in about twenty minutes."

"That's great, I have to pick up my daughter from kindergarten pretty soon also."

She came in and sat down in the great room and Alex offered her a beverage. "Coffee if you have it."

"You bet. I'm Alex Barton by the way."

"Daughter, in kindergarten Alex?"

"Yes," Alex smiled as he knew where she was going with her comment. He peeked around the corner and caught her eye as the coffee pod drained into a cup, and said, "Granddaughter actually. But that's a story for when we have more time."

"Does your wife work?"

"My wife died about seven months ago, so now it's just me and my three granddaughters, Ellie the dog, and old Maurice the cat." And just as if on cue Ellie rounded the corner and jumped into Virginia's lap. "Ellie, get down." He gave her the cup of coffee

"No, she's fine. I had a Westie once, and I still miss her every day." She petted Ellie and looked down with a serious look on her face. "You probably know about my colossal downfall in the movie business." She looked at Alex who nodded with a sympathetic frown.

"I never really understood that whole mess. I never thought you were given much of a defense chance, and then, all of a sudden, boom, convicted and banished before we knew anything. Seemed awful cut and dry…neat and tidy, if you get my drift?"

"I did a three-part mini-series on TV with him, Erick Newsome was his name, we got along famously, and I really liked him. I even went so far as to speak highly of him in interviews and late-night show appearances. We spent a lot of time together and I really thought he was a special friend. I knew he was gay, and it didn't bother me at all, in fact he encouraged me to call him my crazy flaming friend. It was meant to be a fun and special phrase for the two of us, not in public of course. He was very affectionate and would occasionally kiss me on the lips and give me a loving hug. I didn't think much of it, he was thirty-one, I was seventy at the time, I thought we were more of a May-December buddy-buddy relationship. Then one day, after the filming for the series had stopped, he was on TV telling the world that I tried to seduce him and when he turned me down, I called him some derogatory gay names and tried to ruin his career. And of course, he had video of me calling him a crazy flame and of a couple of the kiss cam videos. I realized very quickly he had set me up and had, behind the scenes, done a damn good job of securing friends and photos of his ploy to get ahead at my expense."

She looked out the window with a pensive look. "Worked for him! His career is taking off thanks to all the publicity and support he received after the horny old woman has-been tried to glom on to him and his rising star. And mine is...well, pretty much done.

I'm renting places to try and stay incognito until I get paid and able to get out of here and go back home to Montana and live peacefully, till, I die."

"I'm sorry that happened to you Virginia. And I believe you! I have some neighbors that live right next door, and they are a gay couple who have some chops in this community. They told me some stories about Erick Newsome, now that you've mentioned the name. I would have never put the two together until I met you today. You should meet them; you'd like them a lot.

"Maybe...I might like that."

"OK. I'll see if I can plan something."

"Thank you, Alex. I'm sorry I was a bit vinegary, it's just that people today. But you're easy to talk to, and God knows I did a lot of talking today. I guess I just needed it. So, thank you."

"I really enjoyed it. Thank you for coming over. And...I still think you got hosed on that Oscar!"

She smiled and waved, and he returned the gesture and went inside. He immediately felt a very strong predilection towards her. He made a point of contacting and seeing her every day that week.

Chapter Eleven

The Tantrum

Jennifer Grey had a day off. In her business she worked many different hours and days. She had been working on a couple of cases that had her working evenings and twelve days in a row. She had requested a couple of days off and those had been granted. So, on September 19th and 20th she had two days to herself. On the 19th she slept most of the day and did a whole lot of nothing. On the 20th she decided to go out and do some much-needed shopping for herself. She didn't get to do that very often and today she was going to make up for lost time. She readied for her trip and headed out for downtown Palm Springs. She was walking along Palm Canyon drive going into store after store and decided to stop for a beverage at the Kaiser Grille and sit on the patio so that she could people watch. Little did she know that one of the people she would be watching was Alex Barton and his

5-year-old granddaughter. When she spotted him, he was walking with Laila holding her hand, and they were directly across the street.

She had spoken to him several times. He seemed to really need and appreciate her help. And she did enjoy working with Angie and counseling Daq. As she watched him walk down the street, a familiar feeling of attraction came over her. She admittedly was drawn to him. But he had never really shown the same toward her, not really, so she had not pursued the interest.

As she watched them walk a curious thing happened. Laila suddenly stopped and pointed to a shop behind them. It appeared that she wanted to go back. Alex then talked with her and shook his head and started to move ahead. Laila resisted and pulled her hand out of his and started yelling 'No...No...' Wanting to hear more and watch this scene more closely, she quickly moved to the maître de and handed her a credit card and said she'd be right back. She crossed the street carefully and positioned herself where she was out of sight but able to see and hear all that was transpiring.

Laila screamed, "I said I want to go back!"

Alex replied calmly, "No, I told you we need to get your sisters from school, and we don't have time to go back. And you know the rule about…"

"I don't care, I want to go back for candy!" (Screaming)

"Laila, I said no, and I told you why, so let's go to the car."

"NOOOO! I want to go back!" (Screaming and crying)

"Laila! I said no." Now Laila screamed and cried louder and fell to her butt kicking her feet and slapping her hands on her legs. Alex walked a few steps behind her and just stood while she kicked and screamed. After a few minutes she quieted down, then stood and started walking towards the store she wanted to go to. Alex blocked her way and said, "No, I told you we can't go back because it's time to get your sisters." This time she screamed and cried and started slapping his legs. He dodged and moved so she couldn't make contact and finally she ended up kicking at him which he sidestepped, and she fell hard to the sidewalk.

Jennifer watched engrossed by the exchange and very curious as to its outcome.

Now, Laila just started crying and sobbing and had attracted a pretty good audience. One lady went to her and asked her if she was alright. Alex responded, "She's fine. Please leave her, we're just having a slight disagreement. The lady glowered at Alex but moved away.

After a few minutes of exhaustive crying, she started to quiet down a bit and Alex moved to her and said, "Are you ready to get your sisters now?" She immediately started her unyielding crying again and Alex moved back and waited patiently. After a few minutes more, she stopped crying and just sat in the middle of the sidewalk with a number of bystanders looking on. Alex again went to her and said, "Are you ready now?" This time she nodded her head and Alex held out his hand for her to take, which she did. Once up and walking she held her arms out to have Alex pick her up to which he replied, "No, you can walk to the car." She sniffled but walked to the car.

As they walked to the car Jennifer watched them leave, smiled, and gave a simple nod of her approval. And the feeling of attraction came back.

She would have also approved of the way he handled Laila at home. He asked her to go to her room and think about what happened and then he went in and explained why he did what he did. They talked until she understood, hugged it out and all was good.

Chapter Twelve

Daquiri

Daq and Marcie talked every night. The school had been great to let Marcie attend school with Daq, until other arrangements would and could be made. This made for stories and teenage gossip that was fun and healthy for the two girls. Marcie asked a lot about Alex and the other sisters and Daq drew the conclusion it was because of being envious. Their pasts led to some harsh memories and stories. Marcie had finally admitted that she had seen Jimmy, and that he had promised to take care of her. "Mom and I went to Jimmy's place after he met her in a bar. He and mom went into the bedroom while I stayed in the living room and read a comic book. After, he came out and talked to me and asked me a bunch of questions."

"Like what?' Daq asked.

"Like...how old I was. How long had we been living in the homeless camp. Did I know what He and mom were doing in the other room?"

"Did you?"

"Yea, I don't know much about it, but mom used to do it with a lot of different guys, so they must like it. Jimmy said he could teach me."

"When was this?"

"I don't know exactly, but it was before your dad died." Daq did some math in her head about the dates and came up quickly with the thought...*'that son of a bitch!'*

"He also asked about you."

"What about me?"

"Did I know you? And just that he knew you and we lived close to each other. He told me not to tell you anything about what he had talked to me about, and especially to your dad."

"That's cuz Dad would have killed him." She took a deep breath. "Marcie, stay away from Jimmy, he's a bad guy. He'll tell you how he wants to help you and take care of you…but he won't, cuz he just thinks about himself. So, stay away. OK?"

She nodded her head and immediately looked down.

Daq looked at her and said, "I'm not mad or anything. It's just that you're my friend and I don't want you to get hurt; Jimmy will hurt you, I know cuz he did it to me. And if my dad had found out, or if Alex was to find out now, Jimmy would be executed in a matter of seconds. And I saw Alex in action once, he kicked the shit out of Jimmy and one of Jimmy's goons and never even broke a sweat."

Marcie gazed at Daq and shook her head slowly side to side, "Why you wouldn't want to stay is unbelievable. He is rad, and kind of a hottie also…"

"Ewww!"

"And look where you live now and everything you got. He isn't mean or, you know, trying to do things…"

"No." Daq smiled as she thought of the earlier conversations that she had had with Alex about that very subject. "He actually reminds me of my dad, his son, when Dad was with Shaila and getting off the junk. Those were great times, and I loved every minute, and I kinda feel that way now."

"You're lucky."

"Yea, maybe I am. We better get some sleep." And they crawled into bed and Marcie fell asleep quickly, while Daq lay wide awake with her mind going a mile a minute.

'That goddamn Jimmy! Tells me I'm his girl and come to find out he's poking my friend's mother and trying to get my friend to work the same as me. Bastard…Pops was right. He is all about himself, he doesn't care about anyone else.

Wow, I just called him Pops…I guess maybe I am starting to like what he is. I mean, it is a very nice house and the food, and he lets me cook, he even calls me chef. And his rules...they're not bad, cuz I do think he is trying to protect us and teach us stuff, and he tells us we're doing good and that he is proud of us a lot more than he tells us we're doing something wrong.

I love the way he takes care of Ang and Lai, the way he sings those goofy old songs, how he puts them to bed every night, kisses them both, hugs them a lot...and me too, sometimes. It's so cool that he helps Angie the way he does with her being way smarter than everyone else, and he did get Lai to talk, and she is doing better than I have ever seen her do in a long time. And she loves him, you can see it, it's almost the same as when her mom was alive.

And I guess I do like coming home to see him too. He makes me smile and I kinda want to do good, so he's proud of me. And he was so cool about Marcie...'

She felt herself start to cry. *'And I especially like the dog and cat...'* Then just as she fell asleep, *'yea, I'll probably stay...'*

Chapter Thirteen

Goodbye Neighbor

September 22nd

Burt and Ernie hosted a little gathering at their house. Virginia Belson was the guest of honor for the evening. Alex was there with all three girls (and Marcie) along with a few other neighbors and friends. Alex took the girls home after about an hour and Daq was in charge. Alex went back to the party.

Burt did know about Virginia's plight with Erick Newsome. Burt was very active in the Palm Springs community and had met Erick. He conveyed to the entire group that Virginia had indeed gotten a raw deal, and that Erick Newsome was not a good person, who was now getting ahead in the entertainment industry, but was quite sure his star would soon burn out. Everyone loved having Virginia at the party and she was elated to have this time to forget and be herself even if for one night.

At around 11 PM, everyone started going home and Alex offered to walk Virginia back home, which she accepted. Burt and Ernie said they were going to sit on their patio in the front with another couple for a while and they would keep an eye on the house. As they walked back, she said, "I'll be leaving tomorrow. I am finally getting my money for the series, and I have a flight for tomorrow afternoon to go back home to Montana.

"Oh, you didn't say anything about that."

"You know, I had a great time tonight and I didn't want anything to become the reason people talked to me. Everyone seemed interested in me and just wanted to talk and be nice. It was a great evening, it meant so much to me you'll never know."

"Well, I'm glad you had a good time, you deserved that. And I am very grateful to have gotten to know you even for a few days and, frankly I will miss you."

"Could you come in for a nightcap?" Virginia said with a rather sensual look.

"I shouldn't leave the girls..."

"You wouldn't have to stay."

He looked into her eyes and said, "That would be nice."

***

When he came back to the house around 1:30 AM, Ernie waved and smiled at him and went inside. Alex went inside, checked on Ang and Lei, saw that Daq's door was closed and no noise from her or Marcie so, then sat down in the great room. He didn't quite know how to feel. He had just made love to a very extraordinary woman, who he barely knew but had formed a very strong bond with after just a few days. The intimacy had been very engaging and pleasurable, but also very natural, as if they had been at that for many years. But, in his mind, he had just cheated on Faith. He poured himself a bourbon and stood looking out the front window.

Daq came into the room. "Home kinda late, aren't we?"

"Oh, Hi Daq. Yea, later than usual."

"You with Mrs. Belson?"

He nodded, "I was."

"You saw her almost every day this week. This going to be a thing from now on?"

"No, she's leaving tomorrow, and we probably won't ever see her again."

"Really!? That's not cool, I really liked her. And so did you, huh?"

"Yea. Sit down Daq."

She apprehensively said, "OK." She sat in the armchair and he in the one next to her.

"I haven't felt this way since Faith, your grandma, and I don't know how I feel right now. I feel like I have hurt and disappointed her and that scares me to death. But I really liked Virginia."

"Did you love her?"

"No. It was way too early for that and what I felt for her was not love like I had with Faith, or not even love at all, or maybe it was, kinda...it was just...nice, and I almost felt like I did with Faith. And I think that's what bothering me."

"Did you have sex?"

"I said this before, I'm going to say it again. At thirteen, you shouldn't even have enough knowledge to ask that question, and I hate that you do. But I do realize I'm older, and a little old fashion, and maybe if you hear this answer it will help with your journey, remember the journey?"

She nodded.

"Yes, we had sex. But again Daq, sex is a definition, and I want you to forget the definition and learn about the feeling involved. When I made love to your grandmother, it was because we loved each other more than anything else in the world, that excitement, pleasure and satisfaction was something fantastic for both of us. That's the feeling you get when you are in love with someone like we were. What happened tonight wasn't that, but it was a connection, a connection between two people that had a relationship, brief as it may have been, but still a relationship and knowing we probably would never see each other again, a way of confirming it was special, and maybe saying goodbye with something to remember." He sighed. "I hope I'm making some sense to you."

"Yea, you are."

Sex will be an important part of your life someday. But only if you treat it with respect. I want you..."

"I know. Enjoy the journey!"

He smiled at her, "And sex should not be part of that right now. Not yet! And remember, I'm always here to talk like we are tonight, always." He smiled at her, "And one more thing, remember that I will beat the holy shit out of anybody that tries to touch you! That's a parent's prerogative!" He laughed and so did Daq. Then he gazed out the window at the stars with a wistful look.

"You're thinking about grandma right now, aren't you?"

He nodded.

"You know, I don't think grandma would be mad. Do you really think she would want you to just be alone the rest of your life?" Alex suddenly remembered what Faith had said to him the night she came to him in his dream; *remember that you are still alive...you must live your life...* He turned and gazed at her and realized just how much she looked like her grandmother. "I'm glad you're here."

"You know...I think, I am too." She stood up and he stuck his arm out so she couldn't get by. She sat down into his lap, and they hugged. As she walked to her room, she realized this was the first time she was feeling towards Alex, like she did towards her dad. It kind of felt good.

Chapter Fourteen

Laila's Fifteen Minutes of Fame

Monday morning and everyone in the household was bustling around to get to their appointed destinations. Daq and Marcie were preparing to get Marcie permanently into a class. She had adapted to school very well and was being put into the system as a hardship case and Alex was deemed her temporary guardian. Jennifer Grey was once again helping Alex with the temporary guardianship as there was no word on her mother yet.

Angie was excited for today because she was getting picked up by officer Chen and going to work more on some cold cases. She loved these days. She found the work challenging and rewarding, but she really liked Officer Chen, who had become a family friend.

Now Laila's class was being visited today by a local news channel. They were searching for a kindergarten class to come and visit the morning TV show 'AM Palm Springs'. They were looking for a class that could help them sing a new theme song for the show. Laila's class had been practicing diligently.

So as everyone was in the kitchen enjoying the morning with laughter and excited chatter, Alex smiled broadly and said, "OK girls...let's shoot this fucker!"

All four girls responded in unison, "You bet!" And off to school they went.

Alex sat down with Ellie and Maurice on his lap and petted both. "I think we're doing OK guys; this is finally taking a good positive turn. I know it hasn't been easy, but you've adjusted nicely. I hope you guys feel the same. I know it took a while, but I think the wolf pack mentality really worked. I have to thank you for that Ellie, you're the one who taught it to me. So, thank you. Right then old Maurice jumped off his lap and headed back to his room. "I didn't mean you weren't helpful...come on, don't be like that." He laughed and realized it had been a long time since he had felt good enough to laugh

***

Laila's class got selected to appear on the TV show. She was excited and couldn't stop talking about it. The class was to appear on the program on Wednesday, September 27th at 7AM. They would be singing the new theme song along with the three hosts of the show.

Alex had bought Laila a new dress that she had picked out, it was red and white with a ruffled collar, and she looked absolutely adorable. So, the morning of the 27th, Daq, Marcie and Angie sat on the sofa watching the TV as the kindergarten class marched into the studio set and stood with the three hosts, Moira, Katie and Rod. Alex sat proudly on the arm of the sofa and watched his little girl looking like a happy little princess standing next to Rod, ready to sing her little heart out.

Rod looked at the camera and said, "Now for the moment we've all been waiting for, we will sing our new theme song with the help of our kindergarten class led by Ms. Dalton.

Then all the color drained out of Alex's face as he heard Rod say, "What do ya think Laila, can we do this?"

Barely able to breath, Alex squeaked, "Oh No."

Her response was clear, loud and well annunciated, "You bet, let's shoot this fucker!"

The three girls on the sofa laughed loudly as Alex buried his head in the back cushion of the sofa. He could hear the riotous laughter coming from Burt and Ernie's house while he hid his face.

Across town Jennifer Grey laughed so hard she ended up on the floor.

Rod, being the professional he was, bit his lip and tried desperately to control his emotions but his curled smirk gave him away. But he managed to say between giggles, "OK then, here we go."

The camera stayed focused on the class because the three hosts could not stop laughing. But the song was sung very well, and the show concluded. But from that day forward around the studio, that song became known as the fucker that got shot on the air.

Chapter Fifteen

Intel

Armando had been doing his job. He had figured out routines, where the girls went to school, when they got home, how they got home, what they did after school, and all the time frames that went along with that. He had contacted neighbors and had made contacts and was able to get intel on the family members without ever causing suspicion; he was good at his job.

This Friday morning, he had gotten some timely intel about the family he watched, good enough that he contacted 'the snake' and said, "This is perfect."

Chapter Sixteen

Laila's Lessons and Angie's Date night

After a twenty-four-hour apology tour which felt like he had spoken to every individual in Palm Springs, Alex gathered all the girls around the kitchen table and said, "From this moment on I think it would be best that we do not use the saying 'let's shoot this fucker' anymore. Some people don't understand, and it would be better if we just didn't say it, OK?" Daq, Marcie and Angie just smirked and nodded, but Laila looked at Alex and said, "OK Pops."

Alex picked up Laila after school that day and as he was driving home, he noticed she seemed perplexed about something. Now he had prepared himself for some fall-out from her unfortunate answer to a simple question...on TV. No less. Kids could be cruel and inappropriate at times. He chose not to say anything to her at the time, to see if she would come to him.

He sat in the living room reading shortly after arriving home and Laila had gone into her room. After about a half hour Laila came out and crawled into his lap.

"Hi baby girl."

"Hi." She sat looking down and Alex waited. "Pops, why am I different?"

Not the question or statement he was expecting. He had spoken with her teachers, and they said they would be on the lookout for any bullying or teasing. He thought if anything it would be that someone had said she had a dirty mouth or stupid...but different? He wondered. "What do you mean different? Let me look at you. How many ears do you have?"

"Two." She giggled.

"How many eyes?"

"Two."

"How many arms?"

"Two."

"How many noses?"

She giggled again, "just one."

"How many feet?"

"Two."

"Well, you look the same as everybody else to me. Why do you think you're different?"

"Because one of the boys at school said I'm different because I'm...black."

Alex pursed his lips, raised his eyes to the ceiling, and slightly shook his head. "So, this boy thinks your different because your skin is a different color?"

She nodded her head.

"Hmmm. OK. Let me show you something." He picked her up and carried her into the kitchen and sat her down at the kitchen island. He went to the cupboard and retrieved two cups. He set the first one in front of her and did not let see the other cup. "What is this?" He pointed at the cup.

She smiled sheepishly and said, "A cup."

"How do you know it's a cup?"

"Because it's round and has a handle."

"Good! What do you do with it?"

"You put coffee or milk or water in it and you can drink out of it."

"Right!

Then he set the cup to the side and put another cup in front of her and said, "What's this?"

She laughed, "Pops! It's a cup too."

"How do you know?"

Laughing she said, "Because it's the same as the other cup!"

"That's right!" He pulled the other cup back and set the two side by side. These are both cups, so tell me what's different?"

"One is white, and one is black."

"That is correct! They are exactly the same, except for color! And color does not make any difference in what, or who they are. Right?"

She looked into his face, and he could see her wheels spinning as she thought. Then the expression of apperception came over her face, she smiled and said, "Yea. Yea! I get it."

"So, what are you going to tell this boy tomorrow at school?"

"I'm going to show him the cups!"

"Was he nice to you when he said you were different?"

"Oh yea. We play together all the time."

"OK. Then I think showing him the cups is a great idea."

***

Alex watched Angie as she washed the dishes after breakfast this beautiful Friday morning, September 29th. Tomorrow was the day that the girls would say whether they wanted to stay with him or not. He thought back to the previous days of September and reflected on the progress, the setbacks, the quarrels, the patience shown.

Daq was the most difficult but that was understandable, she was the oldest and she had seen and gone through the most. She had really been unfortunate enough to view and live through the worst parts of Bobby's illness and addictions. Then of course she had the Jimmy experience and that probably was the worst because he had made her feel that he was going to be her savior and give her a life of her own. But the reality of the whole situation was dark and dirty and very confusing for her state of mind. She had fought Alex during the thirty days, but she had also shown a willingness to be a part in the family. She had passions, as he had seen in her cooking, and Alex was sure to let her be responsible developing those passions. She also had become a good big sister, and it was evident that she loved her sisters and felt a protection for them. She loved to encourage Angie and seemed genuinely proud that Angie had the intellect that she does. Daq always took part in the word of the day and was the first to congratulate her on solving cold cases and mysteries. She was Angie's' biggest fan. And when it came to Laila, she was sweet, understanding, caring and always willing to help her learn. And when Laila would act up, Daq was there to reel her in. It felt as if she had accepted or started to accept Alex as a father, as a dad.

Now Laila was different. She had no aspirations of leaving or going somewhere else or being with someone else, she just needed stability, love, understanding and as it turned out, a little discipline. She was going to be a pistol, always thinking, always planning…no, planning wasn't the right word, conniving suited her better. But Alex knew her heart was good and that she would be a great person someday, with the right direction. She wasn't going anywhere, and Alex knew that.

Angie was a brilliant child, an anomaly in the world of normal people. She was a gifted intellect of eight years old that would need to have special education, and she would be way ahead of her peers. But perhaps the most remarkable aspect of Angie, at least in Alex's eyes, was that she was able to be an eight-year-old that fit in with others. She never looked down on her peers and enjoyed all the things that eight-year-olds love to do. And was very cognoscente of her abilities and how to use them correctly.

Alex was feeling very confident that over the last thirty days that girls had come to view this situation as theirs and that they were heading towards becoming a family. He didn't believe that he would have to revert to plan B.

As he watched Angie wash and sing her way through the dishes it dawned on him that in the nearly two months that they had known each other and lived together, he had never really spent much time just the two of them. She was the rock, and in her mind, this was a done deal on the first day they met, and Alex knew that. So, he had poured all his energies into Daq and Laila and had never really spent quality time with Angie. He helped her with the word of the day and had gotten Jennifer to help with her advanced learning and officer Chen with cold cases. He had been there for her and encouraged her, but he had not spent the quality time with her that he had with the other two. He was going to change that.

After the girls were at school, he called a friend that was a client back in his working days. He had in fact bailed him out of a very crucial problem a few years back. The man worked for the McCallum Theatre, and they had an air conditioner problem on the night of a very prominent performer was to perform and they needed help immediately. Alex had taken the time to work on the problem after work and got the air conditioning to work just before the performance. He had told Alex that he owed him one. So, Alex called him and asked for the favor, and after many phone calls and some wheeling and dealing, he was able to grant Alex the favor he had asked for.

Alex then called Burt and Ernie to see if they could stay with Daq, Marcie, and Laila for the evening because he had something special for Angie and himself scheduled for the evening. Burt confirmed that he would be happy to do it, but that Ernie was going out with some friends and wouldn't be back till around 11PM, but he would join as soon as he could. So that was set. When Angie got home, he would take her to the store and buy her a new dress, but he was going to keep the evening a surprise. He turned to go to the car, it was time to pick up Laila, and when he turned to go into the hallway he ran into Marcie. "Oh, hi Marcie, I forgot that you were staying home today. Are you studying hard for that exam?" Since she wasn't a student at the school yet, they were working with her on some extra studies to determine at what level she was at.

 "Yea, I think I'm pretty close to being ready for the test academically. Are you going to pick up Laila?"

"Yes, why don't you come with me? I don't like leaving you here alone."

"Oh, I want to keep studying and you'll only be gone for a few minutes, I think I'll be fine for a short little trip like that."

"OK. But don't leave the house, and let no one in. Got it?" He smiled at her and patted the side of her face.

"Got it!"

He left the house and picked up Laila, came home and made lunch for her and Marcie. After lunch, Marcie and Laila picked up the dishes and cleaned the kitchen.

When Daq and Angie arrived from school (they were riding the bus now), Alex took Daq aside and told her about the surprise he had for Angie. She thought it was a wonderful idea and she was all onboard. Alex then took Angie out to downtown Palm Springs and bought her a new dress which he told her was for a 'special occasion'.

Daq fixed a wonderful meal and told Angie that she and Marcie were going to do the dishes so that she could get ready for her special occasion. She was confused when Alex came to her and asked if he could take her to the theater for a father daughter date night. She excitedly agreed.

Alex asked her if she knew anything about 'The Wizard of OZ'.

"I read the book."

"You read the book? Of course you have. Have you ever seen the movie on TV?"

"Yes, once when Shalia was alive, we watched it together on TV. I think I was about five."

"OK. Just wanted to be sure you knew something about the Wizard of Oz."

"Why?"

"You'll see."

When they left, Burt was there with the other girls and wished her a special night. As they drove to the McCallum Alex watched her excitement grow and knew she was going to enjoy the evening he had planned. As they walked into the auditorium she was in awe of how large and beautiful it was. The stairs leading to the different floors, the decorating and of course the number of people. Alex let her absorb the surroundings and then led her to their seats. His friend had managed to reserve for them a mezzanine box in the very front row. She sat down and Alex handed her a program.

"Wicked?"

"Yes. This is a live theatrical event and it's a story of Glinda the good witch and the wicked witch of the west, before Dorothy arrives in OZ. You can read the story inside." He watched as she read the story behind the show. Just as she finished up, the lights went down, and the intro music began. Her eyes got huge, and her breathing became rapid. Alex smiled; he remembered the first time he had ever seen a live event he had felt the same way. He leaned down to her and said, "We have to be quiet, but enjoy the music and the show." She excitedly nodded at him.

For the next three hours she was absolutely mesmerized. She sat in total attention, laughed and smiled, cried and gasped, and was completely enveloped in the music and settings. At the finale she stood and clapped and cheered and when the lights came up Alex looked at her and said, "Did you enjoy that?" Instead of answering she wrapped her arms around him and just hugged. Both had tears in their eyes as they filed out and a woman sitting behind them came to Alex and said, "I think I watched your little girl more than I did the show. She epitomized the passion of live theatre. So glad you brought her!" Alex thanked her.

As they got into the car, she said, "I can't wait to tell Daq and Lai about this!"

"Well, not so fast. There is a tradition when going to the theatre. You must stop for a drink afterwards so you can discuss the show."

"Like with an umbrella in it?"

"Why not!"

So, Alex pulled into a very upscale restaurant and bar near the theater, and he strolled in holding hands with the beautiful little girl that was glowing in her new dress and night out on the town.

They sat down at a table outside on the patio, Alex ordered two mock-a-Rita and was sure to tell the waiter that those were to come with umbrellas. When they came, Alex toasted her, "Here's to your first theatre experience and many more to come." They clinked their glasses together and sipped their drinks. Alex knew it was way past her bedtime and she would hit a wall at any time. But when the small band that was playing music on the patio started playing 'Dancing in the moonlight' he asked his date for the evening to dance. She accepted rather sheepishly, and Alex stood her on a small wall that stood only about eighteen inches high but was perfect for the fit of the two as they danced. There were two other couples sitting at the table next to them and they smiled at the scene and joined them to dance. After the dance the four introduced themselves as Joe and Sherry, and Harry and Delores and spent a few minutes talking to Angie about the show. And before the evening ended both Joe and Harry asked Angie to dance, which she graciously accepted.

When they had said their goodbyes and headed to the car, Angie was amped and talking about the show, the drink and the new friends. She was elated and as excited as Alex had ever seen her. As they drove home Angie was exhausted and even though she tried not to, she fell asleep in the car. When Alex drove into the garage and parked, he moved to her side of the car and picked her up to carry her to bed. Halfway to the door she suddenly jerked her head up with eyes wide open and said, "Something's wrong!"

Part Four

Abduction

Chapter One

Alex put Angie down and went into the house. He moved quickly down the hallway and came to the horrific sight of Burt lying on the floor near the front door. He had been beaten almost beyond recognition. The coppery smell of blood permeated the house. Ellie stood in the great room and barked at the scene.

"Oh my god!" Alex turned quickly and said to Angie, "Check on the other girls! And stay there, don't come in here." He pulled his phone out from his pocket and called 911, explained the situation and they said a response team would arrive shortly. He checked vitals and saw that Burt was alive but very shallow breathing and a faint heartbeat. He tried to make him as comfortable as possible and then realized he had heard nothing from Angie. He turned to look down the hallway and she just stood there trembling. "Angie, what's wrong?!"

"No one else is here." She quietly said, turning a ghastly pale shade of white as she spoke.

Alex stood up quickly and ran to her. He enveloped her in a hug and said, "OK sweetheart, we'll get through this. No one else is here?"

She shook her head, "I looked everywhere, they're not here."

"Did you look in the backyard?" She nodded. Alex quickly started a search of his own and as he quickly realized that Angie was correct, he felt the panic start to rise in his breathing and heart rate. He went out into the backyard and yelled the girls' names and when there was no response, he closed the door and stepped into the kitchen area and pulled out his phone again. Right then Ellie began to bark at the back door an urgent 'pay attention to me' bark that Alex recognized immediately. He looked at the dog and then suddenly from behind him Angie spoke,

"Marcie had something to do with this."

Alex looked at her and realized she was getting one of her premonitions. He looked back at Ellie still urgently barking at the back door and suddenly he put two and two together and opened the back door. Ellie ran out and Alex stepped out onto the patio and said loudly, "Marcie! Come in here right now. Don't make me come and get you!" Ellie kept barking but slowly Marcie appeared. "Ellie, quiet...now!" She stopped barking. Alex looked at Marcie who was crying and had blood running down the side of her face. "Marcie, one chance only...the truth right now!"

Marcie started to cry uncontrollably and kept repeating "I'm sorry, I'm sorry."

Alex snapped at her, "Stop crying and tell me what happened! We don't have time for your blubbering!"

She took a deep breath and said, "They took Daq and Laila." She started crying again.

He grabbed her shoulders, "Stop this! Now tell me everything! Who took her?!"

"Armando and a couple of other guys! I'm sorry! I didn't know they were going to hurt anyone."

"Who is Armando?"

"The guy that made me give him everything I know about you guys."

"Marcie! Was Jimmy in on this? She looked at Alex and hesitated. "Was he?!"

"Yes! Him and one other guy."

"What other guy!?"

"I don't know his name. He had a big snake tattoo on his neck. He was the one who said he would hurt my mom if I didn't help them."

"Why didn't they take you?"

"They tried. The big guy just hit me and told me stay by him, but I ran outside, and they couldn't find me. I'm sorry, I didn't know what they were going to do so I just told them about the stuff you guys were doing. Before the big guy hit me, I asked about my mom, and he just laughed." She started crying again.

Right then the EMTs arrived. Alex was giving them the information he had when Ernie busted through the front door. "Oh shit! Oh shit! Burt…Burt… What the hell!

Alex grabbed onto him and said, "Ernie. He's alive. Let them do their work."

"What the hell happened!?"

"Somebody broke in and kidnapped Daq and Laila."

"What!? Who, why...what the fuck..."

The EMTs right then started to take Burt to the hospital. Ernie ran to be with him as they took him to the ambulance.

Alex turned back to Marcie. "Marcie, what time did this happen?"

"About 9:00."

He looked at his watch. Almost three hours ago. He needed to get moving, unless he was very mistaken, he only had a few hours to get them back before they would be gone and probably for good. He quickly called Jennifer Grey, and prayed that she would answer, after all it was late.

"Hello?" the sleepy voice asked.

"Jennifer this is Alex Barton, I have an emergency. Daq and Laila have been kidnapped and that goddamn Jimmy has something to do with it. I gotta go right now to find them. Can you come over and stay with Angie, the bastards beat up Burt and he's on his way to the hospital.

"I'll be there in about 15...Alex, get the police involved! Don't try to be the hero that does all this by himself!"

"I'm calling Officer Chen right now. She'll be able to handle the cop side of it. Thanks Jennifer, see you ASAP." He then called Officer Chen. "Nancy! Jimmy and some of his cohorts have kidnapped Daq and Laila! I need your help. There is a girl here that knows a lot about them, can you come and question her and get all the info you can."

"Damn straight. I'll be there shortly, I'll get the department on this also, watch the airport, bus depots etc...where are you going?"

"Looking for Jimmy!"

"Alex, watch out!"

"I will, I have my phone so get me any info you can!"

He hung up and took a deep breath, had he thought of everything? Just one last thing. "Marcie, come here." She started crying harder again. "Stop that!" He gave her a stern look and pointed his finger at her, and she knew to mind what he said. She came to him and took a deep breath. "I understand what you went through, but right now I need you to be brave and very explicit about everything you know. Give Officer Chen every detail that you can...you understand?! Every detail! We'll talk later but you need to help now!"

"I promise." He quickly hugged her and that made her cry even more.

"Anything more you can tell me now? Anything else?

"Armando had said the name Hombre once. Something about Hombre working for a landscape company and that was who he worked for also."

"Do you remember the name of the landscape company?"

"No, he never said."

"Pops." Angie spoke up. " Daq told me that Hombre was the name of one of the guys that tried to talk to us the day you ran them off. They both had shirts on that said 'landscaping'...with a sun above the word." Alex ran to the kitchen and opened one of the kitchen drawers and pulled out the neighborhood information book and flipped to the vendor section and under landscaping looked and found one company called Sunshine Landscaping.

"First stop!" He went out to the garage and retrieved the pistol that Daq had gotten from Jimmy. He had previously bought a box of shells for it and three clips which he had pre-loaded. He stuck the gun in his belt in the front of his pants and the bullet clips in his back pocket. That would have to do. He went back into the house and saw that Jennifer had just arrived. He talked to her for a few minutes and started to walk down the hall to the car.

"Wait." Came a voice from the front door. Alex turned and saw Ernie standing in a T-shirt and cargo pants. "I'm coming with you!"

"Ernie, you don't have to..."

"Why! Cuz I'm gay? Listen Alex, I was a navy seal specially trained for foreign OPS that you don't want to know anything about. Now, I just found the man I love beaten near death, I still don't know if he'll make it, but I do know that if I just sit on my ass holding his hand and do nothing... and he lives; he'll kick my ass all over this neighborhood!"

Angie stood next to Ernie with Ellie at her side. Both looked to Alex with sanguine focus. He nodded at Angie, turned to Ernie, "OK. Let's go!"

Chapter Two

The first stop was the guard shack on the way out. No place was there an address for the landscape company, but Alex knew that the HOA would have it because that was a requirement for any approved vendors with transponders.

Alex jumped out of the car and went to the guard and told him this was an emergency, and he needed the address for Sunshine Landscaping.

"Sir, I can't give out that information." In a rather haughty tone.

"Look, I need this right now, as I said; this is an emergency...life or death."

"For a landscape company! I doubt that!" And guffawed at Alex. A sharp left-hand jab hit the guard directly in the nose. He cried out in pain and Alex grabbed a handful of hair and put the bloody nosed man's head up against the computer screen. "Pull up Sunshine Landscape! Now!" This time there was no argument or smart-ass remark and within seconds Alex had the address and was putting it into the car GPS system.

As the he took off to the address, Ernie looked over at him and said, "That oughta make the HOA newsletter."

"Probably."

When they arrived at the address it was nearing 12:45AM. The house was dark, but two vehicles were parked in the driveway, one had a magnetic sign on the side that said, 'Sunshine Landscape…Let the Beauty Shine Through' with the same logo as the shirt.

Ernie said "Looks like the right place. How do you want to go at this?"

"I'm just going to wake them up."

"Well, if they're involved you ain't going to get much cooperation and some may cause trouble or run out the back. I'll watch the back but stay close enough that if you need help…holler!"

Alex nodded, (how the hell did I not know he was a Navy Seal) then knocked loudly on the front door and continued knocking while shouting, "There is an emergency, you are in no danger, but you must answer your door!" After a few minutes of knocking a sleepy eyed, rather pissed-off Hispanic man opened the door, holding a machete. Alex held up his hands in a surrender motion and said, "I just want to talk to you about Armando."

"Armando?"

"Yes, you've been letting him in to our neighborhood..."

"Ehh?"

Right then Ernie came around the side of the house and started speaking perfect Spanish to the man. As he spoke the man lowered the machete and listened intently. Then there was a back-and-forth conversation for a good five minutes which ended with Ernie giving the man a twenty, a pat on the shoulder and a "Gracias amigo! Buenas Noches. Perdon por la hora tardia." He looked at Alex, "Let's go!"

They got into the car and Ernie said, "He didn't know anything about what was going on. He let those guys in with his crew because they paid him, and they said it was to help him and themselves start a new business. I don't think he cared at all about the bullshit about a new business, he just cared about the money. He takes care of several family members, and any extra cash is a huge help. But he did have some additional information. He knows Armando, not well, but enough to tell me that he is a local fixer. Someone for hire to do just about anything for a price. He's a bit of a ladies' man and likes to spend time in bars. I know where his favorite is. Let's go, I'll give you directions as we go."

Ernie gave Alex all the info about the bar they were going to. Based on the description that Marcie and now the Landscape guy had given them, they knew who they were looking for. If he wasn't here, they could certainly find out about his whereabouts. As they walked into the bar just on the outskirts of town, they scanned the room which had a large bar to the left and tables for seating to the right. There was an old, black Labrador Retriever laying on the floor in front of the bar. Ernie nudged Alex and jutted his chin toward a table with four guys sitting. One matched the description, but Ernie had said that the defining mark was a rose tattoo on the right side of his neck. They moved toward him, and he glanced up. He recognized Alex from his surveillance of the house and stood and moved away. But Ernie had moved quickly to the rear of where he was sitting and blocked his way before he could make his getaway.

"Going somewhere Armando?" Ernie Squinted his eyes and saw the tattoo then shook his head. "We got some questions."

"You got the wrong guy."

Alex came up and stood next to him. "You like spying on my house and kids? You best have some good answers to my questions if you want to ever be with the ladies again. Let's sit down." They grabbed a table in the back. "One chance before you wish you had never got involved. You see I've got nothing to lose. My two daughters are missing because of you and if you don't help me get them back then you may as well kiss goodbye that pretty face of yours, because I will beat you senseless starting with your face and when I finish there will be no teeth, no nose, no eyes and that dog up front will be feasting on your balls; and I don't care what happens to me after that. Understand?"

Right then a tough looking buddy that was at his table came up and said, "Armando? Need some help?" Ernie shot out his left hand and hit the guy directly in the Adams apple and with his right hand grabbed the back of his head and pulled him into whisper range and quietly said, "He's fine...understand?" And pushed him away. Then held up his hands to the rest of the patrons and said, "Nothing to see here folks, just having a little fun." The man retreated to his table.

Alex looked at Armando and said, "Who you are working for?" He accepted the silence for a few seconds. "Who? And where is he? Snake tattoo on his neck."

Armando looked at him with trepidation. "I don't know what you're talking about."

Alex picked up a fork and stabbed it down into the back of his hand. "Let me repeat! I have nothing to lose! So you are about to become dog food unless you get smart and talk; Right now!"

Armando screamed and tried to stand and run but Alex grabbed him and pulled him back to the table and gave him a right-hand uppercut directly to his mid-section. Armando lurched forward under the pain and Alex slammed his face down onto the table. Then set him down in the chair as he writhed in pain, the fork still in his hand and blood dripping from his nose and battered face.

Right then about four other patrons came over to help Armando. Ernie stepped in front of them and Alex started to stand to help Ernie. Ernie waved him off and pulled out a Glock 9 pistol and said, "Gentlemen, we are about done here, so if I were you, I wouldn't get involved, it would just take longer to finish up. And…you probably wouldn't like it much." They backed off.

Alex grabbed Armando by the hair again and lifted his head up and punched his broken nose again. "I'm running out of time Armando, and out of patience! So, talk!"

Armando looked at Alex and said, "Jimmy's buddy has the girls, and the two guys that grabbed her up are with him too. Jimmy left in his pickup and said he meet them at the theatre. They're waiting for Chad! That's all I know."

"Who's Chad?"

"The snake tattoo guy."

"That's not enough to save your ass! Last chance! Where?!"

"Downtown Palm Springs."

"Downtown is very large…where?"

"That's all I know!"

"Bullshit!" He slammed down on the fork in his hand and bent it forward. Armando screamed in pain and Alex punched him in the nose again. "Where?!"

"A theatre! I don't know the name! It's been closed for a while and they're fixing it up."

"The Palace?!"

"I don't fucking know…I swear." He started crying uncontrollably.

"You better be right!" Alex stood and hit Armando in the side of the face, and he fell to the floor, his face covered in tears and snot and blood, with the fork still sticking out of the back of his hand. Alex started out the door and Ernie nodded toward the bartender. Alex went to him and gave him a hundred-dollar bill. "For your help! And silence." Nobody else followed.

The two jumped into the car and started toward downtown. Ernie said, "So, to the Palace?"

"Only place I know of in downtown. And it is being renovated. As long as Armando was telling the truth."

"I think that's a pretty safe bet. Where did you…"

"I trained to box professionally for a few years in a tough circuit; you learn and see things, and sometimes do things, that you're not always proud of…or even think you're capable of." He sat quietly for a few seconds. "Thanks for your help. And, by the way, I didn't know you were…that guy."

"One and the same. The Seals was a long time ago, but some things you never forget and when I saw Burt…"

Alex simply nodded.

Chapter Three

When they drove into town, they parked a few blocks away from the theatre, in case they had someone on the lookout. As they approached, Ernie said, "You know anything about this place?"

"No. I've walked by it a few times, but never been in it. What about you?"

"I was in there once when a group got to go in and view the place as it was then and what the plans for the renovation were going to be. It's quite a place. Big and ornate. When you walk in the front doors the first thing you see is the concession bar, which is in a large lobby. On both sides of the lobby are stairs that lead to the lodges and balcony. On the ground floor there are two entrances to the theatre, one on each side of the concession bar. Inside there is old theatre seating, at least fifty rows that go right up to the orchestra pit and then of course the stage and screen. The ceilings are enormous and covered in paintings and ornate sculptures. There are two seating boxes, one on each side of the screen, that hold six or eight people. Then there's the lodge or mezzanine floor in the back middle and then the balcony above that, both with theatre seating."

"What about a backstage area?"

"Yes, there is one, but I never saw that. So, if there is a door, which I assume there is, I don't know where it is or where it opens to."

"OK. My guess would be that these idiots feel pretty safe because they think no one knows their whereabouts. So, chances are they aren't going to be thinking about someone coming in. I also would guess they are one of two places, in the lobby or in the theatre seating close to backstage. My bet would be close to backstage, with someone watching the doors, back door included. So, whaddaya say Seal?"

Right then his phone buzzed and vibrated. He looked at the screen and saw that it was Officer Chen. "Hi Nancy, any news?"

"Yes. Based on the description Marcie gave us of the leader of this mess, his name is Chad Renquist, AKA the 'Snake'. He's a mid-level trafficker out of LA but has connections and associates in San Diego, Temecula, and the Coachella valley. And a demented, mean son of a bitch, that is connected with some of the largest operations and cartels. And Alex, his thing is young girls, and when I say young...five to six years old."

"Jesus!"

"Listen, we got a tip that he might be staying in the Royal Palms Hotel on Indian Canyon Drive. Someone said they saw him go in there. We're checking on it now."

"OK. We're checking on a location that is supposed to have the two girls in it."

"Where at? I can send a squad there immediately!"

"Not yet. I don't want them to know we're coming. Stay with Angie! Please."

"Goddammit Alex..."

But he had already hung up. He pulled out his gun and Ernie looked at him and said,

"You ever done anything like this before? I mean killed anyone?" Alex shook his head. "Look, I know you're a tough SOB, and probably done some atrocious shit in your life, but pulling the trigger to kill someone is a whole other animal. Hopefully it won't come to that, but remember, don't think! As a boxer you had to react quickly and violently so don't change that instinct, react quickly, and if that means pulling the trigger to drop someone, do it! Let me see that pistol." Ernie took the pistol slammed the clip into it, pulled the slide back to cock it, sighted it, put the safety on and showed Alex how to release it to fire. Put this in your belt, but be careful, pull the gun out before releasing the safety, or you could shoot your dick off. He took a knife from his back and put it in his teeth. He pulled out his Glock pistol and attached a silencer and stuck it into his belt. He held the knife in his right hand. "Remember, pull the trigger if you have to...don't think. Let's go see if there is a back door."

Alex, now duly impressed, just nodded.

Chapter Four

The back door was securely locked and to break in would have meant alerting any and all that were inside. They looked around and spotted some windows about ten feet above the door. The sides of the building had fire escapes, but none were in the back. There was a small ledge just under the window and Ernie whispered to Alex to lift him up to the ledge. Alex formed a step by interlocking his fingers together and Ernie stepped into his hands, and he lifted him so that he could grab the ledge and pull himself up. He got a handhold on the window frame and was able to pull himself into a kneeling position. The glass in the windows was a wire reinforced safety glass. He saw how to unlock the window but no way to get to it. He pulled out the hunting knife and was able to get it in between the glass and the frame and started cutting the wires in the glass closest to the lock. Each time he cut a wire it made an audible snap but there was nothing to do about it. He had finished one side when someone became visible down below. He was a big guy and was carrying a rifle. He was looking around and had a definite air of suspicion to him. Perhaps he had heard the snapping of the wires. He headed toward the back door and Ernie jumped down to the ground directly in front of the door and when it opened, with lightning quick speed grabbed him by the shirt and pulled him into the door opening. "Where are the girls?! Talk or die! And do it quietly"

"Inside, about the middle of the seats. Only one girl, the other is gone."

He fired a single round into the forehead of the man. He tumbled back and lay dead in front of the door which had a chain on it inside. Ernie quickly fired another silent round into the chain, it broke, and he moved quickly inside. Alex stood gapping down at the dead man on the floor. He recognized him as the henchman he had beat up at Jimmy's house.

"Alex! Don't think! Let's get the girls. He said one was already gone, we need to hurry!"

Alex shook his head to clear the thoughts, "Right." They moved silently to the left side of the backstage and peaked around the curtain that hid the backstage from the auditorium seating. Sitting just to the right of the center aisle in the middle sat two guys that Alex recognized as Hombre and the bigger guy that got in his face in the front yard, and there sat Daquiri, but no Laila. Ernie pushed Alex back so that he couldn't be seen. He whispered, "I'm going out there. You stay out of sight so that if they come back here, you'll be here to greet them. Watch me so you know what is happening."

Before Alex could say anything, Ernie had stepped out onto the stage and yelled, "No body move, and nobody will die!"

Both henchmen stood quickly and drew pistols. The bigger of the two, Sampson, grabbed Daq and shielded himself with her. Hombre and Sampson fired their pistols at the same time that Ernie did. Hombre took a bullet to the face sending a spray of blood and his body splattering on the seats behind them. One of the two enemy bullets hit Ernie, and he dropped to the floor holding his shoulder. Sampson pulled Daq closer and started moving to the other side of the theatre. He fired another shot at Ernie which missed but Ernie fired back at him purposely wide to avoid hitting Daq which made Sampson stop firing and retreat.

Ernie said in a quieter voice, "Alex! They're moving to the other side! They'll be coming your way!"

Alex started to move across to the other side of the backstage when he saw ladder rungs leading up to a catwalk above and a little behind the stage curtain. He quickly climbed to the catwalk and moved to the other side just as Sampson came backstage. He was holding Daq close to him and pointing his gun in front. He stopped and looked around expecting to encounter Alex but did not see him.

Just to left of where Alex stood was a lighting bar that housed a number of spotlights. Alex looked at the position of Sampson and Daq, reached out with his left arm and grabbed the lighting bar and swung off the catwalk. Sampson looked up, surprised, which allowed Daq to move forward a bit and Alex, who looked rather ape-like as he hung from the bar, aimed and fired his pistol and hit Sampson in the upper shoulder close to his neck. Alex dropped off the bar and hit the floor, fell to his left and from a lying down position fired again and hit Sampson in the chest. Sampson fell back dropping his pistol.

Daquiri screamed, "Daddy!" She ran to Alex, and they embraced and as she resolutely held on to Alex, he looked at Sampson lying on the floor with a growing pool of blood spreading out around his head. He said to Daq, "Are you alright baby!" He felt her nod her head into his chest and he held her tighter. "Where is Laila?"

"Jimmy took her." She started crying. "He's taking her to that Snake guy!"

"Shit! Do you where?"

"No, he just came and got her and told me that. He was laughing at me!"

"OK. We need to check on Ernie!" They ran to him and the blood was flowing heavily. "Oh, hell Ernie!"

"It's not as bad as it looks."

"Daq! Backstage by the exit door I saw some rags that looked clean. Get them. I'm calling Chen right now. She'll be able to get someone here in a hurry! You hang in there!"

He called Officer Chen who was at the house with Jennifer. "Yes Alex!"

"Nancy, we are in the Palace theatre, the alley backdoor is open. Ernie has been shot and is bleeding bad, can you get someone here ASAP! Also, three bad guys are dead here also." He heard her calling on her radio to dispatch.

"They're on their way! Should just be a few minutes."

Right then Daq came back with a stack of clean rags. "Hold on." Alex said as he pulled back Ernie's shirt and revealed the wound. It appeared that the bullet went through the Lat muscle and left a large, ragged hole. Alex packed the rags on the front and back of the wound and had Daq put pressure on both sides. She was squeamish but did the job.

"Nancy! Jimmy took Laila! Daq said he came in…'Daq, how long ago?'…She says about half hour ago. He is taking her to this 'snake' guy. Is he still at the Palm Royale?"

"Alex! Listen to me! We checked out the hotel and he was there, but he must have got wind of us being there because he's gone. All we found was an eleven-year-old girl. Jesus, what he had done to her, she's at the hospital now. So, he is in the wind.

And we know nothing about Jimmy. So, we have a BOLO out for Chad and Jimmy, and I will get the info about Laila and Jimmy out right away, find out anything you can from Daq, anything they said, or she overheard, anything that might help get an idea where they are!"

"OK. Watch the hotel closely though, if Jimmy doesn't know that the snake is gone, he may go there."

"Already thought of that and we have all the doors staked out."

Chapter Five

Chad had just looked out the window of his third-floor room in the Palm Royale. He watched as the cop in the suit went to the front desk. They always think they're being clever by not wearing a uniform. But he'd been around long enough to know a cop when he saw one. And he also knew that now the cops would know where he is. Old papa bear must have gotten home and realized a couple of his cubs were gone and now all hell is breaking loose. Somehow, they knew about me, probably that Marcie kid. Too bad she got away, but it's not a problem that can't be overcome.

He knew he had to get out of the hotel. He only had a limited amount of time before the cops and papa bear would get here to question him. He was waiting for that waste of life Jimmy to call about the youngest girl. He was going to bring her to him, because Chad wanted her close to him. She was a particularly sweet prize for him, and he knew he would have to groom her properly, so she needed to be by his side...for training purposes.

But first things first. He grabbed the eleven-year-old girl by the throat and looked in her eyes. "You liked what I did, didn't you?" She just closed her eyes as a tear streaked down her face thinking about him laying her face down across the desk.

"Didn't you!"

She quickly nodded her head.

"And if anyone asks, you're going to say you wanted me to do that, right?" Again, she nodded. "Cuz if you don't...I'll find you, and when I do, you'll wish you were never born." She already wished that, but she knew what he meant. Still nodding she prepared herself for what was coming. He slapped her hard across the face and shoved her down into a chair. "And don't forget that little friend of yours, the one you love so much, what did you say, she's like my big sister. How sweet...I'll cut her up into little ribbons and spread her out all over this state." She started crying. "That's right. Now you'll remember." He opened the room door and told her to get the fuck out, but as she stood, she passed out and fell to the floor.

"Fuck!"

He should kill her, but that would not be smart with the cops knowing he was here. Too easy to pin a murder charge on him. No, it was time to split. He grabbed his phone and checked to be sure he hadn't left anything and exited out the door and went down the stairs and out a side door. He moved across the street to a grouping of doctors' offices and called Jimmy. When Jimmy answered, he snapped at him, "Where the fuck are you?!"

"Just coming to get you man."

"Well, I'm not in the hotel anymore. It's too hot right now."

"Don't they have air conditioning?"

"No, you stupid shit! I mean the cops know I'm there."

"Oh, right."

"Do you have the little girl?"

"Yea, right here with me in the car."

"OK. Pick me up. I'm across the street from the back of the hotel in a complex that has a bunch of doctor's offices in it. Just pull up to the side of the street, don't come in the driveway, I'll come out to you. Got it?"

"Yea, of course."

Chad rolled his eyes, "How soon?"

"About five minutes."

"OK. Hurry, but don't do anything stupid like get a ticket for speeding."

"Got it. No worries!"

Chad just shook his head.

Chapter Six

Jimmy and Chad drove to the Palace Theatre only to see numerous police cars surrounding the outside of the building. Chad told Jimmy to park the car a few blocks away and stay with Laila while he went to find out what he could about what had happened.

He found a vantage point that he could view the alley where the back door was open. He saw police and EMT personnel going in and out. He then saw Alex and Daq come out and talk to a cop in a suit. He moved a little closer to the scene, so he was able to hear bits and pieces of conversation and learned that his three cohorts were dead. *'Well, at least they won't talk.'*

But now he knew that what he thought was going to be a simple kidnapping, was a helluva lot more. And he was pissed off about it. This should have been so simple, but the old grandpa had to go ballistic and ruin the whole thing. Now he was out a thirteen-year-old virgin (almost) who could have made him a lot of money. He still had the young girl, which was good, but...there might be a way to make this even better, and ruin old grandpa's life even more. That would be a sweet victory for the 'snake'.

He made a quick call to an associate close by who had been put on alert and told him to meet him and Jimmy in a casino parking lot a few blocks from where Jimmy was parked. He then quickly went back to Jimmy's car and told him to drive to the casino.

As Jimmy pulled into the casino parking lot, Chad directed him to park in a middle row about halfway down the row. Jimmy followed instructions. At this time of the morning there weren't many cars, but enough to hide them. Chad called on his cell phone and told his associate where they were parked and to meet them there as soon as he could. He said he'd be there in a few minutes.

Chad told Jimmy to stay in the car with Laila. Then he explained to the new guy, whose name was Randall, what the plan was that he'd just cooked up in his head. "I'm going over to the old man's house and grab up the other girl. That son-of-a-bitch may get his older kid back but I'm going to have his other two. I can't let some decrepit old geezer get the best of me and kill my people! I got a reputation to uphold, and no way does this go unpunished! And an eight-year-old is prime real estate for my business! He's going to be busy at the Palace for a while, so I should have ample time to get to the old man's house and grab her up. You can take the girl in the car over there, and the dumb bucket of hair sitting in the driver's seat to the motel." Chad directed him to a motel quite aways further down Palm Canyon drive. He had already planned with the owner of the motel, who had an agreement for some of the business Chad and his associates conducted in Palm Springs, and a room would be waiting for them. Chad told Randall where the motel was and what room to go to and to wait, until he arrived. He then went to Jimmy and said, "I'm going to use your pick-up for a few minutes before I get to the motel."

"For what?"

"If I thought you needed to know that I would have told you. Don't worry I won't hurt your precious piece of shit pick-up.

The cops don't know anything about your car, do they? They wouldn't recognize it or have a BOLO out on it, would they?"

"No. I ain't never got a ticket or had any cops around it."

"You're sure?"

"Yea...Daq's the only one that's ever been in it."

"You, stupid son-of-a-bitch!"

"What? You said Daq would be busy!"

"And you don't think that she would have told the cops about your pick-up! They probably have a description and we've been fucking lucky they haven't seen it yet!" He looked over at the associate. "Randall. Any ideas? We need another car. This one could be recognized by the cops."

"Yea. I know a girl that works nights at this casino. Let me call her and see if she's working, I think she does this shift. If she is, then I can borrow her car.

"OK." He glowered at Jimmy and waited.

"Yea, she's working. I'll go in and get the keys and then you can take my car." Randal moved inside the casino.

Chad went to Randall's car and stuck the transponder he had from the landscape company on the headlight of the car, went back to Jimmy's pick-up and got his pistol and stuck it in the back of his pants. He looked at Jimmy and said, "Leave your pick-up here. You can pick it up later. Go with Randall to the motel and wait for me."

"What motel?"

Chad thought about it for a few seconds, but reluctantly decided to tell him because you never know, he might just need it. "OK. I'll tell you but do not make me regret it." He gave Jimmy the information and then looked at him, "and for Christ's sake can you please just do nothing till you get to the motel. I'll see you in about a half hour!"

Jimmy just lowered his head despondently, "Yea…"

When Randall came out, he handed Chad the keys to his car, and they talked for a few minutes, bumped fists and Chad drove off to his destination. Randall waved for Jimmy to bring the girl and himself and get into the car. When Randall got in the car with Jimmy, he grabbed his nose and said, "Jesus Dude! Did you shit your pants?"

"Man, I gotta take a major dump. And with Chad breaking my balls, it's even worse."

"Well, go inside and use the can! I'm not riding with you when you're that damn foul! And be sure you clean yourself! I don't want any lingering smell on you! Hurry up! If you're not back in about four minutes, I'm gone." He watched as Jimmy strode across the parking lot towards the front doors. He shook his head and whispered, "No wonder Chad's going to off him."

Chapter Seven

The EMT's had looked over Daq and Alex and all was deemed OK. Detective Halloran issued to Alex the need for him to stand down trying to take matters in his hands. He had made arrangements to have Alex and Daq driven back to their house since Officer Chen was keeping guard at the house. He had called Officer Chen and told her the situation and she agreed to stay at their house till all was safe. He told Alex that he would have a police car drive them home shortly.

Alex looked at detective Halloran and said, "Thank You. Just be sure you get my little girl back home to me!"

"We're on this and will do everything possible to get her back safely."

Alex nodded and walked over to Daq and said, "The police will be taking you back home. Angie, Jennifer, and officer Chen are there. Take care of Angie."

"You're not going?"

"No, but don't tell anyone. I'm getting back to our car and go look for Laila. I might be able to find out more info by shaking some bushes I know about."

"Alex, I want to go with you."

"Daq, I know but, you would be in danger and I'm not going to lose anyone else tonight."

"I might be able to help. I don't know, like recognize someone, or remember something...I want to help!"

"Daq, listen to me, I have to do this, but I won't put you in danger. Please go back to the house and let me do this, without any arguments. Please!"

Daq turned and headed back towards the police cars. Alex watched her for a few seconds then turned and slipped away to get back to his car. When he got to the car, he slid into the driver's seat and started the car. The passenger side door opened and Daq got in.

"Damn it Daq! I told you..."

"You better get going, I'm sure the cops are already looking for us and if they find us, we'll never get to go anywhere."

He glared at her but drove away. He turned right onto a street going away from the Palace Theatre. He started to admonish Daq, "I specifically told you the reason..."

"That's Jimmy!" She pointed towards the sparsely occupied parking lot at the casino.

"What!" Alex looked to his left and sure enough Jimmy was walking toward the casino entrance." He pulled over the car immediately and parked it on the side of the road. He jumped out of the car and then remembered Daq. He knew leaving her in the car alone would not be the right thing to do, not knowing the situation. "You come with me! Stay close and listen to me!"

Jimmy was just going in the doors as Alex and Daq ran up behind him. Alex stopped and let him go in the doors, and then followed him inside.

Randall was watching as Jimmy headed for the doors and when he saw Alex and Daq run up behind, he surmised that this was not a good development. He knew about Daq and had a basic description and figured that that was her. He started the car and drove out of the parking lot and called Chad, but the phone rang once and did not go through. Burner phones have voice mail but if they are shut off the call just ends. He headed to the motel, not knowing what else to do.

Alex watched as Jimmy headed into the restroom. He looked around and saw that there were not many people around; that was good. He noticed a folding yellow caution sign sitting on a bare floor where the ATM machine was located about thirty feet from the restroom. He told Daq to go get the sign and put it in front of the men's restroom door and stay there and instruct people that the men's restroom was closed for a short period of time. Which she did.

Alex slipped into the restroom and looked around. There was one man standing at the sinks washing his hands and no one at the urinals. He tilted his head and saw a pair of feet under one of the ass-cabins. That had to be Jimmy. Alex moved slowly to the sinks and started to wash his hands. The other man finished up and headed out the door. Alex moved to the stall where Jimmy sat. The door was ajar, he hadn't even bothered to close and lock the door. Alex slammed open the door and grabbed Jimmy by the hair and threw him flat on his face onto the floor with his pants and underwear still around his ankles. Alex winced from the smell but ignored it as he kicked Jimmy in the back of the head causing his face to violently bounce off the bathroom floor.

"Hello JIMMY!" Jimmy rolled to his side and looked into the face and eyes of Alex. His eyes filled with fear as he raised a defensive hand. Alex grabbed the hand and bent it backwards till Jimmy screamed, he then punched Jimmy twice in the face. "Start talking scumbag, where's my daughter!"

Jimmy squeaked back, "If you kill me, you'll never know where she is!"

"Oh, I'm not going to kill you; but in about thirty seconds you going to beg me to."

"I don't know anything!"

"That's it! lie to me; you, stupid son-of-a-bitch!" Alex slapped him across the face then reached down with his right hand and grabbed him by his exposed penis and scrotum. "One last chance! Where's my daughter? If you don't tell me, I'm going to remove these!" He squeezed hard with his hand and pulled equally hard.

Jimmy screamed.

"Talk, you little bastard!" Another hard jerk and a sustained squeeze.

Jimmy screamed again, "OK! OK! She was in the car with me and another guy in the parking lot!"

"The snake?!"

"No...I don't know where he is! He left in another car. The other guy is waiting for me to come back to the car."

"Where?!"

"About halfway down one of the middle rows. A green Toyota Camry. But he might be gone!"

Alex squeezed even harder, "What do you mean?"

"He said if I didn't come right back, he was leaving."

"And going where?" Another hard squeeze.

"To a motel towards the end of Palm Canyon Drive."

"You going to make me ask!?"

"The Starlight Motel, room 361. It's down by the Canyon golf course, on an off street across from there."

"That sounds made up!" He squeezed still harder.

"I don't know what else to tell you! You'll see it across from the parking lot of the golf course!"

"God help you if you lied to me!" He let go with his right hand and then with an open hand slapped hard into his balls. Jimmy doubled over his aching private parts. Alex kicked him in the side of head. Jimmy groaned and rolled to his side and started sobbing.

Alex started to exit the restroom but stopped and washed his hands and then said to Daq, "Laila's in a car here, supposed to be in the parking lot!" They moved towards the doors and stepped out. Alex started looking in the parking lot. "It's a Toyota Camry."

Daq stopped and grabbed his arm. "Green?"

"Yes."

"I saw him leave. Just as we were coming in, I saw him leave, I remember because he seemed like he was in a hurry."

Chapter Eight

Jennifer Grey sat in a chair next to Angie who was holding old Maurice in her lap and Ellie staying close to her feet in a watchful protective mode. The blinds in the room had been pulled down. Officer Nancy Chen patrolled the house, checking all the doors, windows and back and front yards. She had her service revolver drawn and ready. They all waited for some news.

Outside, Chad pulled his car up close to the block next to Alex's house, got out and casually walked up the street towards Alex's house. If security went by, he had to look like he belonged here. He had a lightweight shirt on that had a turtleneck to hide his tattoo. As he approached the house, he hid behind bushes, slipped on a tight-fitting full head mask and nitrile gloves, then viewed the surroundings. When it seemed clear he went to the front window on his belly amongst the bushes and quietly peered into the bottom corner which had a slight opening in the blinds. He saw Jennifer and Angie sitting in the chair. But he saw no one else, that made him pause. It wouldn't be like old grandpa to leave any of his kiddies without protection. Right then he heard steps by the front door. He quickly laid down and went completely still. He watched as Officer Chen looked around only a few feet from him and then went to the front door, opened it, and said, "It's me, no worries." But before she could close it Chad had quickly and quietly gotten to the door and as she closed it, he kicked it hard with his right foot. The door hit her full in the face and she fell into the entrance foyer, he pulled his pistol out of his pants and fired a shot into her chest. He aimed the gun at her head to be sure she was dead when a fist hit him full in the left side of his face that sent him sprawling into the wall. Quick as lightning another blow hit him in the temple. Then a hand grabbed the gun and twisted it from him. Now, gaining some of his faculties back, he swung his hand out and pushed this brawler back. He saw the gun and lunged for it and grabbed on, but whoever this was did not give up easily.

Jennifer held onto the gun for dear life, determined not to let him have it back. She pushed her shoulder into him and slammed him against the wall again. He looked at her and gasped, "A woman?!"

"You're goddamn right!" She started to twist the gun, but Chad managed to get his other hand on it, and he started to win the battle. Just as he was about to pull the gun away from Jennifer, he felt a bite on his wrist that made him scream. The little fourteen-pound Westie was no longer just a bystander. She had jumped up and bitten Chad on the wrist and would not let go and she shook his arm like it was a rodent. Jennifer took the gun away and threw it outside into the bushes. As Ellie hung on his right arm, with his left he hit Jennifer in the face. She fell backwards and then he roughly latched on to the dog's head and pulled her off and slung her into the wall. She yelped with pain as she slid to the floor.

Chad looked into the living room and saw Angie standing by the door that led to the kitchen. As he moved toward her, Jennifer was on her knees and lunged at him and had him around the waist when he kneed her in the chest and when she doubled over, he threw a hard right-hand punch into the side of her face that put her down flat on the floor. He jumped to Angie who was trying to get through the kitchen but to no avail. He pulled her up and slapped her across the face then put his hand over her mouth and said as he pulled her to the front door. "You be a real good girl until I get you to the motel." Lights were coming on around the neighborhood, so he had no time to worry about cleaning up. He had hoped it would be easier than this, but he felt confident that his disguise and garments had prevented any chance of being identified.

He got to his car and opened the passenger door and threw Angie into the car. He grabbed her throat and said, "One wrong move and you and your sisters all die!" He slammed the door, got in the driver's side, started the car and drove out the gate, which was open. He headed toward the motel. He smiled when he thought of Alex arriving home and finding a dead cop on the entry floor, and his mean-bitch babysitter (she was a tough bitch) out cold on the living room carpet. Hopefully that stupid mutt was dead also. He looked at his wrist which was bleeding, but only on his shirt, none had spilled onto the floor.

Now to the motel, pick up my young girl, and we get out of Dodge. *'Live with that you miserable bastard old man! I'll teach you not to mess with me...I got both your young little girls and now you, and that obstinate little bitch you call Daquiri, can try to live knowing I've got both of them and when I'm finished, I'll sell them! And you'll never find them.'* He smiled and gave an evil chortle as he called another henchman to join him at the motel before he took the girls away.

Chapter Nine

Alex and Daq drove down Palm Canyon Drive towards the golf course, Daq started to cry.

"What? What's wrong Daq?!"

"I did all this. This is my fault! If I had listened to my dad, like he wanted, I wouldn't have gotten involved with Jimmy. But I had to go and do just the opposite. Now look! Laila could be gone!"

"Daq, don't do this. This is not your fault. There are a thousand circumstances that led to this moment, none of them your fault. Many are mine, and just plain fate must take credit for a lot of them also. But not you! So, get that out of your head! Let's go get Laila and get home! Alright?"

She wiped her eyes and nodded. She looked at Alex and said, "What did you do to Jimmy back at the casino?"

"That's a story for another day."

"I thought you were one woke dude when you beat up Jimmy and the other guy at his house. Even though I didn't say anything. Did you do something like that just now?"

"Right now, let's concentrate on getting Laila back. But...I enjoyed this time even more than the first."

She looked over at him, nodded and said, "Good."

"You know that first day at Jimmy's? That was the day you completely became my own daughter. The very thought of that piece of shit touching you made my blood boil, and I would have killed him in a second to get you away from him. Now let's do the same for Laila."

Right then he saw the motel sign for the Starlight Motel. Jimmy hadn't lied. He turned down the nameless street and saw the rather run-down motel. It was three floors that appeared to be in a square. The area was desolate with no other buildings around. Alex stopped short of the parking lot, turned off his lights and pulled into the right side of the motel by way of going over the curb and creeping along the barren ground next to the parking lot. He continued around to the back that had overgrown bushes and trees creeping into the parking spaces. He backed the car under a tree that hid the car from sight, but also gave a view of the right side of the motel and the driveway to the entrance. He sat and observed all aspects of his position. He picked up his phone and called Officer Chen

While the phone rang, "Daq, I need to find room 361. You stay here! Do not get out of the car! Understand? Once I find the room, I want to see what I can find out. I'll be back...hopefully with Lai." On the fourth ring a downtrodden voice answered,

"Alex..."

"Nancy?!"

"No, it's Jennifer."

"Jennifer! What the hell is going on?!"

"Someone broke into the house, shot Nancy, and took Angie."

"What! Took Angie! Who... what the hell...Where..."

"Alex! Shut up and listen! He broke into the house and shot Nancy. I fought with him before he got to Angie, but I couldn't stop him, but when I hit him, he jerked his head, and I saw tattoo ink on his neck. I think it was the snake guy. He also said something about getting her to a motel."

"Bless you Jennifer! I think I'm at that motel right now! This snake guy has Laila here right now, with someone guarding her, but I have Daq...get with the cops and tell them everything. The motel is the Starlight Motel across from the Canyons golf course. Room 361!"

"They're already here...I'll tell them!"

"Wait!" He thought for a minute and realized if the cops showed up with lights and sirens and the snake wasn't there yet, he'd lose Angie for sure and possibly Laila. "No, don't tell them till I call you back."

"Why for Christ's sake?!"

"Just trust me!" He ended the call.

He looked at Daq, "I gotta go! Stay put! Here's my phone, if I'm not back in fifteen minutes call the cops. 911…not Officer Chen."

"Daddy! Is Angie gone too? Does the snake have her?"

"Yes. He went to the house and grabbed her. Honey, I got to get Laila. I'll try and be right back with her then we can deal with this snake and get Angie. They're coming here!" He jumped out, locked the doors and headed to the back of the motel. He tried a door in the back, and it was locked. He went around to the other side of the building and saw the stairwell that went to all the floors. He tried the door on the first floor, and it was locked, then to the second floor and it was locked, then to the third, it was locked also. He didn't want to go the lobby because he figured that whoever was there was going to be part of this whole mess and would certainly notify the snake.

He was still in his long Kakhi pants and dress, desert style shirt, but he had put on a tank top under his shirt. He quickly stripped off the shirt and tank top, pulled out his pistol and wrapped it in his tank top. He put the barrel of the gun directly into the lock of the door and fired, he then slammed his left shoulder into the door and the entryway flew open. He stood still for a moment to see if there was any movement from outside or inside. Nothing. He put on his dress shirt, tucked the gun in the back of his pants and glanced at the first door on his left. Room 331, so 361 would be down towards the end of the hall, all rooms were on the left side. The right side of the hall looked over a pool area directly below all the rooms, it had a wooden railing all along. The Motel had obviously been designed for all rooms to view the pool. He glanced down at the pool, which was not in the best of condition, but saw that the pool was surrounded by a black wrought iron fence with black metal, squared pickets approximately 5" apart and each had a fleur-de-lis symbol on the top. The lawn furniture surrounding the pool had seen it's better days...many years ago. He focused back on the room numbers and the very last door had number 361 on it. He stopped and saw that the curtain was drawn, but many times in these older motels the curtains did not line up perfectly as they once had when new. That was the case here. He glanced in and saw a man sitting on the couch and he could hear the TV playing. He couldn't see Laila but adjusted his view a few times and finally saw her feet sitting on the floor just past the couch that the man sat on. He moved to the door. He lightly knocked. He heard movement to the door, "Yea?"

Alex said in a low voice purporting to be Chad's voice, "Snake." He heard the chain come off and the door opened slightly. He slammed both hands against the door hitting the man directly in the chest. He pushed his way in and when the man lifted his face Alex hit him with a right-hand cross punch that sent him sprawling to the floor. He was temporarily unconscious, and Alex quickly closed the door. As he looked to Laila, he knew he would need to get her quickly and out of here. But she was in shock, and it appeared she had reverted into her silence mode for dealing with this situation. He started to approach her carefully, when the phone on the desk rang. Fear completely froze him. He knew he had to do something, but what? He thought for a few seconds and knew he had to answer.

"Yea, hello?"

"Randall?"

"Hmm." His heart was beating so hard he was afraid whoever was on the phone could hear it.

"This is Al from the front desk. Chad wants to know if everything's OK?"

"Everything is fine." Alex grunted. "Why?"

"He tried to call your cell and got your voicemail. That made him nervous I guess."

"I silenced my phone...forgot to take it off." Alex prayed that Al bought the story and didn't suspect that he wasn't Randall.

"Oh, OK. I'll let him know." He hung up.

Alex looked at the phone, put it back on the cradle, and started thinking, *'if that was me, would I be satisfied with Al calling me back? Or would it be better if Randall called Chad? I would definitely want to hear from Randall myself.'* He went to Randall laying on the floor but was coming to from his punch to the head. Alex rolled him over and slapped him easily in the face a couple of times.

"Listen man, I'm just a babysitter, I ain't got nothing to do with any of this!"

Alex took out his gun and put it in his face. "If that's the case then you'll do me a favor. First, why didn't you answer your cell phone a little while ago?"

"I forgot I had silenced it."

Alex nodded, rather pleased that he had guessed correctly. "Get your phone out and call Chad. Tell him you had your phone on silent mode and forgot to take it off, but everything here is OK."

Randall fumbled for his phone, found it and called the last number that had called his phone. Alex put the gun to his temple, "Believable! Tell him sorry for voice mail, had the phone on silent…"

Chad answered. "Yea?"

"This is Randall, sorry about the voice mail. I'd turned my phone to silent back at the casino and forgot to turn it on again. Sorry. But all is quiet here." He listened for a few seconds then said, "OK." Hung up and looked at Alex, "It's cool man. I did what you told me. He's going to be here in a few minutes." He pleaded with Alex, "C'mon man, I been square with you, let me go."

"In due time...till then you'll be smart to shut up and do nothing; and you might just live by doing that. Don't move." He then went to the window and looked at the curtains and saw that they had a cord to close and open the drapes. He made sure the curtains were closed properly, put his gun in the back of his pants and broke off the pull cords, went to Randall on the floor, moved him to the bathroom tied him up, gagged him and reminded him that he would die if he made a sound. He closed the bathroom door and quietly went to the hall to access the situation.

Chad came into the lobby. "Hey big Al, still all good?" As he walked out of the lobby to the stairs that were right of the pool and close to where room 361 was.

"Yep. Still no troubles."

"Good! Real Good. You installed an elevator yet?" He laughed. "I might be needing one pretty soon, not getting any younger ya know!" Another bark of laughter. He started up the stairs.

Alex pulled his gun, went back into the room, closed the door and listened for the knock at the door, but it didn't come. He looked out the curtain and could see no one around. He slowly opened the door and went into the hall and heard voices downstairs. He cautiously looked over the edge and saw Chad walking back into the office.

"Shit! Now what?" Alex whispered as he went back into the room. He knew he'd have to act fast. He went to Laila who was still sitting on the floor sucking her thumb. She looked up without saying any words.

Chapter Ten

Chad roughly slammed Angie into the front passenger seat. "One wrong move and you and your sisters all die!"

As he drove to the motel, Angie started to cry. "SHUT UP!" I don't need a sniffling little shit ruining my victory." He smiled a malignant grin at her. "You should be happy. You and I will soon become real good friends. In fact, if I hadn't taken care of my business earlier, I may have just pulled over right now. But who knows, maybe a little later." He gave an evil chortle. Angie stared at him, eyes wide and mouth agape. Not many eight-year-olds would have understood his meaning, but Angie did. She felt herself becoming sick and she leaned forward and vomited onto the floor of the car.

"Oh great! Now I have to drive with the smell of puke in the car." He rolled down her window about halfway down and his the same. "There's a rag in the glove box, get it out and clean up your barf and throw it out the window!

Angie obeyed the command and said in a very subdued voice, "I'm sorry."

"Yea, Yea." As they drove on, Angie silently cried and shook with fear. Chad took out his phone and turned it on. He called Randall's cell phone, but it went to voice mail. "That's fucking weird." He called the Motel, and the night manager answered. "Big Al! Any problems come up that you've seen? Is Randall there yet?"

"No, no problems that I've seen. And yea, Randall's been here for about twenty to thirty minutes.

"Did he have the little girl with him?"

"Yea. They went right to the room and I ain't seen them since."

"Anybody else show up? Any new customers, or anybody?"

"Nope. Completely quiet. Haven't heard a peep all night. You want me to check on them?"

"Yea, call him. His cell phone went to voicemail. I'll hold." He waited as he drove and glanced at Angie who sat shivering. He just smiled.

"Chad?"

"Yea, talk to me."

"Everything is fine, I talked to Randall, and he said all was good. His phone was in silent mode when he first got here and forgot to take it off."

"OK. I'll be there in just about two minutes. See ya then." He hung up the phone. He thought for a few minutes, then started to dial Randall's number. Right then his phone rang. "Yea?"

"This is Randall, sorry about the voice mail. I'd turned my phone to silent back at the casino and forgot to turn it on again. Sorry. But all is quiet here."

"OK. Good. I'll be there in a few minutes." He hung up just as he was pulling into the Motel parking lot in the front. He parked, got out of the car, and looked around. Car lights flashed from the street in front of the motel. He waved and indicated that he wanted the car to stay where it was but for the driver to come over to him. He opened the passenger door and said to Angie, "You're going to stay here for a few minutes till I get back with your little sister, then we can take off for our new adventure! So, stay quiet and nice till I get back." He grabbed her by the collar and pulled up to his face, "Understand?" Angie sobbed loudly and nodded. He tossed her back in the car and slammed the door.

The driver's name was Jeremy. He worked for Chad in the Coachella valley as an enforcer and a 'get anything done' type of guy. He was big and dumb, but loyal and mean and one tough son-of-a-bitch. Chad didn't think he'd need him, but no sense in taking any chances. "Hi Jeremy. Thanks for coming."

"Any time boss. You know that."

"Yea. Listen there's a girl in this car and I want her to stay there until I come and get her, or I come back to the car and take off. Got it?"

He nodded. "Yea. Should I get in the car with her?"

"No. She's scared enough already. Just watch the car and don't let her out or anyone in."

"OK. I'll stay right here." He pointed to a flower bed by the entrance that had overgrown bushes around it and was close to the car.

"That's great Jeremy. Thanks...you're a good friend." Jeremy beamed at him after hearing those kind words. Chad saw the reaction and humorously chuffed as he walked into the motel office.

"Hey big Al, still all good?"

Chapter Eleven

Jennifer sat and waited for Alex to call. Nothing. She gingerly got up and went out to the front yard. She ruminated for a few seconds, *'what is he doing!? He should have called by now! Maybe I should call him? But what if it disturbs something he's doing? But I have to know! Surely, he would have thought about a call coming in and silenced his phone if it could be a problem. Yes...I've got to call!'* She dialed the phone. It rang three times and went to voice mail. She left a brief message, then said out loud to herself. "Shit! Now what?" She looked at the activity in the house and then spotted something on the floor underneath the entry table. She got a better angle at it and realized it was Officer Chen's stun gun. It had obviously fallen off her belt and gotten knocked under the table during the shooting and altercation. She waited for the optimum time and then picked up the gun and slid it into her belt under the lightweight sweatshirt she had thrown on before coming over. Then quickly she slipped away and got to her car and took off. As she drove through the open gate she headed in the direction of the motel. *'If I don't hear from him in a few minutes, I'm calling the cops.* She sped on towards the Starlight Motel. This was a game of timing and she sure as hell wanted to do it right.

Chapter Twelve

Daq was scared. She sat alone in the car and wondered if Alex would ever come back. She kept watching, hoping beyond hope that she would see him running to the car holding Laila. She saw a car drive in the parking lot, just as the car came in, a light came on, a phone light, and the person holding the phone...looked like the 'snake'.

"Oh hell! What do I do now?" Daq said out loud. "Maybe it wasn't him. But it sure looked like him." She sat for only a second and then jumped out, leaving the cell phone in the car. She moved quickly to the side of the motel and peeked around the corner at the front of the building. There stood the 'snake', she could see his tattoo. He walked around to the passenger side of the car, opened the door and then grabbed Angie. She quickly turned away from the view of the car and slammed her back against the side wall. *'I have to get Angie! I know Alex will be mad, but I can get her and get her back to the car safely. Then I can try to help*

Alex somehow...I can call 911! But I got to hurry now. The 'snake' will be going to the room where Alex and Laila are. Maybe he'll already have her! And when he brings her to the car, he'll see I've got Angie, and we can all leave!'

She looked around the corner and the car sat by itself, but Angie was in the front seat. She moved quickly, keeping an eye on the front doors just in case he came back. She got to the car door and opened it. Angie looked up. A look of terror came over her face that made Daq pull away for a second. Then she realized what the look was all about. A huge hand wrapped around her throat and squeezed so hard that she couldn't even breathe, let alone scream. She was pulled back into the chest of a giant man and while she was subdued in that position, he reached his other giant like hand into the car and pulled Angie out. She started to scream and cry, and the giant said, "Quiet...or I'll kill both of you." Angie quieted down. Both girls were helpless to fight back or try to escape as the giant dragged them both into the lobby. "Get the boss!" He growled at the man behind the counter.

The man behind the counter quickly yelled out the open window to the lobby area and the stairs, "Chad! Hold up and come back!"

The 'snake, who was on the second-floor stairway, stopped and looked back. Upon seeing the giant holding the two girls in the lobby, smiled broadly and started back down to the front desk. When he pushed through the doors into the front desk, he chortled, "Well, Well, Well. What do we have here? Hello Daquiri! Nice to see you again. Where's your grampie?"

She looked at him with hatred in her eyes, "Getting ready to kill you!"

Chad laughed, "Oh, I see." Then his face turned malevolent, "Where is he?"

"I don't know."

The slap made her vision go dark and a bolt of white lightning flashed through the darkness. Then the pain hit, and she slumped down but the giant pulled her back up. Now the tears started to come, she didn't want them to, but oh my god, the pain was horrible. As she started to cry the 'snake' barked an order to the man behind the counter.

"Al, are the cars in the parking lot all that is here?"

"Yea. As far as I know."

"Well go check to be sure! If there are any others, let me know."

Al ran out the front and turned left. In just a few minutes he was back, puffing from his run but able to say, "There's a car in the bushes over there," he pointed to the right, "it's got the door open, and no one is in it!"

The 'snake' looked at Daq, "Trying to be a hero, were we?" He looked back at the giant and the man behind the counter, "He's up in the room. We have to assume that he got the best of Randall. Al, you got a weapon here?"

"Just this." He pulled out a long hunting knife that had a nefarious look to it.

"No gun?"

"No, never needed one."

"Stupid! This will have to do. Al, stay here and let me know about anything! Got it?! Give me a key to the room."

"Yea." He slid the key across the counter.

"Jeremy, bring the girls. And if either one of them makes a sound. Snap their neck!"

Daq looked around and didn't have a clue what to do, *'Oh god, what do I do now. He's going to kill Alex and take all of us away. Oh god...Oh god...*

Chapter Thirteen

Alex knelt and looked at the terrified little girl. "Hey baby girl. It's Pops. I'm here now and I'm going to take care of you, just like I promised." He reached his hands out to pick her up, but she pulled back and turned away. "No baby. It's OK. I'm not here to hurt you, I'm here to take you home. Daq's in the car waiting."

Laila looked up at him, her eyes filled with tears as she pulled her thumb out of her mouth, started to sob and held her arms out to Alex. He leaned forward and picked her up and she wrapped her arms around him as she cried. He stood with her in his arms and fiercely hugged her. He rocked her as he said, "I'm so sorry this happened baby girl. But it's almost over. Daq's waiting for us in the car, we need to go."

He held her tight a few seconds more then turned to head out the door.

"My My...how touching." Chad stood in the doorway with a shit-eating grin on his face. His arms were wrapped around Daq, with the huge knife at her throat. Jeremy the giant had Angie by the throat. "I'll have that gun you got in your hand there." Alex had almost forgotten that he still had the gun in his hand when he picked up Laila. "Real careful like grandpa. You hand it to me holding the barrel." Alex was holding the gun in his right hand and carefully raised his fingers up and held the gun by the barrel with two fingers and the other fingers raised up like he was holding a smelly diaper. He took a step toward Chad and watched as Chad pressed the knife against Daq's throat. He held the gun out and Chad took it from his hand. "Ain't this a cute little peashooter. You use this to kill my guys?" His smile turned mean. "I don't like my guys getting killed. Somebody got to pay for that shit. But nobody's getting killed in this room." He threw the knife on the floor behind Jeremy and pointed the gun at Alex. He kissed Daq on top of her head. "No sir, you're gunna live and so are all your girls here. But you won't know where they are, cuz after I get done with them...you see I gotta break them in. (he winked at Alex) Then I will sell them and they will be gone and no one will know where they are, not even me. But I know one thing, you have to live with the fact that they're gunna be druggies that get beaten and tortured every night, and of course they will be at the mercy of the people that paid to fuck them...any way they want, and what they want you probably don't even want to hear about. You see, the people I sell them to, that's what their customer base is all about." He cackled at Alex.

"You miserable, low-life cocksucker...I WILL kill you, no matter..."

"Oh please! Shut up! Your idle threats don't scare me one bit, so just stow it." He looked at the gun and pointed it at Alex. He pushed Daq over to Jeremy the giant, "Here. Hold onto this one too." He focused back on Alex, I don't want to shoot you, for the reasons I mentioned before, but if I must, I will. Remember that, Gramps."

"If you're the tough guy you claim, then why don't you and I just go mano a mano! I win...I take all my girls home and you go about your miserable life. You win...go ahead with your plan and I'll relinquish and live with the consequences."

"Nice try Grampy. But I don't give up a winning hand...ever! And that's what I got here." He looked at Alex with an air of superiority that made Alex's throat fill with bile. "Where's Randall?" Alex said nothing. Chad moved by him and opened the bathroom door. He chuffed a small laugh. "Not bad old man, not bad." He ambled back towards where Jeremy stood holding the two girls. He looked at Alex and his face hardened into a granite stare, "Put the little one down."

Alex held her tight as he glanced around the room trying to think of something to do, when suddenly he saw something that had not been there before. There in the doorway was the face of Jennifer Grey.

Chapter Fourteen

Jennifer drove into the parking lot of the Starlight Motel just minutes after Chad had moved Daq and Angie out of the lobby and started toward the stairs to go to room 361. She parked, looked around the parking lot, grabbed the stun gun and checked to be sure she knew how to use it. Fortunately, she had been trained in the use of these types of weapons. Her job sometimes took her places that needed protection. After she felt comfortable in using it, she got out of the car and started into the lobby. She called the police and gave them the address and information. When she entered, the man behind the counter quickly looked up and said in contemptuous tone, "Who are you!?"

"I'm with the snake, he told me to show you this. She walked over to the counter digging in her pocket with her left hand, and when the man leaned over to look at what she was removing from her pocket, she zapped him with the stun gun in her right hand, she held the gun to his arm for as long as she could and he fell back against the wall behind the counter and slid to the floor. Jennifer quickly rounded the counter and as the man struggled to get up, she zapped him in the neck and held the gun on him for a few seconds. He went directly to the floor and did not move.

She moved out of the lobby and towards the stairs, constantly looking around to see if there were any others around that could possibly hinder her path. When she got to the stairs, she took off running up the stairs. She thought to herself that she was glad she worked out some, because this would hurt if she hadn't. When she got to the third floor she looked to her right and heard voices and saw an open door. She moved against the wall and proceeded slowly and quietly towards room 361. When she got to the open door, she quietly listened.

"Not bad old man, not bad." Then in a very ominous voice, "Put the little one down."

She laid her stomach against the wall and peered in the doorway. She made eye contact with Alex holding Laila and saw a very large man holding onto Daq and Angie. She only glimpsed the Snake as he was somewhat blocked by the giant. But Alex's eyes told the whole story. He needed her to do something; and quickly!

Chapter Fifteen

As he looked at Jennifer, he said to Chad, "OK, OK. She's scared. Just give it a little time."

"Not a chance Gramps. You move on my orders."

He looked again at Jennifer who was now holding up the stun gun so he could see. Chad had moved into view now and was standing in front of Alex holding the gun on him. Jennifer pointed to Chad and wiggled the stun gun. Then pointed to Alex and then to the large man named Jeremy. Alex understood and gave a nonchalant nod so as not to arouse suspicion with Chad. He turned to his right and put Laila down and scooted her farther to the left in the room, then slowly stood up and saw Jennifer creeping into the room looking at him. This time he nodded vigorously at her giving Chad pause, just enough pause for Jennifer to zap him in the neck with the stun gun. His body contorted and he dropped the gun. She kicked the gun away from him as he hit the floor. Alex didn't waste a second, with all his strength and all his training as a boxer he threw a right-hand punch into the face of Jeremy the giant, he heard the bones in his hand crack but yelled, "Daq! Get Angie and get safe!" She pulled away from the giant, who had let loose of both girls, grabbed Angie and moved to where Laila was standing.

Surprisingly, the giant looked unharmed, a bit shaken but mainly just pissed off. With his left arm he made a sweeping back-handed slap that caught Jennifer full in the face, she hit the wall behind her and fell to the floor. The stun gun fell from her hand and tumbled away beneath a chair. The giant turned and looked at Alex and started toward him.

"Oh, SHIT!" Alex quickly moved to his right as Jeremy grabbed at him with his left arm. He was able to avoid the grasp but noticed that Chad was getting up from his jolt from the stun gun. He made the decision to stay put and kick Chad in the head. The kick put Chad down on his stomach again, but there was a price to pay for that. Jeremy had turned and threw a punch that hit Alex straight in his chest. Alex flew backwards and hit the wall next to the open door and slumped to the floor and rolled into the doorway. His chest felt as if it had an elephant sitting on it and breathing was very difficult. He scooted backwards on his butt into the hallway and looked up into the maniacal eyes of Jeremy as he came through the doorway.

A shot rang out and Jeremy jerked from the pain in his back and turned into the room. Daq stood holding the pistol that only weeks earlier she had held to her own temple. "You little bitch!" He roared. She pulled the trigger again and the bullet went into the giant's chest. This time he fell backwards onto his butt and rolled over to his side away from the door. She dropped the gun and just stood looking at the giant laying on the floor.

Right then Chad crawled into the doorway and grabbed the knife laying on the floor by Jeremy's feet. As he started to get up with the knife in his hand, Jennifer gabbed his ankle and yelled, "Watch out Alex!" Chad kicked her in the neck and clambered up to his knees, lifted the knife and dove at Alex sitting in the hallway. Alex had regained some of his faculties after the tremendous punch from Jeremy, enough to avoid the knife that Chad plunged at him. The knife hit the floor just inches from his side, but

Chad was laying on top of Alex, his snake tattoo mockingly staring at him. Alex hit with his left hand into Chad's face and was able to push him off him and onto the floor.

Alex ignored the pain in his hand and chest and stood and moved down the hallway never taking his eyes off Chad. He watched as Chad got to his knees and then stood and screaming at the top of his lungs charged towards Alex with the knife held above his head in a stabbing stance. Alex backed up quickly down the hallway, past the stairs, and just as Chad got to him and stabbed downward with the knife Alex sidestepped and Chad fell forward. He quickly got up and held the knife in an attack stance and took a few steps back. Alex also was in a fighter's stance with his hands open in front of him.

Chad smiled an evil smirk with his bloody teeth taking center stage of the performance. He swiped the knife at Alex twice, which Alex easily avoided. Alex moved directly in front of Chad still in his fighter's stance and grinned at Chad, "Come on, SNAKE...let's finish this!"

Chad with an underarm thrust with his right arm, stabbed at Alex who quickly blocked the thrust with his left hand and hit Chad full in the face with his right hand. The pain from his broken right hand was mind numbing and he winced just long enough for Chad to stab again with the knife and this time it found Alex's left side just under the rib cage. The pain shot through Alex like an electrical shot but also jolted him into an angered frenzy. He hit Chad hard again with his right hand in the side of the face and then a second time in the ear. Chad's chest lay on the railing when he dropped the knife and Alex with his left hand pushed his head over the railing further and with his right arm catapulted Chad's legs over. Chad fell headfirst but the amount of strength that Alex had used to throw him over caused his legs to flip over and Chad did a full somersault onto the wrought iron fence surrounding the pool. The last thing Chad saw on this earth was the iron fleur-de-lis as it plunged into his Adams apple and the tattoo of the snake.

Alex looked down at the body hanging on the fence, "How's that for an idle threat...Snake!" He saw the cops moving in the lobby doors and held his arms up in the air. Detective Halloran looked up and saw him and said to the others, "He's good!" Alex looked down the hallway and saw Daq standing looking at him as she outwardly cried. He moved quickly despite the pain and enveloped her in a hug, "It's over baby! It's over!"

"Daddy..."

Chapter Sixteen

Alex holding tightly to Daq went back towards the room. Before he made it back Angie came out also crying. She wrapped her arms around him and cried harder. He hugged her tightly and picked her up and she wrapped her arms and legs around him, which hurt like hell, but he didn't care. He held her for a few seconds then walked into the room. Jennifer had gotten up off the floor even though she looked as if she had just fought a world war and was holding Laila in her arms. Alex slowly moved closer to Laila with Angie and Daq holding on to him. He knelt and looked at her and said, "Hey baby girl, you want to be part of this?" She raised up from Jennifer's arms and put her arms around Alex's neck. Daq and Angie both put arms around her and the family of four had a moment that would last forever.

Alex then sat down. He was bleeding from the stab wound, he could barely move his right hand, his chest ached, and his breathing was labored along with other bumps, bruises, and contusions. The EMTs had just come into the room and Jennifer yelled, "Over here quick!" One of them moved quickly to Alex and the three girls shifted towards Jennifer.

Angie and Laila each curled under one of her arms and Daq sat close as they watched Alex get patched up by the EMT. He told the girls that he looked like he would be fine. The stab wound was mainly superficial. Alex smiled at Jennifer, and she returned the gesture. After a while of just sitting and resting, she looked at the three girls and then said, "Wow, today is September 30th!" Daq smiled as she knew where Jennifer was going. "So, girls, anything you were going to talk about today? Since we have a few minutes while we rest, we could talk."

Daq looked at her sisters, "So what do ya think? Should we stay or go? Let's take a vote. Laila...you want to stay with Pops?" She nodded her head. "Ang...what about you?" She nodded her head also. "OK."

Jennifer said, "And how about you?"

Daq looked at Alex, "Well, I do like the dog and cat." Alex smirked at her. "So, yea...I'll stick around." She moved closer to Alex and just grinned and nodded.

Jennifer looked at Alex. "Looks like you won a bet!"

Part Five

Finale

Chapter One

The hospital was becoming more like old home week. Burt and Ernie each had rooms, Jennifer had a room, Officer Chen had a room and Alex had a room after he was released from ICU. All three girls got checked out thoroughly and all three were given a room for the night for observation. When Angie came into Alex's room, he looked at her and said, "So looks like you all have a room here to keep an eye on me." She laughed and moved up close to his bed with Laila at her side. His right hand was in a cast, and he was stitched and heavily bandaged where Chad had stabbed him with the knife. He also had three broken ribs from where he had been hit by Jeremy the giant, who also had a room in the hospital. Additional bumps and bruises made just laying still painful. But he was glad to see the two girls. "You guys are staying here I understand."

"Yep! All three of us in one room."

"OK. But no beer!"

Right then a nurse came in and smiled at the girls and said, "Time to leave ladies. Papa needs his sleep. You can come back and see him in the morning, I promise. They said their goodbyes and gave their kisses and said they'd see him in the morning. Alex watched as they left, and the nurse came in to ready him for the rest of the day. "OK Mr. Barton. The doctor has ordered a sedative for you tonight so you can sleep, you need rest." She administered the sedative into the IV.

"OK. But after I see all my friends that are in here with me. I mean, I was the reason they all ended up here. I have to see them and thank them."

"Well, we'll talk to the doctor tomorrow about that. But for now, you stay here, and you sleep. Perhaps tomorrow you will get the OK to see other people, but for tonight…you're in my prison."

He was becoming increasingly tired, and his words no longer made a lot of sense, he looked at the clock and it said Saturday September 30th 1:00 PM. He smiled, *'30 days hath September'*…and then he slept.

Chapter Two

When Alex woke up, he saw that the sun was still shining. He shook his head slightly, raised up and looked around the room. No one was in the room; he laid his head back down on the pillow again and gathered his thoughts and rapidly began to cerebrate the happenings of that fateful night. He looked at the clock and saw, Monday October 2nd 6:41 AM. *'Wait! What? The last time I looked at that clock it was September 30th...I remember saying 30 days hath September...What the hell?'* He quickly rang for the nurse. In a few minutes the nurse he remembered from the first day came in, he remembered her name as Helen. "Well, well...welcome back to the living."

"What the hell did you give me, an elephant tranquilizer?"

She smiled, "No. But the body has a way of healing itself. You did wake up for a few minutes on our nightly checks, but nothing that you would remember."

"So, what's the verdict? I am living?"

"Yes, but we certainly would tell you to avoid nights like you had a couple days ago."

"Yea, me too. Speaking of that, how are my friends all doing."

"Knew you'd ask so here is the complete run-down. Your daughter Daquiri and her two sisters were released yesterday. Besides a few bruises and scrapes they're fine. Officer Chen was released yesterday also, and she stayed with the girls last night. She was deep bruised but the bullet she took was stopped by her protective vest she was wearing."

"Thank God. For all of that."

"OK, next. Ernie Stevenson. He's still here recouping from the gunshot wound. He lost a lot of blood on a wound that could have been much worse. It was close to a main artery and had it ruptured it he could have easily bled out. But thankfully it didn't. But he is in pain and has a slight infection but should recover fully.

"Can I see him?"

"Yes...but we'll talk more about you in a few. Now, Burt Falmeyer. He is still here and still under close observation. He was close to death. He'd lost a lot of blood and someone his age, or any age really, can't take that kind of beating. He has multiple bone fractures in his face, shoulders, sternum and ribs. He has abdominal injuries and has trouble breathing on his own. He is still in serious condition, and we have him in an induced coma. We've fixed everything, but now it's just a matter if his body will heal. I like his chances, but he's got to fight."

"I want to see him first! And I think Ernie should go see him right away!"

"I know, and we're working on it, but slow down. When you're dealing with a bullet wound in him and your stab wounds, you have to be careful."

"OK. What about Jennifer Grey."

"She's been asking about you a lot. She will be fine, but she is still here also. She has a broken nose and a cracked bone under her eye and a couple of broken ribs and we're just watching to be sure nothing else pops up. Yes, you can see her today. But all this dependent on the doctor giving you the OK to get up and move around. I have to take out the catheter and get you something to eat and see how all that goes. Then the doc will be in to see you later. So, try to be good till she gets here...OK?"

"I'll try." He smiled at her. "So, Jennifer asked about me...a lot?"

"She did. I kinda thought you guys were...together. You're not?

"No...we're not...we've just been working together, you know, for a while."

"Hmmm."

"What does Hmmm, mean?"

"That, I guess, would mean it is open for interpretation." She smiled with an air of empiricism.

"When my kids get here send them in." He grinned at her.

"First things first. Let's get that catheter out."

"Oh, joy."

Chapter Three

After it was determined that his bodily functions and stamina were good, the girls came in to see Alex. The three girls seemed genuinely concerned about his thirty-hour nap but after a brief discussion they all seemed OK, and the conversation turned to the others that were in the hospital.

"Where's Nancy, I thought she'd be here since she stayed with you last night?"

Angie answered first, "She didn't want to interfere with our time together. I told her she was being silly because after what she did for us, she was like family."

"Good for you!" Alex called the nurse and told her to please send Officer Chen into the room. When she knocked on the door, Alex got up out of his chair and answered the door. When he opened it, he didn't say anything just hugged Nancy and whispered to her, "Thank God you're alright! And...thank you for all you did for us!"

"It was my pleasure. I've actually come to think of myself as a part of this family."

"Glad to have you!" He kissed her on the forehead and then said to the group. "OK. Here is the scoop, the doctor has said I can go visit Burt and Ernie, but I must go in a wheelchair. I've talked to Ernie on the phone, and we have a plan. So, I'm hoping that Daq will push me to Ernie's room, and Nancy will go with us. Angie, you and Laila stay here in the room until we come back to get you. Ernie has to be in a wheelchair also, so Nancy that is going to be your job, pushing Ernie to Burt's room. But Ang and Lai are part of this plan so we can get them to his room. OK, everyone ready?" He smiled at Daq. "Here we go gang!" He sat down in the wheelchair and Daq quickly pushed him down the hallway with Nancy in close tow learning the plan as she went. When they arrived at Ernie's room, they pushed their way in and Ernie, knowing what the plan was, hopped out of bed and got into his wheelchair, and Nancy took the controls. They opened the door and then, as if they were having hospital hall races, the two wheelchairs raced back to Angie and Laila. They had been told that visiting

Burt could only be Ernie, and for a short time only. Alex and Ernie had surmised that Burt would respond much better to everyone being there, but getting everyone into the room was going to be the trick...so the game was afoot!

Laila climbed up into Ernie's lap along with a stuffed teddy bear she had picked out at the gift shop and was quickly covered with a blanket with just the bear's head peeking over the covers. Daq was pushing Alex and Angie walked beside them. They all went up one floor to where Burt's room was. This floor of the hospital had two hallways with the nurse's station positioned between them. There were two nurses at work in the station. The elevator opened in front of the left hallway and Burt's room was located in the right hallway, so it meant getting everyone past the front desk. Nancy pushed Ernie to the front desk and over to the right hallway, she stopped and explained to the one nurse what she was doing, and that Ernie was here to see Burt. At about the same time Daq and Alex exit the elevator and while going toward the right hallway, Daq broke down into uncontrollable crying and moved into the left hallway. The other nurse seeing that Daq was going into the other hallway leaves her chair, comes out from behind the station and goes to Daq. Angie, standing in the elevator pushing the hold button, quickly runs from the elevator and squats in front of the station counter. The nurse talking to Nancy, quickly tells them to go to Burt's room and runs back behind the counter and begins talking to Alex, who is loudly saying "Honey, don't do this, it's not helping!". Angie sees the opportunity and slips around the station and goes with Nancy to Burt's room. Alex watched as Angie slipped away and then says, "Sweetheart, this won't help Uncle Burt." Which was Daq's que to stop crying and come back to the wheelchair, which she did, sobbing hard enough that the two nurses sympathetically allowed her to push Alex down the hallway to Burt's room, with Alex's assurance that they would stay in the hall with the other caregiver.

When Nancy and Ernie got to the room, Ernie, Angie, and Laila quickly went in and Nancy stood outside. Ernie took the moment to tell his partner that he was there. "Burt, I'm here. I'm here with you and I want you to hear me...come back home, I love you and need you back! Don't you dare leave me!" Right then Alex and Daq came in the room. The three girls stood together while Alex stood alongside Ernie. He leaned down and said, "Burt, it's Alex I just came here to tell you that you're probably the best friend I have and your job of taking care of me ain't over! So, get well, come home, and get back to work! Oh, and I got a little surprise for you." He motioned for the girls.

Daq stepped up and whispered to Burt, "I love you Uncle Burt, this is Daq, and I want you to come home. Taking care of Alex is not easy and I need your advice and help. But most of all I miss you and your amazing hugs! I love you."

Angie had had Ernie pull up a side chair and she stood on it. "I love you Uncle Burt, and listen, I have a new word game that we can play, and no one here is smart enough to play it with me except you. So come back soon, and I miss your hugs too."

Daq lifted Laila up and sat her on the bed next to Burt. She laid the teddy bear next to him and whispered, "I brought a bear to keep you company. It will be someone that you can talk to. But be sure to bring him home with you so we can play with him together." She leaned in and kissed him on the cheek.

Ernie stood and watched while tears ran down his cheeks. Alex herded the girls out into the hall and said to Ernie. "We'll wait for you in the hall." Once in the hall everyone stood and waited and then saw one of the nurses headed down the hallway towards them.

"Uh Oh." Said Nancy. Alex looked at her and waited.

"Just what is going on here?!"

Alex looked up at the ceiling, and both ways down the hallway, then at the door to the room. "This isn't my room. Girls, I think you made a mistake!"

"Very funny. I'm calling security."

"Nurse. We're sorry for the trickery. But what we did for the two that are in that room right now…we would do again at any cost.

"How Galant. Stay right there."

Right then Nurse Helen from the floor below came around the corner. As the nurse going for security walked up, she stopped her. "What's going on?"

"This group thought it would be funny to trick us so that all of them got into the Falmeyer room. I'm calling security right now."

"I don't think that is necessary, they are all from my floor and were very concerned about their friend. Let me handle this. Were there any effects on other patients?"

"No. But I have no intention of letting…"

"Nurse, don't make me pull rank,"

"OK, whatever!" She strode back to the front desk.

Nurse Helen looked at the group, which Ernie had now re-joined, and said, "Well played! Now all of you get back down to your floor, and no more antics out of any of you!" She was thanked by everybody that filed past her as they all headed back downstairs.

Chapter Four

Daq pushed Alex down the hall to Jennifer's room. "How come you're going in by yourself?"

"Well, you guys already saw her on the day I slept the whole day away. So, I just want to talk to her alone."

"Oh. Are you going to ask her…" Alex looked into her eyes with a touch of apprehension. "To be your girlfriend?" She smiled knowingly at him. And he returned the gesture.

"Perhaps, we'll see what she says."

"I think you'll be fine."

"Why? Did she say something?"

"Oh for god's sake…just go in, I'll wait right here."

Alex stood up and pushed the door open. He stepped in and the door closed behind him. "Hi Jennifer. So sorry it took me so long to get here. But apparently, I needed a bunch of sleep."

When Jennifer saw Alex at the door her heart rate sped up a little and a feeling of affection came over her. She had a bandage/brace covering her nose and a large bandage covering the left side of her face just under her eye. She thought, *'I'll bet I look like Frankenstein. He'll probably run out the door.'* "I completely understand, I haven't been at my best either. As you can probably see." She said, as she waved her hands in front of her face.

"Listen, I don't think 'thank you' would cover what you've done for me and the girls. Since the first day we met you've been a rock of strength that we, especially I, really needed. I would go so far as to say, I may not have made it without you. The advice you've given me, the council you've given the girls, and counseling Daq, and Angie with her abilities...I just can't tell you how much it has meant to me to have this friendship and support. And then add in what you did over the past few days that got you in here...Just, Thank You. Thank You to whatever degree it takes to thank someone like you!"

"You're very welcome. It has been a privilege to work and play with all of you, especially you Alex, you're...a special kind."

"Well, I don't know about that. Uhhh, there is one more favor I would like to ask, one more piece of advice." He moved up close to the bed.

She nodded.

"I've met someone. Someone that I like a lot, and I would even like to explore the possibility of a relationship. But I still deal with the loss of my wife. I deal with the love I have for her and if I would ever be able to love someone else. And, would someone else be able to love me knowing all that, or if even trying is wrong. So, I don't know how to approach this." He lowered his head.

"Anyone you are to be with in the future has to know that the love you have for your wife, will never go away, it will always remain strong in your heart. But I have learned over the years in my job and in my life, that the heart has room for many loves. I remember you when you first met Daq, and she said 'you don't love me.' Your answer was 'like hell I don't! I have loved you since the very first time I held you in my arms when you were just a few months old. My heart opened a spot up just for you and let you in…and you've never left and never will. Don't you ever forget that!' And, in just a couple of months you have made room for two more little girls. It's never wrong to look for more; and whoever this is that you've met, has to realize and understand who you are, and respect what's in your heart."

He raised his head and took her hand, "Do you think you could do that with me Jennifer? At least try?"

"I thought you'd never ask!"

He bent down and gently kissed her lips.

Chapter Five

After a few weeks of recuperation, some of the bandages were coming off and bones were starting to heal. Alex still had on his cast on his right hand and that would probably stay on for a couple more weeks. All three girls were working with Jennifer and other professionals to help them cope with all that had happened over the last three months, and in the months and years prior to that. Alex recognized the need to keep the girls in these programs, mental health is a vital part of growing up and with what these girls had seen in their short lives, it was not going to ever be ignored.

Alex made sure that his newfound family stayed as just that. He resisted the urge to make everyday a fun day, he asseverated normalcy. There was school, homework, house duties, routines, arguments, discipline and a lot of positive encouragement and direction that a house needs to be a home. But there were a lot of fun days also...those were important also.

Daq's 'Chef status' was quickly becoming a passion for her. The creativity she was showing was amazing and Alex gave her his full support, even becoming her sous-chef many times. Daq was becoming a vibrant young lady, full of energy and life, eager to learn and unflinchingly facing any challenges. Alex was so proud of the girl that only few months earlier was ready to take her own life, which she readily admits would have been a tragedy

Angie was the special child that was, and forever will be, the rock of this newfound family. Blessed with abilities and intelligence beyond most people, she remained grounded and in touch with the reality of life. Always looking to learn and experience more, she never neglected her willingness to help others. She also became one of the biggest fans of live theatre...ever. Whenever asked what she would like to do in the future, her answer was always the same, *'Oh, so much.'*

Laila, who had started out silent and scared. Was now a vibrant, outgoing and very outspoken little girl. Someone that could influence a situation by just getting involved and working her charms. She also had an uncanny ability to work out problems by just thinking it all the way through, generally to her advantage. Alex knew that she would need guidance to keep her talents commendable and positive. But he knew her, her heart was good, and her positivity was contagious. He always saw her as a motivational speaker, somewhere down the road.

Ellie had survived the bounce off the wall that the snake had given her, and she and old Maurice were still the same. Plenty of food, each other to wrestle and play with, a place to sleep and now even more people to give them love and kisses. Life was good.

Burt and Ernie were finally back home together again. The girls were very happy about that, and Alex had to advise them on how much time they were spending with them. Burt was quick to tell him to mind his own business, that he enjoyed the girls coming over. Alex had gone over separately one evening and expressed his gratitude for all they had both done. Ernie had walked outside with Alex and thanked Alex for everything he had done for Burt.

As they stood in the front yard, Alex looked at Ernie. "Hey Seal. Maybe someday you could tell me about some stories from your past?"

Ernie looked at him, "Well, you know the old saying."

"Then you'd have to kill me?" Alex and Ernie laughed, hugged, and went back inside.

Now Officer (Nancy) Chen had kept everyone up to date on the police side of the 'event'. (which was what everyone had agreed to call that fateful night of September 30th) Randall, who had been rescued from the bathroom floor was arrested and released the next day after he had cooperated with the police in giving evidence and locations of some of the sex trafficking locations around the Coachella valley. Jeremy the giant who had had surgery and survived the two bullets that Daquiri had put into him, also cooperated and gave several names and locations not only in the Coachella valley but in Los Angeles also. He would have to serve time, but his charges were reduced to misdemeanors for his cooperation. The outcome of all this was that many of girls were now out of the hands of the dealers and pimps and receiving much needed help and therapy.

The young girl found in the snake's room, did not recover.

But the Police were happy with the progress and successes. They were also quick to say that the job in sex-trafficking and drugs was far from over.

Jimmy still had not been found. Officials surmised that he had left town, probably for good.

Marcie now lives in a foster home and is under the supervision of Jennifer. Alex visited her a couple of times and had told her he forgave her and understood why she had done what she did. She had twice come over to the house and spent the evening with Daq and the family. Her mother was found dead laying in the remote desert, but it would never be known as to how she met her end. A funeral service was given for her and was attended by Alex and Jennifer and the girls. It was a farewell that Marcie needed.

Alex and Jennifer were taking their newfound relationship slowly. After recovering for a week after getting out of the hospital they had a dinner date. Alex had picked her up and driven to a nice restaurant had a wonderful meal and then walked around in downtown Palm Springs and stopped for a couple of nightcaps. Then he drove her home, kissed her goodnight on the doorstep and went home. This happened three more times in the same week. One night Jennifer had driven to Alex's house and had dinner with him and the three girls. Then they had game night, and she helped put the girls to bed and after all three were asleep, Alex and Jennifer sat in the living room and talked and cuddled. But she left and went home before the cuddling got too serious. But this led to an evening that saw Jennifer cooking for Alex in her home and the plan was movie night. But the movie never got started and later that night when Alex went home, he sang all the way.

That night he dreamt that he and Jennifer had rented and boarded a sailboat and the person that shoved the boat from the dock was Faith...she was smiling and waving.

Chapter Six

It was Halloween night. And the girls were in costume. Daq was headed to a party at school. It was a class party, so it was supervised, in fact Alex and Jennifer were going later to help chaperone. Now Daq's costume was a white sheet with eye holes cut out and a sign in front that said, 'Big Sheet'. Alex had asked and been assured that the school was OK with the costume.

Now Angie also had a school party for her class, and she had gone with the same theme as Daq except she was 'little sheet'. The two girls were having a lot of fun with the costumes and decided that Laila should be involved also, so her costume read, 'a bit of a sheet'.

It was a neighborhood tradition that any kids or grandkids of the community could do trick or treating to a few specific homes. So Daq and Angie decided they would go with Laila early in the evening to do her appointed rounds. Jennifer and Alex went also and the five had a great time. The neighbors laughed, took pictures, and interacted with the three girls in their ghost costumes. Laila got some treats and the other girls' ooh'd and ahh'd over those and everyone ended up at Burt and Ernie's. Of course, they spoiled them worse than if they had been grandparents. Alex surveyed this scene and thought how lucky he was to have this life, even though three months ago, he didn't know it even existed.

He rounded up the three girls at about 6:00PM. The school parties started at 7:00 so it was time to head back home. They arrived at the front door and Alex said, "OK you party girls! Go get ready for your grand entrances, we leave in a half hour! Laila! Go stash your booty in your room and do not put it where Ellie can get it, because you know she will eat ever last bit of it. Then you get ready also, because you're going to both of their parties with Jennifer and me! She clapped her hands and said, "OK Pops!" Alex watched as the three girls ran inside to do their appointed tasks of getting ready. Jennifer leaned in and kissed Alex before she too stepped in to get ready. Alex stood still for a few seconds and reveled in the moment then heard, "Hey!"

He turned just in time to see the gun mussel flash and the crack sound of the gun going off. He leaned right as the bullet hit and he slumped to the cement floor of the front porch.

Chapter Seven

Jimmy had laid low for the month of October. After all that had happened, he figured that he had to stay out of sight. So, he hid his pick-up and holed up in an abandoned hovel located behind the golf course at a casino outside of Indio. He was pretty pissed off about what had happened and in his peanut sized mind he concocted a revenge plot to take care of Daq's old grandpa. He had bested him a couple of times and this last time he had degraded him by almost pulling off his privates and leaving him on the bathroom floor with his pants around his ankles. That ain't gunna go un-punished, but this time he was just going to kill the old man, no more trying to figure out a way to hurt him…just kill the bastard.

He figured that Halloween would be perfect. He probably would be going out with the kids and not be expecting anyone to be there to hurt him. And it was a pretty quiet neighborhood, so getting in and out would be easy and fast and no one would see him.

So, the night of Halloween, Jimmy had snuck into Palm Spring by way of the local transit bus. Walked to Alex's community, used a box he found to climb over the wall so he could avoid the security gate. He moved over close to Alex's house and watched and waited.

Then he saw them leave the house and were gone for about an hour. He stood on the street and paced back and forth till he saw them coming back to the house. He hid in some bushes across the street and when he saw his opportunity he walked across the street called out to Alex and shot him on his front porch. He then ran away the same way he had come.

Chapter Eight

Jennifer quickly ran back to the porch and saw Alex laying on the porch. "Alex! Oh, God!"

"No, No ,No...I'm OK. Don't scare the girls!"

"What the hell happened!?"

"Jimmy just tried to kill me."

"Jimmy! How did you know it was him?"

"I saw him after he shot me and then as he ran down the street to get away. That's number one."

"What's number two?"

"Only Jimmy could plan to kill me on my porch, get to fifteen feet of me, and miss.

That idiot couldn't hit the ground with his hat!"

Jennifer helped him up and right then Daq came around the corner, "What's going on?"

"Nothing. Sounds like someone lit a firecracker."

She retreated to her room. Jennifer said, "Did he hit you at all?"

"I think it may have grazed my shoulder."

"Let's look."

"In a second, I want to call Nancy and get her on this." He called and she answered, he explained what had happened and gave her all the details he could. She said she'd take care of it. Then he looked at Jennifer. "I do not want the girls to know about this! I'm fine and we are all going to do what we had planned."

"At least let me look at the wound." She pulled up his shirt and looked, it had barely nicked his shoulder. She went to bathroom and got some alcohol and rubbed it on the little mark. "You're right, this kid is a lousy shot!"

"I hope I didn't detect disappointment in your voice."

She laughed, kissed him and said, "It was actually...gratitude."

Alex slipped into the master bedroom bath and cleaned himself up and changed clothes and came out to where the girls were standing in the kitchen in their sheets and signs. All of ten minutes had gone by since the gunshot. Angie looked at Alex and said, "That wasn't a firecracker." Daq came and stood next to Angie.

"OK. Let's move over here because Lai doesn't need to know." Right then his phone rang, and he moved into the great room and answered. It was Officer Chen, who was on duty at the time.

"Hi Alex. He's in custody. Boy, how that kid can put one foot in front of the other is an absolute amazement. He took a bus to get to you. Get this, he apparently thought that you and the girls would be the only people out tonight, Halloween night, because he seemed surprised that he was noticed as he ran down the street. He actually bumped into a guy and the gun fell out of his pocket. The guy picked up the gun without touching it and we have it now. Then, as he tried to get back over the wall, he injured his arm and left blood all over the wall. Then we picked him up, care to know where?"

"Let me guess. Standing in the bus stop, waiting for the bus."

"Bingo!"

"Jesus, he obviously missed the memo about brains being passed out. Is he off the street?"

"Yes. In the back of a squad car headed to jail."

"Thanks Nancy...we owe you again."

"I'll be here to collect!"

"Luvya!"

Alex looked at the two girls and said, "OK big sheet and little sheet. Jimmy tried to shoot me tonight. But in typical Jimmy fashion; he missed. The police have him in custody and everything is fine. I think we can safely say all this crap is over."

"I'm sorry I ever met that piece of shit!"

"It's over, that's the important thing! Let's go to some parties!" The little sheet gave

Alex a big hug and took his hand as everyone headed out to the parties. He looked down at her with a touch of amazement, "You're a little spooky...you aware of that?"

"Oh yea. Just don't try to hide things from me."

"Got it."

They drove towards the school, and Daq had intentionally sat in the front with Alex. Jennifer, Angie and Laila sat in the back. As Alex drove Daq scooted as close to him as possible then leaned over the console and whispered to him. "If after the thirty days was up, if I would have said I want to leave, would you have let me?"

"Nope!" The whispered answer was quick and definitive.

"So, you lied?"

"Yep! That was always plan B."

"What...to lie!"

"Absolutely." He looked at her and her look back at him was a mix of a little amusement, and perhaps a little consternation. "Daq, sometimes you have to do anything it takes to make the right thing happen. And you, and your sisters was the right thing to happen. This...was the right thing to happen. And if I would've had to lie or flap my arms until I could fly...I would have...for this. You understand what I'm saying?"

She nodded and then held out her hand across the console to him, and he grabbed on and held her hand. They held hands all the way to the school like that.

Chapter Nine

Everyone had a great time. Alex had the opportunity to dance with all 'his' girls he had brought to the party. His highlight of the evening was when Daq asked him to dance. She had taken off the 'Big Sheet' and he was contemplative at how beautiful and grown-up she looked. After his dance with her he noticed that there was a young boy staring at her with a big grin on his face. "Looks like there is a young man over there looking to dance with you."

"Oh, yea, he's nice."

"Your first dance?" She nodded. He thought to himself...*'the journey begins.'* "Have fun, but remember, I'll beat him senseless if he tries to get fresh!"

She laughed and then kissed his cheek. "I love you Pops." Then moved quickly to the young man in waiting. Alex suddenly realized he had another lump in his throat.

As they drove home Laila fell asleep in Jennifer's arms. When they went into the house they stood in the hallway and were greeted by Ellie and Maurice as they ran in to see everyone. Alex looked around and said, "We're all here, together, safe and sound...what do you think is in store for us next?"

Everyone just looked at him when Angie said, "Well, there's always Christmas."

The whole family laughed.

Author's Note

Thank You for reading my book. This has been a story I've had in my mind for many years. In fact, I started writing it three different times but never finished it until now. It is a special story for me as I have folded many aspects and experiences into it over the years. It is a work of fiction but has many relevant issues that face society today.

I want to dedicate this book to all the organizations that fight the battle of suicide prevention or the stigma of suicide. Suicide affects all ages, all genders and impacts the entire family and friend network. Supporting these organizations is paramount to the success they can achieve. Thank You to all who work, organize, contribute to and support these valuable organizations.

And please, if you or any one you know, has suicidal thoughts or tendencies, get help by reaching out and talking to a trained counselor. 988 Lifeline.

        The world is better with you in it.

Printed in Great Britain
by Amazon